# Meet Zeke

Bullied in school, the brother of a rebellious sister, without real friends, and stifled by an overbearing father - these incendiary ingredients have ignited 15-year-old Zeke Titcomb, a full-fledged pyromaniac. He has terrorized the small town of Chaldea, Maine by torching his high school to the ground. And the town will never be the same.

But the high school is only the beginning. Zeke's unsuccessful attempts to set the adjacent Junior High School on fire and the neighboring Walloomsac High School strain the efforts of the authorities, desperate to find the culprit, but not before Zeke has further traumatized the townspeople with a burning spree.

Zeke, now incarcerated in the Portland Youth Center, isolated and sulky, withdraws. Dr. Elizabeth Proctor, his appointed psychologist, convinces him to begin writing in a journal. Something strange happens - Zeke begins to open up. In it, he gradually reveals the events that led up to the fires, his feelings about life in Chaldea, and the family anxieties that burden him. Zeke immerses himself in his journal. Only when his parents allow two staff members from his old high school, a former English teacher and the school librarian, to help him work on his writing, does Zeke begin to catch a glimpse of what he has done and who he is.

# Kindling

by

David Cappella

"Of Small Towns" by Baron Wormser from *The White Words*. Houghton Mifflin. 1983. Permission of the author.

"The Visit" and "The Possibility of a Hand-Hewn Education" by Jim Provencher from *The Portland Press Herald/Maine Sunday Telegram*, subsequent Sundays, November 1981. "The Earth Gives Up its Dead" by Jim Provencher from *Yankee Magazine*. March, 1977. Permission of the author.

"Down in Maine" by Jim Bishop from *Mother Tongue*. Contraband Press. 1975. Permission of the author.

Permission to quote lines from the song "Fire" by Arthur Brown, Vincent Crane, Robert Ker, and Michael Finesilver granted by Onward Music.

Published by Piscataqua Press
An imprint of RiverRun Bookstore, Inc.
142 Fleet Street | Portsmouth, NH | 03801
www.riverrunbookstore.com
www.piscataquapress.com

ISBN: 978-1-944393-02-1

Printed in the United States of America

# Acknowledgements

It was Jim Provencher who initially encouraged me to follow through with the voice of Zeke way back in March of 2008 when it came to me while visiting him in Sydney. That spring, in my backyard in Farmington, CT, it was Steve Ostrowski who wanted to hear more of Zeke's voice. My thanks to both of them and to Candace Barrington, Joe Clifford, David Daniel, David Durgin, Tom Hazuka, and Baron Wormser, all of whom read and commented on various drafts of the novel.

# Of Small Towns

It is not so much gossip that absorbs
Them as a fondness, to be found
Even in the children, for measuring lives:
The noting of how many years some wife
Has outlived her husband and how each of the road
Commissioner's four children quit high school
In the middle of the eleventh grade and how
It was twenty years to the day (they are
All addicted to anniversaries) that
A black spruce fell on a one-armed man.
Comparison is insistent—the father who
Is a better shot but not as good a card
Player as the son; the sister who
Writes poems while the other two clean house.
Here, people want to live to learn
Who the next President will be, how many
Games the World Series will go,
Whether the trains will ever come back.
Ceremonious and dutiful to national symbols,
Too many of the sons die in the wars.
The coffins show that faraway places exist,
That you can die quite forcibly elsewhere.
Those who have hoisted themselves up
And fled will say that the finitude
Of small-town life breeds idiocy, that
The imagination turns upon itself, chews
Its substance over and over until it is worse
Than nothing. The surmises that the metropolis loves
To make, the crushes of people whose names you will

Never know, the expansive gestures made
Among incoherent buildings—all that is
Peculiarly urban and self-aware is lacking.
Instead, you have a hodgepodge:
Legends hovering, dreams that lapse into manias,
Characters ransacked like cottages in winter.
Each random movement would become an event.
It is no surprise that every now and then
The attentiveness becomes too great
And some hamlet spawns a horror
Of the first degree. As is to be expected,
The émancipé's letters home are blunt:
"You are all like those vile canning jars,
Lidded and sealed and put away for endless winter."
And yet—it is these towns that dignify the slimmest
Of lives with a history, remembering even dogs
With an earnest pleasure, a rush of anecdote and regret.

— Baron Wormser

# Tinder

*I like flames. I like watching flames grow. I know why, too. It's because...because I know I started them. Me. I get to see how they grow, twist and turn, roll up, swell, snap, then devour things. But I don't have to watch them to know that they destroy, destroy everything, everything completely. Nothing left but ashes.*

*I like how flames slowly overtake things, especially when you know that they cannot be stopped. I feel I'm strong like they are; my power builds with them as they get bigger. I'm invincible when the flames grow. I feel this even when I am not watching them. It's my secret, something special not shared with anyone. Not my sister, not any teacher, not anyone. I fuel the flames when they burn what I tell them to burn.*

*I find ways to get them to burn that no one, not the police, not the principal, not my father and mother, can detect. I want to burn down the damn schools in this damn town. I wish I could burn down the mill. That would get everyone.*

*The schools, easy pickings. They're wood, full of those old books, rags in the gym and the janitor's closets. The floors, the walls. Even the bricks might crumble from the heat.*

When she arrived at her office Friday morning, Dr. Elizabeth Proctor found Zeke's youth center journal on her desk beside his psychiatric file, which she had been reading the day before. The night orderly, she thought. She decided to get a coffee before reading it, knowing that this case needed to be handled with extreme care. The town expected nothing less. Small Maine towns have finicky personalities, ones that can get very tricky to deal with, especially when they spawn unexpected horrors like the burning down of two schools and almost a third in the neighboring town. Let alone three homes and a warehouse. Chaldea, Maine, was no different.

Yesterday, in their second session, Dr. Proctor had asked Zeke to write down what it was about lighting fires that he liked so much. Zeke had seemed preoccupied. The pudgy, pale-skinned fifteen-year-old had refused to look at her or engage her. He had played with the laces of his left sneaker, which rested squarely above his right knee, untying them and retying them over and over as he sat in the worn easy chair facing her desk. He had only mumbled "I dunno" down at the floor and continued to play with the sneaker laces.

Dr. Proctor said, "Well, Ezekiel, since you're obviously somewhere else, why don't you write me something that I can read. How does that sound?"

"I dunno...yeah...maybe...I guess so," Zeke spoke softly to the floor.

Dr. Proctor knew that Zeke liked to write in a journal. That's why she had suggested he start a new one when he began his two-year stay at South Portland Youth Center. Maybe if he wrote she could use his words to get him to talk.

Dr. Proctor sipped her coffee as she looked down at Zeke's first journal entry after their session yesterday. Though interesting from a clinical perspective, getting into the deep waters with a disturbed adolescent wrenched her emotions every time. Zeke's new journal was the first step on another troubled journey into the murky depths of a teen's psyche. Troubled teens. Adolescence, what an ordeal, she thought, glancing over the sentences that made up the paragraphs. The tight a's and o's, the tiny e's of Zeke's small, painfully neat handwriting gave the word "blaze" an anger, an anxiety. So did the word "match," let alone how he wrote the word "hate." The harsh "f" in "father," a word repeated several times, almost ripped through the page. Dr. Proctor took a sip of her black coffee and reread Zeke's journal entry.

# Chapter 1

*You want to know what I remember best? Mr. Resnick. Mr. Resnick was the best. I used to go to the library to help him with stuff. I'd organize shelves, stack books behind his desk, clean up the magazine and newspaper rack. I would try and hang out down at the library whenever I could. I felt safe there, calm.*

*The light coming in through the windows made everything quiet and still. Sometimes when I looked up from stacking a book, I noticed the dust caught in streaks of sunlight. Or I'd notice Mr. Resnick sitting at his desk, leaning over an article he was reading. Often he had a pen in his hand, and I knew that he was writing something. The look on his face when he was doing that was serious, even more serious than when he was reading and that was some kind of serious. When he was writing, his eyes seemed to be boring through the paper. I'll never forget that look.*

*I never thought of him or the library when I torched the school. Maybe I should have. But I didn't. No. I did not think about books, about the gym or the cafeteria. What I thought about was what difference does it make, really? I suppose it makes a difference to everyone but not to me. I know why. Who cares what I think anyway. I thought about a bunch of things, but I'm not going to talk about them now. Why should I?*

*The fires changed everything. I knew they would. It made a difference for me. The second the fire took was the second I began to be...I dunno. Everyone says I'm a pyro. Anyone can learn how to burn stuff, but I'm more than that now. You've got to plan to burn down a building. When I planned the first fire, I bet I looked a lot like Mr. Resnick looks when he's writing.*

*When that friggin' school burned down, I smiled. But I smiled inside a long time. I kept thinking about all those friggin' football players, especially Billy Atwood, and all those kewpie doll girls who were so friggin' rah-rah in their blue and white cheerleader uniforms. I thought of them and all those stupid announcements about G period rallies and school spirit, how Chaldea was going beat Dirigo and how we were the best school with the greatest students. What bull. We were no better than any other friggin' school in the middle of nowhere in a dumbass nowhereville state.*

Morris Resnick startled awake. The house was quiet. Janice slept fitfully beside him. He heard Webster, his old mutt, breathing heavily. It was cold upstairs, the stove fire having burned down to coals. He stared through the skylight overhead into the night, clear and star-filled. They threw down their spears in that familiar white silver he had come to know on these sub-zero January nights. He had lived upcountry for over twenty years. He knew the place. Maine was a long way from Baltimore, for sure. Here he was, caught between stove embers dying downstairs and the eternal stars above. Caught in his dreams. With *the* dream.

For the past few weeks he had this recurring dream about Zeke. This kid who lit fires seemed beyond absurd to him one moment, but then, in the next, he understood completely about being a teenager up here in rural Maine. Up here life was a little more socked in emotionally. He knew the kids; he knew their families. As the librarian at Chaldea High School and as the school district's librarian, he knew almost everyone in the town though he lived a few towns away. Few people wanted to live in

Chaldea, and the young people certainly did not. "I hate this town, Mr. Resnick," was the refrain he heard as students marched in and out throughout the day, some getting books for class, others stopping in just to waste time on a bathroom pass, others simply hiding from bullies, and a few others, too few, skipping class to do what most students hated doing – read.

Nobody ever said upcountry living was a bed of roses, Resnick thought as his breathing slowed. The details of his dream now came into clear focus; he knew them by heart. He awoke from the dream at the same point every time. The phone ringing interrupted these middle of the night dream thoughts.

That is what had happened on that unusually cold early morning in November. After the third ring, he had found the phone. "Morris! Morris! You there?" It was the principal, Tom Rowell. "Get over here - to school! Quick!"

"What? What's wrong?" Resnick tried to sit up in bed. His wife woke and turned toward him.

"Morris, the school's on fire! Get over here!"

Resnick hung up, stood and fumbled with his pants, which hung on the chair next to his side of the bed. "There's a fire at the school, Janice. I'll call you as soon as I can." He grabbed his shirt and raced downstairs. "Call David, please," he yelled back up to her.

"Watch it going down the road. Remember the culvert beyond the old maple tree is washed out!" Janice called.

Resnick worked the notchy gears of his Subaru as he half slid down the old logging road toward the town road, which was hard packed, graded gravel. He negotiated the slippery culvert. His mind wasn't on the road. Instead, Resnick was thinking about books, about the school library, about all those carefully chosen acquisitions over the years. The new English teacher up from the city, Mr. Coccinella, had said the school library was a gem, a diamond hidden in the western hills. Whenever he would come down from his classroom to the library, he found what he was looking for. If he didn't, Morris would get it for him without fail in two, maybe three days max. Resnick thought about this as he sped through Narratunk, over the Kennebec Bridge toward Chaldea. The books! Were they burning? A horrible thought for a librarian, especially one who was a poet about to have his third collection published in the spring.

# Chapter 2

*You know what I think of Mr. Rowell and most of the teachers? I hate them. I hate most of the kids in this town. Only Rowell is more of a bully in a way. His big loud voice. He's got this smirk when he talks and tells you that you've been doing something wrong. I hate the curl of his lips that says he's so much better than you. That's one thing we all agree on, that Rowell is an asshole.*

*I thought about that smirk when I was doing the plans for the first fire. Sometimes, when I was lying on my bed staring up at the ceiling, I wondered how Rowell and the teachers would act toward all those flames. But Rowell's a pissant. Like my father.*

*Billy Atwood's a pissant, too, and all those guys that try to get into my sister's pants. The druggies and even those guys from the mill. I hate it when she flirts with them. I know, because I've seen her do this when she walks down by the entrance to the mill when the shift changes. The young guys look at her like they're stalking deer. The looks on their faces. Those dirty looks.*

*A flame is heat's body. It sucks up air and all the energy it can. I love how flames curl and give off heat. So intense. I feel like my insides are one flame living off every feeling I have.*

*I suppose I've got to tell you about my family. My father is Mr. Know It All. Mr. Moral. Mr. I've Heard It All Before. The Foreman of the World. You cannot tell my father anything. He wraps whatever you say into a neat package that fits into his little world. If he treats the guys who work for him on his shift at the Mill the way he treats me and my sister, and even my mother at times, they must hate his guts.*

*My father, Deacon Titcomb of the Baptist Church, town meeting moderator...whoop-de-friggin'- dooo! Got his nose up to here in the town's, in everyone's business, especially me and my sister's. No wonder she is so screwed up with drugs and guys. Mr. Goody Two Shoes knows what's best for us all; he's always got an opinion. He's a real stand-up guy for his own ideas. Like when he pushed for the town to plow up past the dump so he could park his truck closer to the trail that goes up to Little Tom Pond, so he could go ice fishing. He's so straight, so uptight about everything, he squeaks.*

*I'm from a real small town family, for sure. I hate the place, and I hate my family, too. I can't talk about it now.*

---

Tom Rowell, principal at Chaldea High School for two years, rarely dreamed, but when the phone rang, he was climbing Katahdin. In fact, he was beginning the hike along Knife's Edge. He had never climbed the mountain, only hiked around its environs in Baxter State Park. Afraid of heights, the thought of walking Knife's Edge scared him. In the dream, he breathed quickly and did not look down at the drop to either side of the trail. He was still feeling this dream nervousness when the voice of Bob Mosley, the chair of Chaldea's school committee, filled his ear.

"Tom, your school's on fire. The department is on the scene. Meet me over there. Call who you need to call. I have a feeling it will be a long night and a longer day."

"Oh shit. What the hell happened? An electrical fire in the cafeteria? That building is as old as God's old dog, for Chrissake." Rowell sat up on the edge of the bed. "I'll be down in fifteen minutes. The road's blocked off, right?"

"I assume so. I'll meet you at the Exxon, and we'll walk up."

Rowell stood, rubbed his face and hair, and began dressing. His wife, Aida, awake during the call, looked up at him from her side of the bed. "Jesus, Tom...this podunk town."

Rowell walked to his Dodge pickup and into the predawn autumn cold. He noticed Orion blinking low in the sky. Why me, he thought. Why does this fire have to happen now? The school was old as hell itself. The town needed a new school, for sure and certain. Maybe now he could get the computers and resources that the teachers had been desperately asking for. Maybe not. He really didn't care. He had mailed his application for the principal's job back in his hometown of Rumford yesterday.

He climbed into his truck, cranked her up. As he backed out of his driveway, he reminded himself that he had to change the oil. "Damn school, damn town," he said aloud, his breath clouding against the windshield colored by the amber glow of the dashboard lights.

# Chapter 3

*It was easy to light the first high school fire. No problem. When I was in G Period Study Hall, I used to look at the auditorium curtains. They were dusty, old and purple faded things, hanging down from each side of the stage, and I'd think, "Man, those are old, those are dry as a bone, and big." They must have been thirty feet high. There was a lot of material there, velvet or something like that. You know that soft stuff with little bumps that you can brush forward and back and it looks like the wind blew through it like it does to the cornstalks in Davis's cornfield in August before it's chopped for silage.*

*I started thinking one day, as I sat there not doing my homework. Everyone was goofing off as usual. Atwood even smiled at me. Only Mr. Coccinella was on duty with us, as usual. He can handle us; he actually talks to us. I even think he likes us. That's good for a teacher. He and Resnick hang together. Coccinella was always in the library talking to Resnick. They both read a lot. They write and talk poetry all the time. They are different.*

*Anyway, I was thinking how if I lit these curtains from the bottom how the flame would grow up and up in no time at all. Then from there the whole auditorium would go up since it's all wood. Then the rest of the school. Bam! Just like that. You see, the auditorium is an inside space in the school. So those flames, as they snaked their way up the curtains, would build up some serious heat and that heat would feed the flames even more.*

*I was just daydreaming this fire at first.*

∽∾∽

"Hey, numb nut, rise and shine. Guess what?" growled Eben Titcomb, peeping his head around his son's half opened bedroom door. "You won't believe what happened." Eben Titcomb shut the door and headed back downstairs without further word.

Zeke was exhausted. His body felt like lead. He couldn't shake the cobwebs out even as he swung himself up into a sitting position. He sat on the edge of his bed and let the chill of the room tingle his arms and legs. His father's words began to register and a wide grin spread. He straightened his arms and pushed himself up off the bed. He dressed quickly, eager to get downstairs before his father left. "Ayuh, breakfast should be very interesting," he thought, "and the whole day should be good, exceptional even."

Zeke came bounding down the stairs and into the kitchen. "Where's Dad?" Peggy Titcomb, in her checkered kitchen apron, was flipping pancakes in the cast iron frying pan.

"He's gone to get the paper, dear. He'll be right back."

"Mom, please don't call me that, okay?" Zeke sat at the kitchen table. He loved coming down to a warm kitchen on a cold autumn morning, not winter yet despite the inch or two of snow on the ground and the below freezing temperature. The wood stove cranked away and the radiating heat embraced him, snuggled around him real good. The sun streamed in the windows through curlicues of frost etched around the corners of the panes. Zeke noticed they hadn't melted yet.

"Oh, Zeke. You're my one and only, my special son."

"Mom, yeah, okay, but I'm in high school, in case you forgot."

"You're so sensitive. I'm just happy to see you, that's all. Mr. Ezekiel. How's that?" She put a stack of blueberry pancakes in front of him.

"Very funny, Mom." He poured maple syrup on the stack.

"Did you-know-who come home last night?"

"Ayuh, she did, but very late. I heard the kitchen door in the wee hours. She's sleeping. I checked on her when I got up to light the stove." Mrs. Titcomb sighed. "Zeke, do you see her in school at all?"

"Mom, she avoids me like the plague and, if you want to know the truth, I avoid her."

Mrs. Titcomb added some pancake batter to the pan. She remained silent, watching the batter begin to slowly bubble. She used a corner of the spatula and began to break the little floury bubbles as they rose. Her mind was elsewhere. Finally, flipping over the pancakes, she looked over at Zeke and said, "Your sister is not a happy person."

"I'll say. She's messed up. And, she's stubborn. And...." He just stopped.

"Things are so much more complicated than that. So much more.... Maybe, she'll settle down. Some people just have to live harder than others in order to learn their lessons."

"Tell that to Dad," Zeke snapped.

"Don't talk to me like that, young man. And don't go blaming everything on him, either. Michelle is old enough to know better." Mrs. Titcomb set another short stack on Zeke's plate and gave him a kiss on the top of the head.

"Aw, Ma. I don't like them goin' at it all the time. Dad scares the hell outta me sometimes. Most of the time."

"Zeke, don't swear."

"Hell is not a swear word. Even Dad uses the word. He's always telling one of us to go there, isn't he?"

"Finish up your pancakes." Mrs. Titcomb turned to the stove to pour a cup of coffee. Just then, Eben Titcomb walked in.

"Hell, it's cold out there and it's only the first week of November." He looked at his wife. "Did you tell him the news?" he asked.

"No, you said that you wanted to tell him."

"Why, what's goin' on?" asked Zeke.

"Get this, mister man, your school has burned down. Totally gone. A complete loss. No school today." Eben Titcomb sneered. "How could someone do such a thing? That's what I want to know. We've got to find this pyromaniac and punish him. It's reprehensible."

Zeke cut his pancakes, deliberately. He chewed each bite slowly. But inside, he was laughin' real loud. Inside, he was splitting a gut. If he only knew, Zeke thought. If he ever had a clue. Zeke loved seeing his father so pissed and helpless. Serves him right, he thought, as he chewed his last bite of pancake. He'd shit a brick if he found out, Zeke knew for sure. Well, he'll never find out. He scooped up the last bit of maple syrup from his plate and sucked it around his tongue and mouth before he swallowed. He loved the maple syrup this year. He remembered that his mother said it came from Strong. Man, Zeke thought, that place is so nowhere. It makes Chaldea seem like Portland.

# Chapter 4

*I was patient and I waited for nighttime. No one really worried about watching the school at night. Who even cares about the stupid school? Who's going to break into a school? Once in a while the football guys might try it to steal a few jerseys. It means a broken window and sprung door. Big deal. They get caught because they brag about it the next day and before long someone tells the principal who calls the guys in his office, tells them he is going to tell the AD and the coach and the police, but when the guys leave his office, everyone is smiling and shaking their heads, even stupid Rowell, because what are we gonna do with you boys, you gotta cut out these stupid pranks and grow up! Even the secretary shakes her head and smiles at the lunkheads.*

*Setting a fire is no prank. It has to be planned. You gotta want to light it. A fire has to be felt inside the person who lights it. And I felt like a fire that night. I was totally burning up. Because I knew I was really going to do it. I was going to be destroying something the town cherished. Chaldea friggin' High School. I burned it down, down to the friggin' ground.*

Morris Resnick drove through the predawn dark of Central Maine in a sad yet edgy state. The thought of all those books, his books, since he'd bought them, organized them, built the library from scratch into a first-rate operation, a high school library that was talked about and recognized throughout the region, burned up, kept rolling around his brain. The bleak landscape spread out before him lay shrouded in the white light of a waning moon. It was unusually cold, and the Subaru was slow to warm. What was he going to find once he got there? All those books—gone. All the work to give the district resources—gone. Twenty-five years of maintaining literacy—gone.

Resnick downshifted hard as he turned onto Main Street in Chaldea. He pulled into the corner Exxon just as Tom Rowell and Bob Mosley were turning to walk up the street to what was left of Chaldea High School. Morris beeped at them. They waited as he parked and hurried over.

The owner of the gas station had opened up as soon as the news reached him to provide a warm place and coffee for the firefighters, police, journalists, teachers, and townspeople, all who came and went now as the long night gave way. Resnick noticed that the bright lights of the station threw an eerie florescence on the two men and now on him. Outside the sphere of the gas station lights a dusky pink rose in the east. Dawn was coming slowly, thought Resnick, as he greeted the two men with a nod.

None of them said a word as they walked up toward the school.

# Chapter 5

*Spooky, how the flames crawled, wiggled their way up the curtains. Those old curtains stood still as flames engulfed them. I remember an Edgar Allan Poe story from Coccinella's class and from talking with Resnick when I went down to the library to help him out. But, I never thought of an actual person when I lit the fire. Just how the flames seemed so alive, like some yellow-orange dragon that suddenly appeared, squirmy alive as soon as I flicked on the Bic lighter. When I lit the first curtain, it seemed to slide up toward the ceiling. I saw it in slow motion. But by the time I ran to light the other one, on the other side of the stage, I could hear the rushing sound of the first flame grow louder. When I lit that second curtain, I had to leave quick because everything started to happen fast. The flames were becoming monsters with minds of their own, devouring everything! I felt so good. I felt that something inside of me was disappearing.*

*It's hard to explain how I felt. Setting the school on fire wasn't some Stephen King trick. I'd read most of his books because Resnick and Coccinella told me to. That was back when I was in my completely clueless phase. Coccinella and Resnick, I think, sort of ganged up on me. Anyway, they got me to read* Carrie. *It was cool enough. But when I lit fires, I wasn't some girl who used her mind to ignite people she didn't like. I mean I was really picked on but she was really, really picked on. She wanted to get even with those dumb kids for making a fool out of her. These same types of kids that pick on me and others like me, they make fools out of us in their eyes, sure. But, in my eyes, they're losers big time.*

*I'm no Carrie. Nothing out of the ordinary had happened to me that day. The only thing I felt was that I was choking, like everything was closing in on me. At home, it was Zeke do this. Pay attention, will you? Zeke, get it together. At school, it was where's your homework, Zeke? Or, "Hey, Zekeoid, you mung, why'd you quit as football manager? Just because your dad told you to, you mung. You're just a mung."*

*My sister was doing this guy at the mill, getting stoned with who knows and putting everything into her body she could find and stealing to do it. My father, Mr. Pillar of the Community, telling me to do the right thing, to stand up straight, to tell the truth, to behave myself. Every time he hit me upside the head for saying something he thought was stupid I felt like I couldn't breathe. And there was my mother, Mom, trying to keep us all together, pretending that she was this Mrs. Country Homemaker with her damn apron, looking like Betty Crocker on the cake mix box. No, Mom was no Betty Crocker. Life ain't no cake mix. I dunno, maybe it is. I didn't fit in the mix; that was the trouble. I couldn't please anyone, even myself. Except when I thought about lighting fires.*

There it is, Resnick said to himself. The remnants of Chaldea High School. A pile of smoldering ruin. How does one capture an achingly sad scene, the horrific rural trauma of a small New England town? Poets can do it, he knew. Morris Resnick had accomplished the feat in one of his early poems, one that became quite well known, even translated into Russian, not that anyone in town had read it or even known about it. Except David Coccinella.

Does one describe the weather, notice the setting moon over the western mountains, the deepening salmon and pink colors that tinge the faces in the crowd? Does one describe the burned down building, the heaps of bricks, blackened and soaked with foam and water? Does one describe the charred beams and planks that were once joists and floors to classrooms, the smoke rising from them? Does one describe the complete emptiness of the site, the void that stared the onlookers in the face as they gazed at the spot where a school once stood and now, oddly, could see up and over the ruins to the athletic fields that stretched behind where the school once was? How does one tell the psychic loss of the townspeople who still see the school, a school where they themselves graduated, alive and real in their minds, even as they crane their necks to see past the police cordoning off the site and past the firefighters inspecting the site as they trudge around and through the mess, lugging hoses on their shoulders, carrying axes and other equipment back to the trucks? What is there to say, what can be said, in the face of such pure destruction that the fire left in its wake? Resnick cleared his throat as though trying to shake off such questions.

Mosley, Rowell, and Resnick made their way to where all the teachers had gathered across the street on the Litton's yard, which faced the school straight on. Irene Holmgren, an English teacher, sobbed gently and held a tissue in her ski-gloved hand. Carlton Allerton, who taught tenth grade history, sipped coffee and swayed from one foot to the other, looked up at the site, then down to the snow-covered ground.

Everyone's frozen breath rose and mingled in the still dawn. The reek from the paper mill, the sulfurous odor that perpetually enveloped the town, hung in the air, weighing down further the already weighted down crowd. It was Irene who first noticed the three men, and she called, "Morris, everything is gone, completely destroyed. Nothing is left. I feel so…." She began to weep.

Tom Rowell left to speak with Police Chief Avery, who was standing by one of the fire trucks talking to the Fire Chief, Renee Corson. Bob Mosley noticed two school committee members talking beside the police cruisers, their lights strobing across the men's faces as they conversed. He walked over, wondering what they were talking about. Money, probably. How would the town fund a new school? What would the state kick in, a real concern that he would have to discuss with the committee? Despite the mill, this was a depressed area. The mill gave something to the town, not enough as far as he was concerned, and it wouldn't bail them out on this.

Morris turned to Irene and asked, "When did you get here?" The image of a half-burned book lying open, burnt pages fluttering in a breeze, appeared in his head as he gazed beyond Irene at the space where the library used to be.

"Maybe a half hour ago. Judy called me. How she found out I don't know. She was here somewhere. I could barely stay on the road on the way over," she said.

"You barely stay on the road on any day, and it's Route 2!" Morris wondered if the teasing was appropriate.

"I guess you're right about that," Irene sniffed. A wan smile crossed her face. "But you must feel awful. All that work for the library, all those books. Our books!"

"I don't feel much of anything right now except maybe numb, like everyone else. No one ever expects the unexpected." Resnick gazed at the site as he said this. A mindless comment, he thought. But then again, he was staring mindlessness right in the face at the moment. He was noticing how strange, how awkward the junior high school now looked, solitary next to the smoldering mess when he caught sight of David Coccinella leaning against an Exxon pump, gazing up to where, Resnick supposed, he used to teach.

# Chapter 6

*I left no trace. I wore gloves. I left my shoes outside the window. It was perfectly planned. The school burned to the ground. It was great. There was nothing left. The damn place was so old, built back before the Civil War almost, well, over a hundred years ago. It burned hot and it burned hard. I wish that I could have seen it all. I caught the flames from the woods, but I had to sneak back home and into bed. Trust me, it was a great fire. A conflagration, as Mr. Resnick might say.*

*It's funny how I think of Coccinella and Resnick at times like this. I mean, to think about words sometimes when I'm talking. Because I never once thought of them or books burning when I lit the first fire. I just thought of the flames, of how they would build and grow. To watch a flame expand, to watch it eat and wrap itself around what it is burning. I love watching that. I love watching the logs in a fireplace or a woodstove burn. The flames lap and lick, snap and pop. I am captivated...mesmerized, that's the right word. Hypnotized by the movement of the flames. I should write a poem about flames. Resnick would love that. Coccinella would go off on how writing a poem is a creative way to deal with emotions. He'd be so psyched.*

*I went and saw the results of the fire. The old return to the scene of the crime. I walked by slowly, eyeing everything. Nobody gave me a second look. Cars slowed down as they drove by. Mostly outsiders from away, you could tell. The police had the site all roped off. One cop sat in a patrol car. There was nothing left! Nothing! Bricks, piles of them, some burnt pieces of lumber, some old equipment sunk in these piles of bricks and wood, bent and misshapen by the heat, from the shop and the home ec room. The shower pipe and head stall from the AD's office stood alone next to a toilet. That was weird. The results of a fire are totally unpredictable. But I could care less about that; I care about the fire. It's the fire that's everything.*

*When I was standing in the woods behind the baseball field that night, watching the flames that I had set less than ten minutes before rising up, billowing out of the windows of the school, I knew that I was going to start another one. So I thought, as I walked by the place, why should the Junior High School stand there all by itself?*

David Coccinella spotted Morris Resnick staring at what used to be Chaldea High School and headed toward him. He had raced along Route 2 from New Eden immediately after Janice had called. His commute usually lasted twenty-five minutes or more, but he had hoofed it over to Chaldea in under twenty this time. On the drive over, he thought about the tough breaks that inland towns like Chaldea get up here, the tail end of the Appalachians and butt end of the rural poverty line that stretched all the way from Georgia. He remembered Morris had written a poem that caught as much of the disease of small towns in America as any poem he had read. Now, here was the disease right before him, metastasized into burned out rubble in a town that had nothing much except its pride and the reflex to help each other out when the going got tough.

"Any news?"

"No. Tom called me and told me to get over here, but I have no idea what for. The gang is all here. Perhaps we should all slip down to The Anchor and drink with the workers finishing up the graveyard shift." Resnick shrugged his shoulders, "Who needs a school anyway? Who needs books nowadays? Certainly not

Chaldea, Maine."

Resnick looked at David and then down to the ground.

# Chapter 7

*My father is a Grade A asshole. Everyone in town knows that. With me, he's so strict. Do this like this, do that like that. No, I said do it THIS WAY! It's always like that. He knows, no one else does.*

*I was criticized for every little thing that he saw me not doing his way. Once, when I put back the yard rake in the shed, I left it leaning against the wheelbarrow instead of hanging it up on the racks on the wall. I was in a hurry, I guess, I wanted to have lunch, go outside into the woods. Well, Dad came home from wherever he was. I had left the shed door open and he must've seen the rake leaning against the wheelbarrow.*

*Just as Mom put a toasted cheese sandwich on my plate and just as I was about to take a drink of milk, he storms in the kitchen, grabs me by the bicep, yanks me up, without a word, and marches me out to the shed. "Where does that rake belong, Zeke?" he says to me. "Where the hell did I tell you to put it? Put the damn rake away where it belongs! Now!" As I was hanging the tool up, he punched me in the back of my head. Hard. I think I told this one to Mr. Coccinella. He's the only teacher I ever said anything to. I only told him about one incident, a long time ago, and this one was it. I keep quiet with people. I like Mr. Resnick too because he's real quiet. I don't talk to him much about myself though. I loved hanging around the library because he kept it like himself – quiet.*

*My father doesn't cut my sister any slack either. He's kicked her out of the house twice. Mom keeps getting him to let her back. She gets angrier each time she returns. I have never seen him hit her though. Well, that might not be true. Once when she came home really drunk, he grabbed her, but she screamed, "Don't you ever touch me!" He froze. He was waiting at the kitchen door for her. The lights were off, so she didn't think anyone was up. When she stumbled through the door, he flipped on the lights and flipped out. Mom started crying, yelling, "Leave her alone, Eben. Let her go to bed. There's tomorrow." But he reached for her anyway. When sis screamed, he stopped immediately. Man, the look in her eyes. Pure, pure hatred. I was watching the whole scene from the hallway.*

*He treats my mother the same way he treats us, only he never touches her. He just shits on her when he doesn't like what she says or does. Sometimes he's real sneaky about it, too; he's "subtle." Coccinella and Resnick both use that word.*

*There are other words for how he treats my mother, especially when he's pretending he's being nice to her. He's mouthy with her, though it's a restrained mouthy. He's sarcastic and nasty. To use another Coccinella & Resnick word, the guy is "snide." Mostly, I notice this at the dinner table. But he does it with her anywhere. He doesn't care if he embarrasses her or me and my sister. He's oblivious that way. Don't know where I picked up that word. Probably in English class. There was one dinner table incident that is really funny. Ayuh, the incident of the dinner table was totally ironic and my father was his usual asshole self, saying stuff like, "No doubt the guy was abused as a child, all that kind of psychological crap."*

*I can't remember every detail, but almost. It's the night after the high school fire. Naturally, it's the talk of the town. Everyone has their two cents worth about it, about who did it, and why. Naturally, my father does, too. Times ten. We're sitting for dinner. It's dark, a little after five o'clock. My father had to eat at five o'clock, no matter what his mill shift. Every day. Even weekends.*

*My sister is not home. What else is new? Dad is mad about that. Mom is on edge because Dad is furious about this.*

*It's so quiet at the table you can hear your ears ring. I'm thinking all hell is going to break loose, but it remains silent, only our knives and forks plinking on the plates and our chewing can be heard. I stare at every forkful of mashed potatoes, keeping my eyes lowered. I'm bracing for some serious crap.*

*My mother is also looking down at her plate, slowing cutting a piece of pot roast. "Cut me another piece of meat, will ya, Peggy?" says my father. Mom pushes up from her seat to cut him a thick slice. I wonder why he can't do it himself. She takes his plate and puts the meat on it.*

*He chuckles, "I'll have more of your lumpy potatoes, too. Ever since I've known you, your potatoes have been lumpy." As he grabs his plate from Mom, my father pumps up his chest and looks over to Michelle's empty place mat.*

*"I can't believe they can't figure out who lit that fire. Bunch of incompetents. Avery's an idiot, but I thought those fire marshal people were supposed to be so good at figuring out clues."*

*Mom offered, "You know, Eben, they can't figure out a reason for it because it did do so much damage. That was one serious fire."*

*"Peggy, you only know what you read in the papers. That's what the papers said. You believe them all the time?"*

*Mom kept eating, looking down at her plate.*

*"I was down at the site as soon as the trucks were called. I was talkin' with Avery, with Corson, and I watched with 'em as the school burned down to the ground. I heard all the talk about the investigation then, about the strategy for sifting through the debris, hoping to find something. We had that big selectmen meeting today."*

*He looked over at me.*

*"If they catch this guy, they should really stick it to him. Imagine torching a school. A person has to be crazy to do such a thing." He noisily cut another piece of meat, stabbed it, stuffed it in his mouth, and chewed loudly. This is the ironic part. I mean there I am sitting three feet from the guy. He's clueless.*

*"Even Michelle wouldn't do that. By the way, where the hell is she? Again. That little bitch will be the death of me."*

*I said nothing; I didn't even look at him.*

*"Don't call her that. She's your daughter," Mom shot back. That was a*

*surprise.*

*Dad took off on her in his deliberate, quiet way. He sat straight and he looked proper when he said it. The guy was never out of control.*

*"Yeah, Peg, you always defend her. Don't you see what she's doin' not just to herself but to us, her family. She's making a fool out of us. After all we have done for her? She is totally selfish. And you let it go. You try and talk to her. She needs to be punished. But you'd never do it. So I end up looking the idiot when I send her on her way. For God's sake! Let her get out of here and go on her own. The way she behaves, she's not my daughter. She's yours. You were just like her. The apple never falls far from the tree, eh?"*

*Mom did not look at my father. It was quite a scene. Three people, silent, chewing on their food, staring straight ahead. My family, without Michelle. She was the smart one that night. Who knows where she was.*

*Then, after about what seemed like an hour but it wasn't, as we finished up our meal in silence, my father said, "Peg, you've got a soft heart, that's for sure, but it's your soft brain that causes the problems."*

*Mom got up and brought some blueberry pie to the table. She began cutting it. "Do either of you want some ice cream with your pie?"*

After the fire, the town calmed down back into its typical seasonal routines, which is to say, it settled into its own obscurity. The mill shifts ran, the dairy farmers fed their herds, the loggers logged, and families did what families do - they lived each day as best they knew how, sometimes with love and kindness and sometimes with bitter recriminations, often with both. Winter began its insidious invasion of autumn.

The students of Chaldea High School were shuttled across the Kennebec River to Walloomsac High School. They attended this school during the second shift, from two in the afternoon until seven-thirty in the evening. No one was happy about this turn of events. Though homework was given, detentions assigned, meetings held, and students were still bored, everyone's life in and out of school was totally disrupted, but the small mill town suffered its indignity with New England stoicism. Thus, despite everyone's biological clocks running a bit abnormally, their lives, though a tad skewed, went on.

The Maine Fire Marshall's Office had finished its inspections and inquiries. They could not find a cause for the fire. The spokesperson who was the chief investigator said that his people had never seen anything like this. There was no rhyme or reason for the fire. It was one of a kind. Fires usually were set for a purpose. There didn't seem to be a purpose to the Chaldea High School fire. He had said as much to the local and national papers. "It is all very strange," the chief investigator noted.

The same held true for Police Chief Avery. He had nothing to go on, not a trace of anything incriminating.

Down at the mill, the gossip flew as fast as the paper machine turned out the print for the Sunday Magazine of *The New York Times*. While the men, and some women, could not really gab during the shift, except for a few minutes here and there, whether eating in the cafeteria or on coffee break, the workers were never at a loss for opinions. Eben Titcomb certainly had his.

Eben Titcomb had worked his way up to foreman. It took him years because of the history of the mill, because of the paper industry in Maine, really. When the mill reopened in the early 80's, he had gotten his old job back. The one he lost when the prior owners from New York skipped town one night in the 70s and he arrived to closed gates and no job. Eben and the town shrugged their collective shoulders. Still, Eben was done hard by the closing. He was brought up by a stern, hard-drinking father, an honest farmer too willing to trust others, too often burned by them, and too quick to put a whipping on his son.

Overnight, Chaldea became a ghost town for close to a decade. Boarded-up stores and an empty downtown except for Auberchon's

Hardware, Brown's Feed and Supply Store, and Putnam's grocery. The town's economic funk eventually alleviated itself when a Finnish company, with the financial backing of *The New York Times,* came in, retooled the old machines and installed new German ones that could make paper with almost any type of pulp. The town rejuvenated then, as far as a Central Maine town can rejuvenate itself. The Finnish company made money and *The New York Times* had its special, shiny paper for its magazine section and no more worries of a strike. The Kennebec River continued to flow.

Eben Titcomb sat at the row table and sipped his coffee along with several coworkers hunched over their steaming cups. It was their last break before finishing up the shift and heading home. The florescent lights cast an eerie brightness that sharpened colors and cast stark shadows. Everyone was silent; only the buzz of the soda machine hung over the group.

"Well, at least they've started to clean up the mess," Eben offered. "The new school, when it comes, is going to be out off of Route 41." That'll start something, he thought.

"Can you believe they didn't find a cause?" Bill Orcutt asked no one in particular. "Why would someone do such a stupid thing?"

"At the Selectman's meeting," Eben added, "I told Edda Harlowe that it must've been some crackpot from outta town. There are always weirdos traveling through, up to Sugarloaf or up toward Coburn Gore, probably carrying drugs."

"I dunno, Eben," Iona Corbett said. "Lots of people from away pass through to go skiing all the time. You can't tell who could do such a thing. Anyone could've done it. You always hear on the TV about some horrifying act done by the nicest person who lives next door."

Eben chortled. "You're not saying I'm a suspect, are you, Iona? Well, we'll catch the guy. And he'll be punished for sure. People like that have no morals."

"Hey, Eben, no one's above doing something wrong. Even you, you know," added Raymond Harris. Ray didn't really like Eben's highfalutin' attitude at times and he thought Eben might be headed in that direction now.

"Yeah, why don't you take those softie views of yours and put 'em where sun don't shine. The guy that set that fire did major harm to all of us, to the whole town. It was a pernicious act. It was immoral. He'll have a real chance to do hard time down in Thomaston, for sure."

"If he's caught," noted Norman Turcotte.

"Oh, he'll get caught," Eben said, "Guys like that always get caught,"

"What if he doesn't get caught? That happens, you know. You make the world black and white, good and bad. It's a little more than that, I'd say." Ray took his Styrofoam coffee cup with him as he got up to go back to work, tossing it in the trash. "Jesus, I hate Styrofoam. You'd think a paper mill would have paper coffee cups," he added as he walked out.

Eben hollered after him, "You're wrong, Ray. The Bible says, "An eye for an eye. The bastard will get caught and he will get punished. Mark my words."

# Chapter 8

*I made a good firebomb with a quart milk bottle, a rag, and some gasoline. Or kerosene. Sometimes, I made 'em on Halloween and then tossed 'em out on a street away from where I live. I loved the way the bottle would break and the gasoline would explode into an orange puddle of flame. Very cool. To see that made me smile, made me feel there was nothing I couldn't do.*

*It was late Monday night when I snuck out of the house. I had made the firebomb in the afternoon and stashed it behind the shed. My parents are clueless. They go to bed early. They check on me to see if I'm watching TV or in my room, then I'm on my own. Parents see what they want to see. They don't know me; they don't know Michelle. I wonder if they even know who they are.*

*I walked through the woods toward the Junior High. It was real late, and cold. My ears hurt. No one was around. No one is ever around this town. Even when everyone is around, no one is around. I'd burn it all down if I could. Chaldea, what a joke. I live in nowhere.*

*I skirted around the floodlights at the Junior High and stood in a shadow close to the principal's office. That was the easiest window to hit. The firebomb was heavy because I put a quart of gasoline in the bottle. It was a great toss. I mean it was world class. I took a three-step running start and threw the bomb overhand like a pitcher who throws a high hard one. Smash!*

*Right through the window. I watched a yellow light send shadows in the office, then I saw a tongue of flame come up above the sill. I turned and ran back toward the woods.*

*I was really tired and out of breath when I got back home. Gasping, I slipped in through the kitchen and slunk upstairs to bed. I pulled the comforter up over my ears and thought how the flames would move from the principal's office, how they would devour the wood and the cafeteria and the crappy smell hole old gym that was no bigger than Mr. Resnick's library used to be. That would be two schools. Two schools that were right next to each other. Very cool.*

Benson Tibbets's back bothered him all the time now, so when he unlocked the door to the principal's office in Junior High School on this cold Tuesday morning, he made sure to stand straight up and let his arm and hand do the work. He figured all he had to do was empty the waste baskets, but he brought the mop and pail just in case the linoleum floor around the secretary's desk and into the principal's office was scuffed.

When he walked into the office, a blast of cold air hit him. "Shit," he muttered, "someone left a damn window open." The window by the secretary's desk was shut and frosted. "Hell, John must've smoked a cigar last night before he left and forgot to shut his." He walked into the adjoining office and flipped the light switch. As soon as the florescent lights buzzed on, he stopped dead in his tracks.

"Jesus H. Christ!" Benson said. Strewn across the throw rug in front of the principal's desk lay the shards of a broken milk bottle and remnants of a burned rag with a basketball-sized burn under it. He picked up the principal's phone and dialed the police station. Cold air streamed in from the shattered window. A pain shot through Benson's lower back. He smelled gasoline.

# Chapter 9

*I couldn't believe the Junior High did not burn down. I thought the flames from the firebomb would crawl to the desk and all the paper on it. When I woke up Tuesday morning, I expected to hear all about it from my father. But when I came downstairs, he had left and Mom was busy scrambling eggs.*

*I didn't talk to her much that day. Finally, I ate some lunch, gathered my books, and headed out to the bus stop for the strange ride to Ammon and Walloomsac High School, S.A.D. 45. We were S.A.D. 47. School Administrative District. Ayuh. And the schools up here are "sad." We weren't like the schools down on the coast that had lots of stuff and did lots of things because of the taxes on the homes of the summer people and the rich people that had moved up to enjoy the view of the ocean and to be "in nature." Summer people drove through Chaldea; they never stopped. Maybe for a beer at The Anchor after skiing. Sometimes.*

*All that afternoon at school I thought about the damn Junior High School. I sulked through every period. Coccinella even asked me what was up. I told him I was preoccupied. He loved that. He laughed, then asked me what was preoccupying me. I said, "Oh, my sister." I said what he wanted to hear. It got him off my case.*

*It really bothered me that the Junior High wasn't destroyed like the high school. The flames had betrayed me. They had deserted me and they wouldn't do what I asked them to do. The commander of the flames had to assume tighter control of them. That's what I thought, and that's what I decided to do.*

*By the time school was out it was dark. I hated that. I walked out to the bus, head down, thinking about the Junior High. Who should come up to me?*

*"Hey, pip squeak, you look so down. S'matter? L'il baby having a bad day?" I looked up and saw my sister. I told her to cut the crap. She's usually not like this with me, but when she is, she can really bust on me. Just before I stepped onto the bus, I asked her if she was going home. "Naw, not now. I'm going out with Joy and Marsha. We might go to Piss-Cat. Don't tell." She knew I never would tell. I never told on anyone for anything.*

*I got on the bus. Most of the seats were taken. There was one up back, and wouldn't you know it, who was sitting there but Billy Atwood. Man, I get no breaks.*

ༀ

Chief Avery surveyed the office and scratched his head. He knew that the head selectman, Wendell Davis, had already left a message at the office. "What do you think, John?" he asked.

John Stepkovsky had been principal for five years. A former history teacher at the high school, he had made the move not just for more money, something hard to come by in central Maine, but because he thought he could help the faculty and kids, and heaven knows, teachers and school children needed all the help they could get up in this neck of the woods. "This is too much, Lionel. What's going on? Is this the same person? We've dodged a bullet. The damn Molotov cocktail fizzled out. Jesus! Imagine if this place burned down?"

"Well, something is going on, that's for damn sure. I just don't know what! And I am getting very worried. I am floatin' in the breeze. And no one in the town will want to know that. Are there any kids that are really pissed at you?"

Stepkovsky laughed. "You know, Lionel, the answer is 'no.' You know why? The kids do not stay ticked off. But their parents, that's another matter. I have parents pissed at me every friggin' minute of every friggin' week."

Chief Avery nodded as he peeked into a file cabinet. "We were lucky on this, you know? Just keep alert about anything." He looked at the throw rug and the burn hole. "Any teacher problems?" Avery asked, looking up at the principal.

"Aw, come on Chief, name one teacher who is this screwed up. Hell, if any of my staff was really pissed at me, they'd come in here and bawl me out or punch me out. One or the other. Maybe both."

"I know. I'm just asking. I have to," said the Chief. "Hell, this is one serious mess. Maybe it's simply coincidence. I have no idea."

"Well, the building is standing. We only missed a day of school. The attempt was made and we lucked out. That's it."

"I hope you're right. I really am. Because, I tell ya, we do not need any more of this stuff. You know how folk are around here."

"Ayuh, I know full well how folk are." John looked at the Chief. "I'm going home for the rest of the day. Benson said he'd stay until six."

"Is he okay? How's he doin'?"

"He's fine, a little thrown off but not too much. Still had his sense of humor. Told me that he'd bring his shotgun to work from now on."

Chief chuckled. "Jeez, I remember his wife's funeral. That was one sad occasion. I thought he wouldn't survive her death."

"Well, he's alive and kickin'," said Stepkovsky."He's got his daughter and her kids down in Portland. He's down there twice a month. Says he wants to retire in Rockland and go fishin'."

"God bless him." The Chief grabbed his hat from the principal's desk. "You can toss that rug."

"I hated that rug. Ugly little thing. Benson found it in a closet by the library. It had never been used. First thing Agnes did as secretary was to it put down to spruce the place up."

"Damn glad it was fire retardant." Chief Avery turned and headed out the door, back to his office and to his expected phone message.

# Chapter 10

*I was pissed that the Junior High didn't go up the first time. Really pissed. It's like I had lost a girlfriend, not that I ever had a girlfriend. I thought a good firebomb would make real monster flames. I had no choice but to wait and try again. And I did, for over two weeks, keeping my urge inside like everything else.*

*I'm a master at keeping things quiet. I'm a good learner when I want to be. Everything that happened at school, I kept inside. Every problem I had with so-called friends, I kept inside. Not that I had many friends. Every stupid incident with my father or my sister, I kept a secret. When you keep things inside no one suspects anything because they don't know what you are thinking. They can suppose that they know, but they don't. C & R word here: surmise. People can surmise what is going on in your head but they cannot know unless you tell them.*

*And that's just your mind. No one can ever know your heart. I felt in my heart. Funny, I couldn't explain what I felt. I felt like there was a wild fire down there. A real rip-roarer like those fires out west that no firefighters can control. And it is nasty. You do not want to tangle with it. It is pure meanness. That's what I felt was inside of me. But also there was this other feeling, too.*

*I do not like to think about how I feel deep down. It gives me a headache, sometimes it makes me so upset that I cry. I prefer to keep it a secret. Sometimes I bury it so deep, I forget what I am feeling. That way it doesn't hurt me. Except for the times when feelings surface and I think about them. They rise up in me like the flames in the High School rose up the curtains and how I had hoped the flames in the Junior High would rise up out of the firebomb.*

*These crappy feelings hurt my stomach. They make me ache inside, so I get all down. I start thinking how everyone else acts in school, how everyone has a real friend to talk to at lunchtime, how everyone always is going to meet someone. I don't have anyone to meet. After school, I go down to the library, mostly. Maybe to Coccinella's room where there are usually other kids. The kids talk to me there because everyone respects Coccinella and they know he likes me. With Coccinella, you gotta treat everyone with respect or he gets very angry. The kid's say it's that part of him that bothers them, but they always go to him when they are in trouble or want to talk or want some help, so that part of his personality can't tick them off that much. Boy, there's no getting around someone who cares, especially when it's a teacher.*

*When these feelings get to me, which they usually do when I'm at school and feel alone, then I go to Resnick or Coccinella. But I never tell them about how I feel. One kid called me the Pillsbury Dough Boy. I'm not really fat, just a little pudgy...or, as the kid said, doughy. Then he poked me in my stomach, to imitate that damn commercial. The poke hurt, too. It was a mean poke. C & R would not use mean. They would use the word "malicious."*

*Anyway, I tried to burn the sucker down a second time. I pouted most of the time, which really ticked off my father. Once, at the dinner table, of course, in front of Mom and Sis – yeah, she was home and at the dinner table, if you can believe that – he said, "For Chrissakes, Zeke, what the hell is going on? You been hang dog all week long. You in love or something. Gotta girl there, buddy? That would surprise me, you having a honey." As usual, I looked down at my meal. That's me, always eating my supper at the dinner table with my eyes on the plate.*

*I wanted Mom to tell him to lay off. Or Sis. Usually Sis would be all over him like July flies on manure, but no one said a word. My father just chuckled. And I, naturally, looked down at my plate. Again, the sound of forks and knifes on plates with no talking.*

*When I snuck back into the Junior High school, I kept nothing inside. I found the copier fluid easily. I figured if gasoline wouldn't do it from a milk bottle – too small an area, maybe too concentrated – then maybe if I poured that copier fluid over everything, the desk, the cabinets, the paper, then my flames would behave themselves. Then my monsters would really go crazy. When I left the school, several flames were bluish and they were getting fatter, yellower, and so I left. And smoke formed. I left before any of it got into my clothes.*

*On my way home, I felt relieved, as though I had explained myself to the world. I felt as though I had let out secrets and I was listened to for once. They didn't judge me. They just ate and grew. Sort of like me at the dinner table. The flames had their own secrets.*

∽∾

Chief Corson followed the truck down Main Street toward the Junior High, siren blaring, lights flashing. His mind spun. "Som'bitch," he muttered under his breath as he came to a stop behind the fire truck parked on the front lawn of the Junior High School.

His lieutenant, Randy Holmes, in full fire garb with his coat and boots covered in ash and grey mud, waited for him. His face was flushed. "Chief, it seems the lighter tried to use copier fluid this time. Spread it in John's office, lit it. The flames must've rose quickly with that stuff as a starter. Like a giant cigarette lighter, I'd say. In any case, the sprinkler didn't work right away. The principal's office is lost. Smoke and water damage. Everything else checks out."

"Okay, Randy, thanks. Any clues about our lighter?"

"Not a gosh darn thing."

Chief Corson spit on the new fallen snow. November was coming in harsh, he noted for a second. He looked over and saw that Lionel Avery had arrived. The stolid expression on the Police Chief's spoke volumes.

"Jeezum, Lionel, you look like the Old Man of the Mountains,"

Corson said as he walked over to him.

"Tell me what you know." Avery sighed as he looked at the building.

"I just spoke with Randy who was first on the scene. Said the guy used copier fluid. Lit up John's office like a stogie."

"When's the state Fire Marshall coming?"

" Soon as he gets here. I called him before I left the station."

"Let's all meet at my office after you've done what you've gotta do. I'll be there."

"Hey, about your other comment. This is a problem, but we do not know yet."

"Thanks Rene. I won't be sleepin' at all after this one. Shit, the Junior High school a second time. Same damn place. That is too friggin' strange, isn't it? I wonder who this person is."

"Don't know if it's the same person. Could be a copycat. What's got me is the proximity of both of these attempts to the High School fire."

"You mean the copy of a copycat?" Chief Avery smirked.

"Maybe, just maybe, but most likely not." A smile flashed over Chief Corson's face, vanishing as quickly as it had appeared.

"Are we talkin' about one lighter? What are we talkin' about?" asked the Police Chief.

"I wish the hell I knew. Let's wait and see what the Fire Marshall has to say."

"Ayuh, we got no choice in the matter. This situation is beginning to give me real indigestion."

"You're in a Pepto-Bismol job, my friend."

"Thank you, sir. I'll see you later...unfortunately."

# Hot Spot I

*Flames are peaceful. I feel so calm when I watch a fire. The sight of one grabs a hold of my insides and just settles me down. It's as though I find myself on a deserted island, listening to the surf roll in. I've only seen the ocean once on a field trip, but I remember the waves and the sound they made. Coccinella took us to somewhere near Portland. I remember how excited we were. I remember him fighting with the principal about going. Of course, Rowell didn't want anybody out of the building. The teams and cheerleaders sure, but us, the type of kids in our class, no way. I remember hearing Rowell, late during last period days before the trip, say to Coccinella, "Why do you want to take those gorillas to the ocean for?" I never heard Coccinella's reply.*

*It's about the starting of a fire, too. That's pure fun. It's intense. Once I had fixed on a target, I'd begin to plan how to do it. Planning to set a fire is like a puzzle to me, a hard puzzle. I remember that Mr. Resnick was always doing the puzzles in* The New York Times. *I can still picture him. He'd be sitting behind his desk in the library, swivel chair pushed back and turned slightly away from the entrance and toward the file cabinet. His legs were crossed and the puzzle page rested on his thigh. He would be rubbing his forehead with his left hand and holding a pen in his right, ready to write some strange word only he would know.*

*Resnick and Coccinella fascinated me. They loved words. The way I loved fire. They played with words. I played with fire. Fire is my language.*

*I don't speak good. I mean, I don't use good words all the time. I use C & R words to explain myself exactly. That's what Resnick would always say to me, usually on afternoons when I was helping him in the High School library, stacking books and putting away magazines and newspapers. He'd tell me words were special, that they had a life of their own and when you learned their meaning you gained power over the world, you could explain how you felt and you could describe your experiences so someone else could understand. I knew what he was trying to tell me. I never saw anyone get so excited about words. He actually knew where words came from! He said they had histories, that most of them were older than any family in Chaldea or Maine.*

*Coccinella was just like him. He would quote poetry in class. He didn't care. If he liked something or had read something somewhere and thought we should hear it, he'd read it to us. If he had his way, I'm sure he would read to our class everything that he ever read! He loved words. One day, he went off on the word 'linoleum' just because he liked the sound of it. He talked about the word for an hour it seemed, about the sound of 'l' and 'm' and then about their sounds together. Doing things like that made the kids shake their heads and think he was crazy, even though they liked him.*

*In a way, maybe I hung around them sometimes because these two guys were like flames. They were like flames because they could suddenly go off on almost anything you were talking about, hunting, guns, the mill, the river, Chaldea, Maine, America, hell, they could discuss anything. Like flames they could grow off of fuel. Words fueled them.*

*Their ideas would grow and grow until whatever subject they were talking about was totally consumed! They were like that. They fascinated me in that way. And why can't people be like flames? I certainly saw flames as like people. Really, I saw them as my friends.*

ڪ

Dr. Proctor knew the judge would show little mercy on Zeke. Though he was underage and there's only so much the judge could do. Thank God no one was killed or injured. There hadn't been a serious crime in this town for fifty years. Figures it would happen to me, she thought.

At least he's been writing in his journal while here. She had to try and get him to talk more, but it would be tough. The journal was helping. She knew she needed much more time with him.

The phone startled her. Police Chief Lionel Avery spoke slowly. He was tired. The fires had burned him out and everyone in the town, too. "Well, how's it going?"

"Not enough time with this kid, Chief."

"That's something none of us have. We've got to finish this up and get on with life. The town's had enough, I'd say."

"I know."

"In any case, the prosecution is connecting him only to the two fires where we found his prints."

"I'll be informing your office about the status of my report in a week or so. Knowing the court's proceedings regarding juveniles they'll want all the facts, as much information as possible, so they'll want my extensive evaluation."

"Don't you just love your job, Dr. Proctor?"

Dr. Proctor smiled. "I'll see you at the church supper on Saturday." She hung up, sighed. Zeke's parents sprang to mind. She'd have to talk to them. She did not look forward to that session. That Eben Titcomb was a beaut. That whole family....

She picked up the file on Ezekiel Titcomb. She thumbed through it, then dropped it back on her desk. She rubbed her eyes. When she squeezed them shut, she saw stars, only the stars were the words of Ezekiel Titcomb. She picked up his journal. The new entries needed to be read, analyzed, and discussed with the patient.

# Chapter 11

*Mr. Coccinella would tell us stories from books that he had read. There was this one that I really liked, a story from Dante about two souls in hell. The souls were flames. They were wrapped around each other forever. That was their punishment – to be flames and continually wrapped around each other. So, they burn each other up.*

*I keep wondering how flames can touch one another. Do they? Don't they sort of melt together, become one? It doesn't make any difference if it is a big flame or a small one, I don't think. Two flames burn toward each other then, all of a sudden, when they touch they're one big flame.*

*It's great to picture, two flames burning, wrapped around each other. But I don't know if I've ever seen two flames like that. I must've when I gazed into the woodstove in the living room because it has a glass front so you can watch the logs burn. I must've watched a zillion fires since I was a small kid.*

*What gets me is that Dante made their souls into flames. They're alive, flames are, so why shouldn't they have souls. I wonder if every time I light a fire, I am bringing a former sinful person up from hell to burn in my world.*

Walloomsac High School, like any other high school in rural Maine, was no architectural dream come true. It was a sprawling, square brick building in the style of the sixties. It could be a nursing home, a State Office building, or a warehouse. Which is what it was on a good day now that the building was used by two separate sets of high schoolers from grades nine to twelve. Still, it was kept neat and clean. Otis Stearns, one of the two custodians on the premises who worked from three until eleven Monday through Friday, handled the library and main offices and the classrooms along the south side of the school. Artemis Bailey handled the north side, which included the auditorium, gym, and science classrooms. The two had worked together at Walloomsac High School for over twenty years. The kids knew them and they knew the kids, though the kids' behavior and language could make them scratch their heads sometimes. Their own kids were all grown and their grandkids were almost grown, too.

Otis, with his half walk, half limp, trundled into the school library to empty the wastebaskets in the reading area and beside the two desks in the librarian's office. He left his large waste bucket on wheels outside the library entrance. A few trips back and forth with the wastebaskets would get him an extra ten, maybe fifteen minutes, toward coffee break. He and Artemis liked to have their coffee together in the English Department office. They could sit and look out toward the "mighty Kennebec" as Artemis called it, the once important logging river now reclaimed and used by fishermen, kayakers, canoers and campers.

After emptying the wastebaskets in the library, Otis ambled over to the librarian's office. As he reached down to pick up the gray basket, he smelled an odd odor that he thought was gasoline. He surveyed the office and saw nothing out of line. There were two crooked piles of books strewn on one desk, library cards and magazines lying around the two piles. There were no bottles or cans on the desk. He sniffed again. That's gasoline, he thought. "Well, I'd better get Art," he said aloud. And off he shuffled to the other end of the building. Artemis was coming out of the chemistry lab when he spied Otis.

"Hey, old man, it ain't break time yet," he said.

"Nope, it ain't. I want ya to come over to the library. I think I smell gasoline."

"You gotta be kidding."

"I wish the hell I was. Maybe it's all in my head. I dunno, but I think I smell it."

"Then let's go see."

"Shit, Art," Otis said as he turned to walk with his friend.

The two men stood in the librarian's office. They both scanned the room, looking in file cabinets, under the desks, in the two small book closets. Nothing. Artemis sniffed the air again. "Ayuh, I smell it, for sure. It's gasoline."

"Where the hell is it coming from? She's gotta be comin' from somewhere." The two custodians looked over the office space again. Otis walked out into the large reading area. "I don't smell anything out here. It's gotta be in there," he called.

Artemis looked up at the square, acoustic ceiling tiles."You know, we should buy stock in the company that makes those damn tiles. They must be in every ceiling of every office and every school in the world, let alone the country," he said to Otis who was now back at his side.

"That company and the one that makes the orange cones and barrels for road construction," Otis added. He chuckled and Artemis chuckled, too. "Does it seem that the smell is coming down from the ceiling, Art?," he asked.

"Hell, how would gasoline or something soaked in gasoline get up there?" Artemis wondered. They looked at each other, and their eyes widened.

"Call the sheriff's office, Art. I'll go get a stepladder," said Otis. He shuffled off with what seemed a little haste, a slow gait like a reluctant black bear that had been shooed from a raspberry patch.

# Chapter 12

*I am my own flame. So we're all separate ones. My idea is that if we're all flames then we can burn each other. In real life, the big ones devour the little ones. In Dante's hell, there's a big flame that is two souls. Coccinella once described it to us. It was the soul of Ulysses twisted around another soul. I can't remember who the other soul was. I felt sorry for a Greek hero being in hell. But it sort of seemed okay, too, because, you know, at least his soul was swallowed in a whopper flame with another one forever, even though it was in hell.*

*I'm talking about being consumed. I feel like I am always being consumed by other people, especially my father. I seem to be gobbled up by every other flame in the entire world. When I light a fire, it's my turn. I do the consuming, but I really don't do it. I let the flames do it for me since they are a part of me. They do what I want them to do usually.*

*The flames I create do not have a soul. They are alive but they aren't human souls like Dante's. Mine are soulless flames whose only job is to destroy. I love it when they destroy buildings. Hundreds of feet high. I feel invincible.*

"Lionel. You better get here to the high school. I'm on my way right this minute. Someone smelled gasoline." Chief Avery had known and worked with Ammon's Sheriff Milton Nichols for ten years. The man was all business, fair, levelheaded, and bright in a crisp, no nonsense way. Chief Avery liked him. He also knew that, if it came to it, two heads, two departments, were better than one.

As he drove over the Kennebec toward the school, Chief Avery realized that things in town were going to get out of hand. When word of this incident, whether serious or not, got out - and it would get out, that was a given - all hell would break loose. People would talk, talk some more, there would be a growing concern, then even more talk, meetings, gossip, and ultimately a low-grade panic would settle over the town like winter fog over the river and the low-lying land bordering it. Small towns do not like mysteries, and they like fires even less. When small towns panic, everything goes haywire.

Any unfamiliar face gets scrutinized, maybe even harassed if it stays too long. Insipid ideas gain credence, and those ideas usually lead to stupid actions – keeping guns loaded at all times, riding around looking for suspects, being afraid of every little thing out of the ordinary. Small towns were good at knowing about the little things. They were especially good at nurturing fear.

These thoughts bogged down Chief Avery as he unbuckled his seat belt and got out of his cruiser. "Good timing, Lionel," said Sheriff Nichols, who stood with two other of his men by his vehicle.

"I hightailed it."

"Let's go in and see what's what," said the sheriff.He walked along with Chief Avery; his two officers preceded them and disappeared inside quickly. Sheriff Nichols stopped at the entrance. He turned to Chief Avery. "Wait a sec, Lionel. Let's talk for a minute."

It was dark. Stars filled the clear November sky; the Milky Way coursed above, a cloudy white river running north to south.

The yellow school lights spilled out of the windows of the main office. The two men watched their breath roll into balls and eventually disappear in front of them. A cold one tonight. "Hunting season will be over before you know it," said Sheriff Nichols.

"I even haven't been out. All this business," said Chief Avery.

"Me neither. My son comes up from Portland to go for deer. He stays with us for a few days before Thanksgiving and goes. I don't go much now. Lost the taste for it."

"Milt, this thing tonight, if we find something, will cause quite a stir. Is that what you wanted to talk about?"

"It will."

"Did you call the Fire Marshall yet?"

"Nope. I wanted to wait. Talk to you. See what's up. People over here are still talking about the Junior High School and that second try at it."

"People are a tad on edge. This will tip the cart. I appreciate you waiting to talk with me though. Really."

"Not a problem. If this is what I think it is, you will have your hands full, that's certain."

"Well, let's see what's what."

Inside the librarian's office, several ceiling tiles were strewn on the carpet. One of the two Ammon police officers had climbed the ladder and was peering into the crawl space above the tiles. Only his legs showed. The other officer held the ladder and peered up at his partner. The two custodians stood away from them, behind one of the two desks.

"I got it. Looks like a plastic can. The cover wasn't sealed tight." The officer's torso was still hidden as he spoke. Slowly, he stepped down carrying a white plastic pail. He set the pail on the floor. Sheriff Nichols and Chief Avery stepped over to look at it. "Put it in the cruiser, Boyd," the Sheriff said, "We'll check it for prints back at the station."

"There won't be any prints, I bet," said Chief Avery to the Sheriff.

"Agreed."

"How the hell did he get that bucket up there?"

"Damned if I know. This guy is slick. I wonder how he was going to start the fire."

# Chapter 13

*Walloomsac High School was the pits. All of us from Chaldea hated the place. Who wants to be in someone else's school? It didn't look right, it didn't smell right, and no one knew where to go half the time, at least at first.*

*After a week or two, I felt these feelings burning in me again. I could say that the black bear inside me growled but that would sound stupid. But, actually, that is what happened. A real big animal flame was building up inside me, growing and growing. Maybe it was because I felt as invisible in this school as did in Chaldea. Maybe it was because Jeremy Tompkins called me Zeke the Beak. I hate that name. I don't have a big nose. He and everyone else says it just to hurt me. They know it gets under my skin. Most things get under my skin, actually, even though I don't show it.*

*I had to feed this animal flame in me because I felt like I was going to explode. This feeling overtook me on a Saturday night when my father had a real blowout with Michelle. By Sunday, after all the family crap, I was a mess and the animal flame in me growled like hell. I had to get right inside myself or I'd go crazy. I had to burn Walloomsac High School down to the ground. It's weird to talk like this, but it's how I felt.*

*Naturally, my father started the whole thing with Michelle. But Michelle really started everything by just being Michelle. I should let you in on her. She's tough. She takes nothing from no one, not even from Atwood and his crowd or the prissy cheerleaders and college bound kids.*

*And she's smart. Not just common sense smart. She knows things I would never suspect she would know. Things like the second law of thermodynamics. I mean, come on, who knows that in high school? Who knows that at all? I have no idea how she knows this stuff. I saw her once come out of the town library on a Saturday afternoon. I damn near fell off my bicycle.*

*But Sis is ornery, as my parents would say. Whatever side you take, she'll take the opposite, just to piss you off. If you say that G Period Study Hall is a waste of time, she'll come out and say something like, "You know, it actually makes sense to have a study hall at the end of the day so that we can unwind, do some work, maybe get a pass to get out early and go to work or go down town." You know she hates the study hall and wants out of it, but she'll argue for it. She does what she wants to do. This includes dating older men and doing drugs. She could care less about her reputation.*

*Oh, I forgot to mention one other thing. Michelle is beautiful. She has a body on her. I think this is why everyone at school is afraid of her. She looks like she is twenty-five. Really. Her hair is strawberry blonde and shoulder length. She is five feet ten inches tall with serious legs. A real tall drink of water, a looker. I am proud of her beauty, but I am embarrassed by it, too. I guess that I am afraid of it like everybody else. I mean she attracts attention. Once, after biology class, I noticed the new men's phys. ed. teacher from Orono checking her out in the hallway. She was walking like she knew he was staring at her. I looked away before he saw me watching him. That ticked me off. I started thinking bad stuff like the kind that happens between teachers and students. You hear about it all the time. I've heard some stories about teachers and students in Chaldea, but I don't like to mention it. But it's there; it's always there, underneath everything. Just like my feelings lie underneath my smile.*

*Anyway, let me tell you about Michelle and The Titcomb Explosion. The C & R word to describe what happened is "incendiary." And it was Michelle who ignited the fuse to the bomb. The bomb being my father. One Saturday afternoon, maybe a week before Thanksgiving, Michelle comes down from her room and walks into the kitchen.*

*The house is really warm so it's not like you had to wear layers of clothes. Our wood stoves are great, as I said. I love them. Wood heat is the best; it's real heat. The heat soaks you, not like the fake heat from oil or gas that tickles your skin but doesn't warm you. If city people knew how true and deep wood heat is and how it warms you to the bone, they'd all have wood stoves. There'd be a pall of wood smoke over every city.*

*Anyway, Michelle is wearing a see-through halter-top with no bra, a pair of skimpy panties, and no slippers or shoes. Her hair is mussed, and she looks as though she has had quite a night. Her eyes are half closed and she is moving slowly. I have no idea why she does this to herself.*

*Mr. Holier than Thou has just gotten back from a selectmen's meeting about the incident at Walloomsac, so he's in no mood for crap from anyone. He's sitting at the kitchen table reading* The Sentinel. *Mom is at the sink washing some of the good plates to use for Thanksgiving. Mom, she's always one step ahead of things. I love her for that. I'm standing by the wood stove about to head up to my room to look at a map of my street.*

*Just as Michelle pulls the Tropicana out of the fridge, my father looks up at her, his eyes staring at her over his reading glasses. He looks her over, up and down, puts his paper down and calmly says, as though he is announcing the arrival of a train, "The tramp has arisen!" Then silence, a very loud silence.*

*Michelle calmly filled her glass with orange juice, set it on the kitchen table, put the juice back in the fridge, slowly picked up the filled glass, walked over to dad and said to him. "You're a friggin' asshole."*

*My father jumped up and slapped her face so hard she went sprawling across the kitchen against the hutch, spilling and breaking glasses and dishes. "You bitchin' whore!" he said, "Don't you ever…."*

*Mom turned from the sink and screamed, "Eben, what are you doing? Are you crazy?" She ran to Michelle and stooped down to help her. Michelle was crumpled up on the floor. She is way too proud to cry, but tears swelled in her eyes. She just stared at him from the floor. Mom helped her up.*

*My father, Mr. Big Stuff, stood by his chair, chest out, eyes popping out of his head, and screamed, "You are not my daughter. You're the town pump. You screw every goddamn guy you find. You hang around with those hippies over in Grimes doing drugs. You parade around town, cheap. You're a nothin'. Worse than worm dirt. If it weren't for your mother, you'd be outta this house! You hear? You're an embarrassment to this family. Friggin' tramp."*

*Mom was holding Michelle around the shoulders. Mom started crying really hard. Michelle was shaking and quietly sobbing. She finally broke loose from Mom and ran upstairs to her room. I went upstairs, but I didn't dare go near Michelle though I wanted to. I went to my room. I wanted to give Michelle a hug, and tell her that I hated the guy, too. But I didn't. I kept everything in, like I always do.*

*I sat at my desk, leaning forward on my elbows with my hands over my face. I heard the terrible fight downstairs. It was screaming and yelling, but it was muffled. You couldn't really make out the words, just the sounds of the words. I could tell the difference between the words coming from my mother and those coming from my father. They each had a different pace so that this fight sounded like angry music. Coccinella told our class once how Robert Frost said listening to the sound of words in a poem was like listening to a conversation in the next room that you heard but you couldn't make out the words. Or something like that. All I knew is I did not want to know the words to the fight my parents were having. But I sure as hell could hear the sound of their words and I could pretend what sense they made.*

*When the fight ended, I sat up, listening for something else. Silence. My heart was beating fast. I was mad. I didn't feel good in my stomach, either. The Titcomb Explosion. Every time I survive one, I dig a little deeper into the hole of myself. What else can I do?*

Margaret Titcomb pushed her way down the cereal aisle. Wheaties for Zeke. Cheerios for Michelle.....when and if she eats. Maybe some Raisin Bran for Eben, even though he won't eat it. Hippy food, he calls it. If it isn't bacon and eggs, it's hippy food. She'd like him to eat some granola for his health. The whole grain kind down at the natural food store run by the Seventh Day

Adventists is quite good, she'd heard. As she continued contemplating breakfast food, she heard the sound of a shopping cart approaching from the rear.

"Did you hear? What happened over at Walloomsac? It's scary, I think. There's an arsonist on the loose, I'm sure of it." It was Jeanette Lowe, local busybody and part-time secretary in Town Hall. "Imagine hiding gasoline to use later? If Otis Stearns hadn't smelled it who knows what would've happened. It's funny, an old-timer like him saving the school."

Margaret smiled, but didn't speak. She reached for a box of Muesli and began reading the small print. Eben would never eat this. "Well, no one really knows much of anything, right at the moment. Eben says the police and the fire marshall's office have no clues about who might have put the gasoline up in the ceiling."

"I'm scared. Who knows what will happen next? What happens if there are people in a building when it burns down?"

"Look, I have no idea what will happen. The best thing to do is to keep your eyes open. Let the police and fire departments do what they are supposed to do."

"I'll watch, all right. I told Mildred Ketchum that it's gotta be somebody from Skowhegan, definitely."

"Why on earth would you say such a thing? How can you possibly know?"

"You know how people are in that town. They're jealous of the millwork and they think we're bumpkins. Always have."

Margaret put the Muesli back on the shelf. You can't teach an old dog, she thought. Then she laughed quietly to herself since she realized that she was referring both to her husband's eating habits and Jeanette's mindlessness.

"I dunno why you're smiling at a time like this," Jeanette Lowe added. "Something bad will come of this. You wait and see." She pushed her cart to the end of the aisle and turned left toward the frozen food.

# Chapter 14

*I told you that I like keeping secrets, and I have thousands of them. My whole life is a secret. I'll never tell anyone how I got the bucket of gasoline up in the ceiling. I'm really sorry that I didn't get to use it in the library. It was a great place to start a fire, and would've done some serious damage, because of the books and magazines and it being in the middle of the school. Mr. Resnick would have been hurt again. But it wasn't his library this time, so maybe that would make him feel less bad. But come to think of it, he would have been hurt twice. He would have been...get this..."scorched." That was sick, I know. Coccinella and Resnick would like it that I can play with words like this. They would not like what I was doing even though playing with words is like playing with fire.*

*I like it that the fires create a scene in town among everyone. Even potential flames create a scene. I know because there was this sense of fear now at Walloomsac. Everybody felt a little on edge. I felt so in control compared to everyone in school, even the teachers, who were talking about the gasoline, about where the next fire would be. Even Atwood and his crew were talking it up. I heard them near the Walloomsac gym once as I was trying to sneak past them. "The guy's whacko," Atwood was saying to one of his sidekicks, "He's got some problems. I'd be glad to beat those problems outta him, if I knew who he was." His friends laughed.*

*"Hey, Beak, you couldn't even lift a bucket of gasoline, could you?" Atwood said as I walked past. He looked like he was going to come toward*

*but instead he turned his back to talk to his friends. I smiled to myself as I walked down the corridor.*

*It wasn't only kids and teachers at school who were talking now about the school fire attempt. The newspapers mentioned it. Not just* The Sentinel, *but also* The Portland Press Herald *had an article. Our Social Studies teacher, Ms. Brown, read it to us. I heard Coccinella and Resnick talking about a journalist from Boston coming up, but they stopped talking when I walked into the classroom.*

*Flames get attention. And if you're the lighter, you get attention, too. But it's a secret attention. That's the best kind for someone like me. Knowing this makes me feel satisfied. I feel a kind of popular in a reverse way, if that makes sense. I need a better word. It's hard to find the right word, but I think the word might be... "prominence." I feel secretly prominent. I feel important to myself.*

"Hey, Mr. Coccinella, what do you think of all this stuff?"

David Coccinella turned from the blackboard to see Maddy Turcotte standing in front of him. "Oh, hey, Maddy" he said, stalling for time, "Well, what does one say about arson? Fortunately, no one has been hurt. Not much else to say."

"I thought that you would say something like that. You and Resnick have been pretty quiet about the whole thing."

"We're worried like everyone else, but what is there to say? We don't know anything. And, I think I can speak for Mr. Resnick on this point, it is not good to discuss something you know nothing about."

"But we all know a lot. We know what happened."

"A few simple facts. That's it. You do not know more. So, you can talk about facts, which are already obvious or you can surmise and wonder. That is what I call gossip."

"But aren't you bothered by all of these facts?"

"The facts exist. They simply are there. They do not bother me.

How can facts bother? What I am bothered by is the act of arson. There is something very sinister about setting fires. And to schools no less. Such symbols. Schools are our community."

"Yeah, right, a suffocating culture for us." Maddy smiled.

"Okay, kiddo, off with you. I've got work to do. "

Coccinella looked at the essays on his desk, shook his head, and decided to head to the library to say hello to Morris instead of getting a start on them before heading home. As he walked into the back office of the Walloomsac library where Morris worked now, he gazed up at the ceiling. He could hardly tell that a whole new ceiling had been installed.

Morris Resnick sat checking the *Library Journal*. He was always looking at reviews and articles for books that the district should own. He kept the best library system in the state on a shoestring budget that was aided every now and again by extra funds from the superintendent's budget and by the Mill.

"Ciao, Morris, how's the aroma in here nowadays?"

"Yeah, cute, David. I have spent days telling students that, no, it is not gasoline that they smell. Lots of fun, you know."

"Ah, I see that your day has been filled with bookish endeavors. Listen, you want to come over for a beer this afternoon?"

"Why don't you drop by on the way home? Stay for supper," said Resnick. He got up to put a stack of books back onto a book cart. It was then that he noticed Zeke standing in the doorway. Coccinella put his hand on the kid's shoulder. "How are you, Zeke?

"Fine, Mr. Coccinella. I came to help Mr. Resnick."

"Good man," said Coccinella as he left.

"You can shelf these books for me, if you'd like," said Resnick.

"Great, thanks. What else can I do after this?"

"Get those done first, and then we'll see. Okay?"

"I can stay as long as you want."

"Thanks, Zeke. I appreciate it. I really do."

Zeke smiled a warm smile, turned, and pushed the cart out toward the stacks.

# Chapter 15

*It was the Sunday after The Titcomb Explosion when my insides really started getting upset. Michelle wasn't around all day and night. I have no idea where she was. My father and Mom were not speaking.*

*Lots of plates being slammed on tables. Lots of muttering under the breath. Lots of "Ask your father." and "Ask your mother." Lots of avoiding each other. I avoided both of them by staying in my room.*

*I spent lots of time drawing a picture of our street. It's a street where we live even though it's called a road. It's a road because of the farms further up the hill, but it's a street down here because the houses are so close together even though the backyards peter out into the woods. I tried to draw a real detailed map of my part of Blackstrap Road. I tried to draw the yards of each house, I tried to remember what was in each yard, and if I did then I would draw it on the map. I was totally into it. I'd known these houses and this road my whole life. I knew a lot about each house. Everybody knows their own neighborhood.*

*I'm not going to say anything about what you want me to say. I knew what I was doing and I knew how to sneak around my neighborhood. I'll say this: I was taking a break from my map, lying on my bed. I was curled up on my side and after a while, I noticed that I was rocking back and forth. I didn't realize what I was doing at first because I started thinking about my father and The Titcomb Explosion. I started thinking how he must've hated Michelle and me. And even Mom. That's what I started thinking.*

*Then I realized I was rocking back and forth to beat the band. I stopped when I realized what I was doing. It was just when I stopped that I realized that the only place on our street that wasn't an old large house was the trailer that had been put on the vacant land there when I was about seven. Everyone was pissed about the trailer but nothing could be done.*

*I turned over and stared up at the beams in the ceiling above my bed. I decided the trailer didn't belong. Also, I decided that I could send a signal to my father by getting rid of the trailer. Maybe it was a way of telling him that I had no use for him. Imagine having no use for your father.*

*The flames would wake him up. The flames would announce to him that he was being watched, that he had to pay attention to others. To me. My flames would tell him who I was. Flames deliver messages. They are my messengers. They inform the world that I'm real.*

Blackstrap Road curls away from Route 32, one of two main roads that lead into Chaldea, and heads up Bailey's Hill. There are several houses, including the Titcombs home, that stand fairly close in a small half mile area at the beginning of the road when you immediately turn onto it. After that half-mile, hay fields, pastures, and woods border the road.

Mabel Stuckey's trailer sat directly on the road leaving about five yards between the front door and the macadam. In summer, her four kids were always playing out front and everyone in town wondered how none had ever been run over as they would dart out into the street without mind to traffic, even the rare logging truck that sometimes would take the road as a short cut.

Mabel had been in the trailer since her firstborn, and it was beat up, secondhand beat up, but the plumbing worked and so did her wood stove. There were no outside lights to put on at night, so it was dark around her place. Mabel didn't feel safe because of no outside lights but she couldn't do anything about it. She was jobless now, living on the dole, trying to raise four kids between the ages of six months and four years. Mabel's ex never came by or helped her. He had moved up somewhere in Washington Country, and even his family hadn't heard from him two years. He'd left after the last child, telling Mabel that she had gotten too fat and the kids made too much noise.

Mabel was standing in her nightgown, burping her little one near the kitchen window, when she noticed a strange orange-yellow light that seemed to come out from behind her trailer. Frightened, she picked up the phone to call the police. She forgot that the phone had been disconnected, so she grabbed her kid and hurried outside to see what the matter was. The flames had already climbed up to the roof of the trailer. Mabel screamed. She started to run next door to the neighbor's house, but then realized her other three kids were asleep inside. She ran back inside. Half the trailer was in serious flames just as she hustled the kids outside.

By this time, Mrs. Emery, her neighbor, was outside on her lawn. "Mabel, get the kids over here fast," she yelled. The trucks, sirens screaming, roared closer then suddenly appeared. "Get 'em inside, Mabel. Quick."

"Come on kids. Philip, get going. Terry, hurry. Gene, take your sister." The kids, in their stocking pajamas, trotted up on Mrs. Emery's porch where her husband gathered them in the house. The kids, too scared to say anything, trotted inside.

The fire scene was loud and hectic. Chief Corson watched his men hose down what was left of the trailer. It was a total loss. "Formaldehyde," he said to Lieutenant Holmes. "The whole construction is soaked in that stuff. Thank God she got out with the kids, huh?"

"For sure, Chief. I'll finish this job up. We'll wet down the Emery's just to play it safe. You gonna call you know who?"

"Oh yeah. Me and the fire Marshall's office are family. Damn. Randy, we gotta really check this out."

"We'll check the place out tonight before we leave. But you see for yourself, there ain't much. Complete destruction. A quick, hot fire."

Chief Corson sighed and looked at the wet mess, barely smoldering. The acrid smell from the fire dug into his head. He turned toward Emery's place where Mabel stood on the porch, draped with an overcoat provided by Mrs. Emery, stunned. Her little Emma cried in her arms.

"Mother of God, what will happen? What can I do, Mrs. Emery? I have lost everything, clothes, food, furniture. The car. I got nothin', Dot. I had nothin' to begin with, you know, but I got less than that now."

"You'll stay with Herbert and me until we figure things out."

Mabel looked at little Emma. "What're my kids going to eat? What'll they wear? There's no breakfast." Mabel Stuckey burst into tears that burned her face. Mrs. Emery put her arms around her shoulders and brought her inside. The sharp November air stung her eyes.

Other neighbors gathered on the street. Dot Emery had called Peggy Titcomb after she had Herbert call the fire department. She'd heard Mabel's screams, run to a side window by the pantry, seen the flames beginning to devour the back end of the trailer. Peggy came down the street after the fire trucks had shut down. She had a bag of groceries and some of Michelle and Zeke's old clothes. She didn't knock; she simply walked into the Emery's house. They'd been neighbors for forty years. Dot and Herbert had watched Eben and Peggy move onto Blackstrap Road, have kids, and had watched the Titcomb kids grow up.

"I've got some breakfast food for the kids, Mabel. Dot, I brought some flour and mix for you, just in case. I brought some clothes, too. Eben says he can bring two cots over once the trucks leave," Peggy said as she walked into the foyer that led to the kitchen.

Mabel cried harder. Dot Emery smiled and went to Peggy to

help her with the bags. Herbert Emery stood in front of the large living room window. He turned from gazing out at the goings on outside and nodded to Peggy. Then he looked back out at the fire trucks. They were wrapping hoses, putting back tools onto side compartments. The fire had burned itself out. The firemen had doused it good and checked for hot spots in the rubble.

# Chapter 16

*I stayed in bed. I pretended to sleep through the incident. I wanted nothing to do with what happened. Flames, that's what I thought about lying there in bed. I thought about how when flames got big no one could really deal with them. You had to have firemen put them out with water and foam. They had to hack at doors and walls with axes and other tools to stop the flames. Flames, really then, are unstoppable. I feel unstoppable when I make the flames.*

*When my father hit Michelle that Saturday afternoon, I wanted to stand up and yell. I wanted to shout, "I am the great flame creator. I am Ezekiel the bringer of fire. I am your worst nightmare. I will consume you and everything you touch." Of course, I could never say. Like I said. I keep everything to myself.*

*Besides, I could never, ever talk to my father like that. He'd kill me. He'd make what he did to Michelle look like a love tap. Every time he hit me, I made a promise to myself that he, or anybody for that matter, will never know who I am. I know who I am.*

*My full name is Ezekiel. You know who Ezekiel is. He's a prophet. Prophets know about the other world. They have visions. They warn people about destruction. That's me. I warn people. Prophets can even threaten people when they do the wrong things. That's how they remind people that they need to get straight.*

*I would never threaten anyone. How can I? I'm invisible. I'd like to threaten my father, Atwood, and all those cheerleader Barbies who walk by me and look right through me, if they even look at me at all. I don't use words; I use fire.*

*Ezekiel means "God is strengthened." I strengthen God whenever I bring flames into this world. I'm sending a message to my world.*

*I would never say any of this stuff out loud. But I think it all the time. I think it when I am in church. I sit in the pew next to my mother. I keep my head bowed. I try not to look at her. I try not to look up much. Once in a while, I look up at the altar. And I try to never look at my father, even when he is doing the deacon stuff that he does. When I am in church, I am Ezekiel.*

Lieutenant Randy Holmes was just about to put his eight of clubs on the red nine of hearts, when the call came. The warehouse on Blackstrap Road was on fire. The lieutenant, a seasoned fire fighter, dressed and rushed to the garage area.

Chief Corson had arrived, his equipment on, and had started Engine One, the water truck. Two other volunteers already sat inside the cab. A third raced the motor of Engine Number Two. Lieutenant Holmes jumped in it. Sirens blared as the two trucks rolled toward the fire. It had been a week to the day of the Stuckey trailer fire. Same area.

The fire blazed. Deep orange flames rose from the second story warehouse windows, rolling up toward the night sky. "Okay, men, get the hoses up to that second floor. Randy, take two men around back and get inside, if you can," Chief Corson shouted. Three more trucks arrived, their drivers in full gear.

"Hey, guys, around back with Randy. Hurry up," Corson barked. There was no sense calling Skowhegan. By the time they got here, the warehouse would be gone. The fire intensified. As Corson looked up, a section of the warehouse roof caved in. Flames, smoke, and sparks billowed higher.

Corson got on the walkie-talkie. "Randy, you guys okay?" he asked. After a few seconds of static, his lieutenant's voice replied. "Yeah, Chief, we saw it coming. We backed out. It's a loss back here. We're watching the wind, too. It's gettin' breezy, Chief. You notice it?"

Corson looked across the street at a stand of white pines. They were swaying gently. Jesus H. Christ, he thought, that's all we need. "Ayuh, I hear you."

He continued to watch the men spraying the warehouse with water. "Get that smaller hose over there, will ya Jeff," he ordered. Jeff Mullins, a young, dependable volunteer who worked day shift at the Mill, ran to the water truck. As the kid lugged the hose, the wind gusted. Chief Corson watched the fire. The flames sprouted from every window now on the first floor, ranging from the middle of the building now that the roof had collapsed and the tar shingles were burning. Smoke roiled up. It looked like hell itself; it smelled like hell itself. Sparks squiggled high enough so the increasing breeze could catch and carry them. Large sparks.

The fire spread. Jeff Mullin caught sight of a small blaze on the Emery's back porch. The Emery place, which stood a good fifty yards, maybe seventy-five, of lawn from the burning warehouse, was a magnificent Victorian farmhouse that the Emery's had carefully restored over the years. Mullin hollered over to Lieutenant Holmes, "Randy! Look! Sonofabitch!"

"Oh God," answered the Lieutenant, "Get over there! I'll get the Chief."

Chief Corson's face contorted in the flashing blue, white, and red lights. He watched Chief Avery and his two men govern traffic and keep stray onlookers, people who followed the police and fire talk on their CBs or short waves, at bay. The neighbors who lived on Blackstrap Road milled around at a safe distance. None of them could see the little fire that had started on the Emery's back porch. When he received the call on his walkie-talkie from his lieutenant, he noticed Eben Titcomb standing on his front lawn with his hands on his hips.

Eben Titcomb could not believe what he saw. Flames towered in the dark. Why would someone torch the warehouse? Something was going on and he wanted to know what it was. He'd try like hell to find out. At least it's only the warehouse this time. Maybe someone would come in, buy the parcel and build a house, enhance the neighborhood. Someone'll definitely buy the Stuckey land, he felt.

Secretly, he was happy that place burned down. Eben had led the neighborhood charge to keep that good for nothing Keith Stuckey from dumping that piece of crap between the Emerys and the Crowells. A trailer between houses. There goes the value of everyone's home.

No Stuckey was hurt. Good riddance to that tribe anyway. Eben was sick of Peggy yakking about and helping out that fat shrew with the snotty-nosed, half-clad kids. Hell, he thought, they are right out of one of those damn novels about rural Maine. Like that damn book, what was it, *The Beans of Egypt Maine*, by that cussed woman from down west of Portland who wallowed in her poverty. She had come up to read on her promotional book tour at the town library and Peggy had dragged him along. He thought she might have been a secret trust-funder. He'd read the book, though. Thought it was crap, to write that way about living up here. Why don't they just leave us alone? But the Stuckeys, they made the characters from the book seem real. Well, it was a mite nippy, and he needed some coffee. Eben Titcomb turned to head back inside his house.

He missed the sudden flare of flames from the Emerys' back porch. Jeff Mullins and two other volunteers desperately tried to douse them, but sparks had landed on the roof and it was beginning to smolder. The back turret's roof burst into flames and the men backed off. Sirens neared.

"Here comes Skowhegan, I bet,' Jeff said. Chief Avery appeared. "Hey, Chief, we've lost pressure here," Jeff told him.

"I know. We're just about out. Randy is headed to the hydrant up on the main road."

"That's a ways away."

"Ayuh." Chief Avery looked up at the flames that now engulfed the whole back side of the Emery house. The breeze rose and pushed the wall of heat into his face.

Two Skowhegan trucks roared around the corner to find the warehouse fire under control and the Emery place ablaze from top to bottom. The Skowhegan water truck began pumping water and two firefighters directed a hose onto what looked like a Disney version of a Victorian house on fire, flames roaring out of every window on every floor lapping up the shingles and barn board. The water did not stop the flames, only contained them.

When the house collapsed, the onlookers screamed and cried out, the firefighters scrambled and yelled orders to one another. After the creaky tearing loose of nails and ripping of joists, the noise of the crumbling structure subsided, and the firefighters surrounded the burning heap. They did not get too close; one wall stood. The refrigerator, stove, and kitchen island stood exposed to the cold. The collapse had caused a cabinet door above the stove to open. Chief Avery saw canned string beans and tomatoes that Dot had put by at harvest time less than three months ago.

Dot was hysterical and crying into her husband's chest. He squeezed her shoulders. Herbert Emery stared blankly at the home he and Dot had lived in, had preciously restored for the past thirty years. His mind captured the images of devastation: a winterized flowerbed overrun by trucks and hoses, trampled by rubber boots; a wheel-rutted backyard garden; a totally gutted house, a black smoldering mess. They stood alone, huddled beside Chief Avery's station wagon. The strobe lights from police and fire vehicles pulsed into the night.

"Everything's gone. Everything," Dot managed to say, her words muffling into his flannel shirt.

"You never liked the kitchen. Just this morning you were

complaining about space." As he looked down at her, he smiled gently. When she looked back up at him, he added, "You've got plenty of space now."

"Dear Lord, how can you at a time like this?" Dot managed a weak smile. Then she turned toward the catastrophe. "What on earth," she said, staring at the open cabinet above the stove.

"I imagine we're going to rebuild. Unless you want to move to Florida."

"You're a crazy ole man, Herbert Emery. Have been ever since I met you." She continued to stare into the exposed kitchen area. "Do you see those jars of vegetables above the stove?

"Ayuh. You brought them up from the cellar for Thanksgiving Saturday morning, didn't you?"

"I sure did. I wonder if they're salvageable."

"What?"

"I know. I was just wondering about the vegetables, that's all."

# Chapter 17

*Flames bring attention to themselves. People respond to them. They are afraid of them. I wonder how fire was invented. Well, invented is not the correct word. "Tamed" is a better word. Maybe "domesticated," like an animal. I remember once our social studies teacher told us about a movie called* Quest for Fire. *Kids weren't supposed to go because there was sex in it. All the teachers were talking about it, but no one went, except Coccinella. He said it was silly fun.*

*They wouldn't show it in the theaters in Waterville, except at the hippie art theater. Michelle wanted to go, but my father, of course, forbid it. They had a fight. He said something about sex having nothing to do with fire. Michelle yelled at him that he knew nothing about anthropology or about what the film was trying to represent. Anyway, she snuck off and saw the movie. She said it was silly, too. I remember thinking how strange it was that Coccinella and Michelle felt the same way about something.*

*Anyway, I like the title of the movie because it has the word "quest" in it. A quest is an important search. Like that knight from the Round Table. His name was Percival, I think. He was a squire at first but King Arthur made him a knight because he was so brave and honorable. He ended up going on a quest for the Holy Grail. It was a serious mission. Imagine going on a search for fire like in the movie.*

*I don't have to search for fire.*

*Flames are inside me and I let them out any time I want. They exist as a secret inside me. So, in a way, my quest is inside myself, I guess. But I have it easier than Percival. He had to wander strange lands. I do not have to wander anywhere to find flames. I carry them until I let them out.*

ஒ

"So. I'm going to drive up to a place called Chaldea, Maine. Godforsaken country. I can imagine what the people are like. All married to their cousins and have a rural underbite." Chip Arnold chuckled into the receiver. He knew he was being condescending.

"You're bad. I hope you're kidding. And if you are, you should know better," said Susan Whitcomb, Feature Editor of *The Boston Globe*.

"I know, I know. I've been up there, to Vinalhaven Island a few years ago."

Actually, he had been to Maine only once to the island to visit friends who summered there regularly. His friends kept talking about the locals and the relationship they had with the summer people who were mostly academics, artists, entertainers, and wealthy business people.

They'd explained how the locals needed the summer people for taxes since the summer people owned, for the most part, the best land, the deep-water land, the land with the ocean and bay views. Vinalhaven Island was a lobstering community of less than 800. The wives and children of the lobstermen often worked for these summer land owners cleaning house, landscaping, painting, doing other odd jobs like getting ferry reservations for cars, picking up arriving visitors at the ferry terminal and such. Chip never bothered to really think about the economics or the social issues of the beautiful island. He just sat out on his friends' deck sipping his martini and watching the postcard pretty sun set over Carver's Harbor.

"Listen, Chip. Going up to a Maine island in July for a week is not the same as the western mountains of rural Maine."

"Yeah, yeah. Appalachia North and all that. I know."

"No, I don't know that you do. The townspeople are scared, very upset, and they do not take much to someone like you 'from away.'" Susan Whitcomb's grandparents were born and raised in Farmington, Maine, a fair sized town west of Chaldea, and they still lived up there in summer. Susan had spent her childhood summers with them and continued to go up there throughout her college life and her graduate study.

"Wait a minute. Calm down. I'm teasing."

"I know you. You're half teasing. And with that attitude no one's going to give you the time of day, let alone talk to you about this arson outbreak. These are good, honest people. If they suspect you're insincere, they'll close up tighter than...well, as my grandfather would say, tighter than a cow's ass in fly time."

"Aw, for God's sake, don't make this all about me. You're the one that tapped me to go up there. By the way, that's quite an image from your grandfather."

"Look, maybe you shouldn't go up. I can send Sally. In that way..."

"Susan! I'll go. I'll do the job. They can't figure out what's going on up there. If it's one arsonist, they have no idea who it is. I've already made preliminary calls to Chaldea's fire and police departments and to the state Fire Marshall on the case."

"When'd you do this?"

"Yesterday, when you said you might want me up there. Just some prep work, just in case. I'd like to talk to some townspeople and some teachers from the school as soon as I get up there."

"That's what I love about you, you jump right in."

"Then it's a go?"

Susan Whitcomb sighed. "When can you leave?"

Maine is one deceptively large state, Chip Arnold thought, his gaze wandering out of the car window to the dark fir woods that bordered the turnpike. About a half hour ago, just before Lewiston, he noticed that the deciduous trees were becoming sparse, that the fir trees were encroaching on the highway. A colleague who had lived in Maine for several years had told him about the mythic Route 11, a road that was the basis for the country song "A Ribbon of Ice." Locals said there was a tombstone every mile.

Route 11 was a 'Downeast' road that wove its way through the Haynesville Woods, where the fir trees were so tall that the sun couldn't get to the road to melt the ice. Truckers hauling logs hated the perched road for its steep shoulders that fell away fast. It was dangerous driving an overloaded vehicle down to the Mill at Stinkin' Lincoln, where the air continually reeked of sulfur from the paper mill in the middle of town. The air was so acidic that it eroded the paint from vehicles and stuck the taste of metal to the roof of the mouth.

But the Maine turnpike, pleasantly boring, was clear. Traces of early November snow that had laced the woods at the beginning of the highway had now become a solid cover. Chip Arnold figured he had about an hour and half left. He decided to stop for coffee once he made it Skowhegan.

"What can I get you, hon?" The waitress smiled.

"Coffee. Black."

"Sure thing. Comin' right at ya."

No one else sat at the counter. Two old-timers sat and chatted at a booth, their breakfasts half eaten. It was late morning and the smell of eggs, home fries, ketchup, and toast hung in the air. The waitress, placing the coffee in front of him, asked, "Where ya headed?"

"Up to Chaldea."

"Oh yeah? Ain't much up there."

"I take your word for it. I've never been there before."

"I got cousins up there, but I don't see 'em much. They and theirs come down here on the Fourth of July for a family cookout." The waitress kept chatting. "Supposed to snow again. Ain't seen so much snow before Thanksgiving. Good for hunting though."

"This is deep winter back in Boston."

"Closer to the pole than to the equator. You're up here to write about them fires, ain't ya?"

"Yes," said Chip, taking a deep breath.

"Good luck to you. There ain't nothin' much to write about from what I hear. Nobody knows nothing about who did 'em. Everyone's scared. Two families lost their home. A damn shame, for sure." The two old-timers raised their heads, stopped chatting for a moment, and turned toward the conversation.

"Well, the paper wants a story."

"We had a *Sentinel* guy from Waterville up here a week or so ago. He said he talked to the fire and police chiefs. He said they were flummoxed. But that was before the last fire."

He hadn't heard that word in a while. "There's been another already?" he asked.

"Well, I heard someone tried to fire the grocery store in town, and the firemen got there before anything could happen. It seems that ole man Putnam forgot his wallet and he went back to get it and saw a bunch of cardboard boxes and wood crates on fire out back. He called the Fire department right away. They came over and found him putting water on the flames. I think he used to be a volunteer himself back when he was nimble."

"I need to get going," Chip said. "Thanks for the chat and the information."

"Wasn't much. You ain't goin' to get any more than what I gave ya anyway. There's nothin' figured out. Besides, to get anything out of people in Chaldea is like pulling teeth."

"We'll have to see, I guess."

"How long ya stayin'?"

"Longer than I'd like."

"It's supposed to snow hard they say. You don't want to drive in the snow."

"Thanks," Chip said. He walked outside. The cold air bit him. High thin clouds moved in smudging the blue sky. "Snow...sure as shit," he said as he opened the car door.

# Chapter 18

*I feel the strongest I have ever felt. I'm not talking about having muscles like Billy Atwood and being able to lift weights. I am talking about feeling important, feeling confident. Inside I have a big grin. I'd never show it outside. No way. My father would smack me because he would figure that I had something going on. Which would be correct.*

*I looked Mrs. Emery in the eye the other day, no problem. I said hello to her when I was walking home and she was walking from her car into Putnam's. She said, "Well, hello young man. I haven't seen you for a dog's age." "Hi, Mrs. Emery." I kept on walking. I didn't want to give her a chance to talk with me. I wanted to get home. I was making some big plans. But that was a secret for now.*

*They are still having counseling sessions for all the high school kids in Chaldea. I don't know why they need counseling. No one got hurt. Everyone got some excitement out of it. I don't see what the problem is. Why should somebody get messed up because of a fire?*

*If you stare at flames long enough, it's like you get hypnotized, or mesmerized. And when you're mesmerized, you're not yourself. You are so fascinated by something that you forget who you are. Flames have that effect on me. They turn one thing into another. I think they must have that effect on everyone, if only they were given a chance.*

*Once, when I lit the wood stove down in the family room, I watched the flames grow and gobble up the kindling. The fire popped and crackled and the flames wiggled up and around the kindling so quickly. I felt so excited that I wanted to let them out onto the rug. I wanted to let them free to play. But my father came downstairs before I had the chance to release them. He was checking on me to see if I got the fire right and if I was doing my homework.*

*He put some logs on the fire then went back upstairs, and that changed the flames. They quieted down and stayed the same steady size, wrapping themselves around the logs. I started staring at them. I looked at this one flame that burned only on the right side of the logs. It was a deep orange and it seemed like there was another, smaller flame inside of it that was right next to the log. This smaller flame was bending into different shapes. It seemed all excited. I got excited, too.*

*Then something strange happened. Inside this smaller flame, three bright little stars burned. They were like sparks shaped like stars and they burned bright yellow-white inside the smaller flame which was inside the larger flame. And these star sparks were not directly on the wood either. It was like they were suspended in the two flames and unattached to anything. It was so beautiful and so strange. I thought that the star sparks were alive.*

*I crawled on the carpet, toward the fire. I know this sounds crazy but I heard them talking. At first I thought they were just sizzling. You know how flames can sizzle, how a fire can make noises. But it wasn't that. These star sparks were speaking. And I knew that they were speaking to me.*

*I looked through the glass door at the star sparks. They were like the souls of people that Coccinella had talked about only these were small. The more I stared at them the clearer their words became. I don't know if I should tell you what they said. It's a secret. And I have to keep these secrets. You keep secrets with your friends.*

*Anyway, as I was staring at the star sparks, Dad came back down stairs. I didn't hear him and he startled me so that I almost jumped off the carpet when he said, "Zeke, what the hell are you doing?" I turned quickly and said, "Nothing. Just looking at the fire." I got back up and went back to the couch and my homework. "You are one strange kid,*

*Zeke," my father said.*

ঌ൙

Audrey Lothrop lived on West Main Street. Her kitchen was warm and the smell of fresh brewed coffee filled the air. She sat down with a thump, lit a Camel, took a long, deep drag, exhaled a plume of smoke. "I didn't sleep a wink last night," she said. "Kept hearing things outside. Jacob told me to relax. He loaded his 30/30 last week and put it by the bed. It's been there ever since the attempt to fire the grocery store. He says no one's comin' round our place without an invitation. You know how Jake is."

"The whole town's on edge. Everyone's prickly," Ida Howell added. "Never seen anything like this in Chaldea. Not in my lifetime."

Ginny Bartlett added, "The Todds put up new yard lights. Betsy's scared to death what with two small ones and Malcolm working graveyard at the Mill." She took a sip of her tea.

"I feel horribly about what happened to the Emerys. Poor Dot, gracious sake's alive. She worked so hard on that house. She loved having her kids and their families back up for the holidays. What kind of Thanksgiving is she gonna have now?"

Audrey chimed in again. "I saw Dot the other day at Putnam's. She was glassy-eyed, poor thing. She said that she and Herb were thinkin' of moving down to Portland to be near their son. They're going down there for the holidays anyway. They've got nothin' up here now." She coughed hard, then flicked ash into the tray beside her coffee cup. "I gotta stop smokin'."

"Aren't they stayin' with the Withingtons out in Athens?" asked Ginny.

"Not that I now of. Naomi Crowell took them in. She's alone and has the space. I wonder how they feel seeing their burned out place every day. I couldn't face it." Audrey crushed out her cigarette. "More coffee, Ida?"

"No thanks. I gotta run. Jim wants to go over to Farmington to talk to the agent about fire insurance."

"We got fire insurance," Ginny piped in.

"Lotta good it does. You lose everything and you fight to have them cut you a check worth half the value of what you lose. And that's monetary value, not emotional value. Dot lost all those antique pieces of furniture that her mother had passed down to her. Imagine that." Audrey Lothrop shook her head. "God bless that woman. I don't know how she can stand it."

"Maybe she can't," said Ginny.

Dusk had settled over Chaldea. The clear sky, a Maxfield Parrish blue-green, canopied the town. Lights yellowed the windows of a few buildings and a few homes along Tucker Street. The Town Hall was empty, except for two men waiting for the other selectmen. They were early for the meeting, the second called in as many weeks.

"Maybe we should form a patrol," offered Eben Titcomb. "They could drive around at night. Work their way from the town outward. Divide the town into quadrants."

"Come on," responded Clint Wood. "You know Avery's not going to buy in to that. He doesn't need that kind of help."

"We can do it without his permission. It's a free country. He can't stop us."

"Yeah, but you're askin' for trouble, far as I'm concerned. You know damn well that most men are riding around with their deer rifles loaded now. All it takes is one idiot mistake by someone who misreads a situation, who thinks something is goin' on when somethin' ain't really goin' on. That's all we need is a chance for idiots to be more idiotic. Someone will get hurt."

"Hey, Clint. We've got no High School. Almost lost the Junior High. Twice I might add. Walloomsac almost lost their High

School. Then there's my road: Stuckey's trailer, the warehouse and the Emery's. Putnam's place almost went up. That's hurt enough, don't ya think?"

"We're all upset and rattled. But who wants a vigilante group riding around? You can't control people, Eben."

"You sure as hell can try."

"Yeah, I can imagine if this patrol of yours gets in the papers. That journalist up here will sniff that out like a coon dog. How do you think that will be if this patrol of yours ends up in the paper?

"Good, I say. We've got to catch this person and punish him. If some flatlander journalist wants to write it up, so be it."

Voices echoed up the stairwell.

"Ayuh, and here we go with another round of nothin'," said Clint.

"Geez'um, Clint. What do you expect? People need to talk. We need to take control of the situation."

"Listen to me. What's to control? We've got a lunatic arsonist on the loose. We've got no clues. We've got no cause. Let the police and fire people do their job. For God's sake."

"I'm not gonna sit back and watch nothin' happen. I'm gonna do something. And I think the others will agree with me." Eben Titcomb turned to greet the other men. "Well, if it ain't the Town Manager. Evenin' Thomas," said Eben.

Clint Wood shook his head, a look of exasperation on his face.

"Eben Titcomb is the bane of my existence. He sticks his self-righteous nose into everything, and I mean everything. Did you hear what he's aiming to do?" Chief Avery pushed his chair back from his desk and walked over to look out the window of his office. Sugarloaf Mountain, frosted white with snow, stood in sharp contrast to the clear blue sky. This is going to be one helluva Thanksgiving.

Chief Corson leaned back in his chair. "Lionel, he's a bother, that's for sure. Let him prattle on. He's a blowhard; everyone knows it."

"Ayuh. Well, I've got to find this arsonist. Somehow. We've got no leads, no hints. We've spoken with just about everyone. We're beginning interviews with the high school kids again."

"The Fire Marshall has nothing. His men still cannot determine a reason for the fires. It's a real mystery. I am more than perplexed than ever. Helluva thing this is."

"It's as though the whole town has gone crazy. Last Wednesday, around eight o'clock in the evening, one of my deputies found two guys with their rifles out sneaking behind the hardware store because they thought they saw someone prowling behind the alley. It was ole Sherman Tuttle, drunk as usual, trying to get back to Main Street. That's all I need is for someone to get shot."

"The journalist would have a field day with that, wouldn't he?"

"So, how was your interview with the illustrious Mr. Arnold?" asked Chief Avery.

"Oh, you know. He was polite enough. But like most people that come up for a quick visit he doesn't really know what to make of us. The place unnerves them. He wanted more from me than I could or wanted to give. He'll get plenty from other people in town. Eben, for instance."

"Ayuh, I didn't offer him much, either, not that I had much to offer."

"Hard to believe we're making *The Boston Globe*."

"I wonder if the arsonist reads papers."

# Chapter 19

*Flames give me courage. It's not like I talk out loud to them or anything. Sometimes they make music and I can hear their songs, which is like listening to a choir. They're like angels when they sing to me. It's better than church. The candles lit in church, the ones on the altar are lonely and quiet. I feel sorry for those flames.*

*I can tell you for certain not having any real friends is not much fun. And, if you want to know, but probably don't want to know, it hurts. I don't have close friends, except the flames. I have some so-called friends. There's Jimmy who everyone calls a douche bag. He is this scrawny kid who looks like he's never eaten a real meal. He has this bad habit of burping at unexpected times. Most kids hate him. Guys at school punch him on the shoulder on their way down the corridor. I don't know how he stands it. I tell him he's got to stop burping.*

*Then there's Bernie. He's fat. You can imagine how that works at school. Plus, he's pimply. He's got this small face and he looks like a weasel. That's what the kids at school call him, too. The Weasel. His real problem is that he doesn't wash much. I tried to tell him, but he started crying and told me to shut up. I told my mother about this once, last year, and she told me that he's got real problems. And I've heard things. Things I can't quite figure out about who his father is and who his mother is. I'm not going to say any more about it because it makes me sort of nervous.*

*I do know this about Weasel. Not too many people know what I'm going to say. It's a secret I've kept ever since it happened. One morning last September, just after school started and before the fire burned it down, I went to school real early. Why I did that is my secret. But I was at school around the time Coccinella and the athletic director arrived to go running, which they did almost every day before school. I stuck around, walking around the school grounds. Well, around seven or so, I see Weasel come walking up to the back door by the gym and I see Coccinella meet him there. I follow them inside. The AD is there with Coccinella and Weasel in front of his office. I hear Coccinella tell Weasel, "Get undressed in there. There's soap and shampoo. And a towel." Weasel says he doesn't want to shower. Coccinella says, "Bernie I told you that a shower will help you feel better. Being clean is good for you." I can't believe what I'm hearing, so I try to get closer to the office.*

*I slip closer since the door is shut, but not completely. I hear the shower on. Then the AD says, "Dave, I'll leave for a bit. That'll help." So I scoot back to the hallway by the machine shop. Luckily the AD heads toward the gym. Then I go back to the door to the AD's office. I hear Coccinella say, "How's it going, Bernie? Clean yourself good with soap. Lather it up. You okay?" I hear Weasel say, "Yeah, okay. I'm scrubbing." "Okay, good Bernie. After that, shampoo your hair. It's in the green tube. Okay?" "Yeah," says Weasel. But he sounds like he's crying. Maybe it's the water, I think. You know the sound a voice can make in the shower. I hear the AD coming down the hallway from the gym, so I leave and get back outside.*

*So, Coccinella made Weasel shower! Can you believe that? To this day, I can't figure out how he got him to do it. I never asked Weasel. But that shower day I remember I was eating in the cafeteria with Weasel and Billy Atwood came over. I looked down at my plate and waited to get dumped on. I had my hands on my tray, ready to lift it and get out as soon as I could. But Atwood stood over Weasel and said, "Hey Weasel, you don't stink today. That's good. Keep it up!" Then he laughed and, naturally, everyone at his table laughed. Other kids in the cafeteria just looked over our way then turned away after Atwood walked back to his table.*

*So, if you can call Jimmy or Bernie a friend, they were who I had.*

*The flames were better. More reliable. But at least Jimmy and Bernie would talk to me normally. I felt like a real person around them. Not because I was smarter. Actually, they were pretty smart guys but they never did any schoolwork. When you have problems, you can't really do too well in school. I guess.*

*I should talk. I don't exactly apply myself. Now I sound like Holden Caulfield. What a great character. When we read that for Coccinella in freshman year, I loved it. Especially when ole Holden told his history teacher that he didn't apply himself. Great. What was also great was the fact that the town went bonkers because Coccinella taught the book. The town wanted to fire him. Really. But that's another story.*

*I can't really hang around with Jimmy and Bernie because I never see them outside of school. Only sometimes. I tried to see them, but I gave up. Jimmy had to help his father milk cows and Bernie's house was so weird, I was afraid to go near it. It was all old and looked like a shack and the plastic blinds, yellow, ripped, and faded, were always drawn, and I was afraid of knocking on the door. That place used to take a beating on Halloween.*

*I can't trust Bernie or Jimmie. I trust flames. Flames are friends that stay friends. You don't actually control them after they come alive; you don't have to. They just do what flames do – they burn. I know people think flames are fickle. You can argue that they can turn, change direction, spin and whirl in ways that you can't imagine. But that's because they must do what they have to do – which is feed. They need air, sustenance. Like us. In a way, they are human.*

*No one flame is the same as another. Like snowflakes, like us. When you light a fire, you never know what kind of flame will appear and you never know what it will do. You can guess, and you might be right sometimes, but you can never know. Same with people. You never know what to expect from them.*

*Like my sister. If she were a flame, she'd burn this whole damn town down. The thing of it is, she would never even think about doing something like that. She's so cool, she'd just move away and forget about the place. She'd completely ignore it, which is what she does anyway. I love her for that. She just does what she wants and ignores the rest. Like flames, oblivious to the world. They just exist. That's what I want to do, too. Just exist. Alone. And watch flames. So I wouldn't really be alone. I guess it's me and flames.*

⁂

Thanksgiving in the mountains of western Maine is a quiet celebration, homey, warm, and, in its way, solitary. There was a good foot and a half of snow on the ground. The locals said that the coming winter was going to be a rough one. And cold.

Dutifully, families gathered. Kitchens bustled with activity. Foods, prepared with old family recipes, cooked on the stove: Grandma's stuffing, Aunt Rachel's creamed onions, Cousin Gert's giblet gravy. Living rooms and dens hummed with conversations: who shot the biggest buck and where, fixing and tuning up snowmobile engines, the bureaucracy of getting a trapping license, whose child had grown so fast, whether the niece who was attending college in Boston would last the year, and, always, the coming winter.

Of course, everyone in Chaldea, friends from away, visiting family and locals alike, had the fires on the mind. When families sat down to dinner, during the saying of grace old and young alike wondered whether they would hear sirens during the meal.

The Titcomb driveway was packed tight. Relatives from Augusta and Kennebunkport, friends up from the Cape, and Mrs. Crowell and the Emerys made for the biggest Thanksgiving dinner in a long while. Peggy Titcomb bustled from kitchen to pantry and back again, her sister helping. They had cooked big meals for most of their lives and this one was no different.

Eben Titcomb held court in the living room. "We can find this piece of crap through vigilance. The town isn't that big. We should be on guard."

"You think the town isn't?" asked his brother Austin.

"We could do more."

"Aren't the police on it?" asked Tucker Merrill, Peggy

Titcomb's brother, a lobster fisherman from the coast.

"Let's just say they leave a lot to be desired," answered Eben.

Herbert Emery listened patiently, leaning against the doorway into the living room, a neat whiskey in his hand. He thought for a second before speaking. "Chief Avery is a good man, a smart man. He is doing the best he can. He has the town's best interest at heart. So does Chief Corson. These are two very professional men. I have total confidence in both of them and in the state fire marshall for that matter. The arsonist will get caught." He took a sip of his whiskey.

"I hope you're right, Herb. But I personally don't feel all that secure. And I think a lot of townspeople feel the same way I do." Eben Titcomb raised his glass to Herb, then he walked over the bay window and looked out at the yard. The sky, a deepening grey in the west, darkened. "Looks like we might be in for some weather," he added.

"I'm glad we're staying over. I don't need the drive back to the coast, especially on a full stomach," said Tucker Merrill.

"As long as the snow stops before dawn, so the deer tracks are clear," said Austin. "I've got tomorrow off and I'm going out early."

# Chapter 20

*I want to love my sister, I really do. Michelle is older than I am. She'll be eighteen before she graduates. I just turned fifteen. Everyone says I'm young for my age. I don't know what they mean. Do I look young for my age? Do I look like I'm twelve or something? Or do I act young? I don't think I act like a twelve-year-old. I act like myself, and I'm fifteen. When I'm teased at school, I'm not teased for acting twelve. I'm teased for just being me.*

*She's a nice person, Michelle. She's just independent. And stubborn. I think she hates the world, especially my father. He's a problem for us all. But Michelle: just when I think that I am going to go from liking her to loving her, she messes up. I don't know if that's because she is beautiful and can't deal with it. I've heard about that. She's smart so I figure she doesn't screw up because she's dumb about stuff. She's sharp, and so it's her tongue that scares just about everyone. It sure scares me.*

*She goes and does things that make me not like her much. I never hear what she does from her, either. I hear it from the kids that tease me at school. They use what Michelle does to make fun of me. When she does something, I get it thrown in my face as though I was responsible for what she does.*

*The funny thing is I don't know if my sister is embarrassed by what she does. She doesn't seem to be. If she is, then she hides it well. Of course, my whole family is good at hiding things. But with my sister, the things I get told really embarrass me because this town finds out everything about everyone. There are no secrets in a small town. Well, that's not quite true. The secrets that are kept are deep ones. But even the deep ones seem to rise up from the ground like old rocks in the spring when the ground thaws and moves what's buried up to the surface.*

*This image is from a poem that Coccinella gave us one day. We had to copy it down in our poetry journals. He dictated it to us. He was always doing that. He was always giving us poems about Maine and about living upcountry. I never forgot it because it is so true. I mean anyone that lives a life up here knows what the poem is about.*

*Here it is:*

*Earth Gives Up Its Dead*

*A friend who lives in Maine*
*found a small white granite gravestone*
*washed up in his back pasture*
*when he was burning brush one spring.*

*This kind of natural fact*
*makes the word cower to the world.*
*I rub my hands over and over the stone,*
*trying to feel the child swimming up.*

*One month given –*
*the green world*
*taken away.*

*Earth gives up its stones.*
*I pick and pitch them*
*into the woods, across the pond.*

*Earth gives up its dead.*
*In spring they rise,*
*skimming over the pasture pond,*
*skimming to the other shore.*

*I guess Michelle was seeing Jack Tatum for a while. I know this because one of the cheerleaders came up to me in the hallway as I was walking into Coccinella's class. It was Deborah Oakley, a big mouth gossip who thought she was prettier than she was. "Hey, Zeke, your sister sure gets around, doesn't she?" I didn't know what she was talking about, and I told her that. She then said, "Well, she's doin' this guy at the Mill." Then she giggled as did three of her cheerleader friends who were standing a ways away by the stairs. I turned and walked into the English classroom.*

*I knew who it was because a friend of Bill Atwood, Sean Black, had already told me that he saw Michelle drinking down at Wilson Lake a few weeks ago with Jack Tatum and a friend of his. She was laughing and he had his arms around her waist and was kissing her neck. But that's not the bad stuff.*

*Lots of kids go to the lake and drink and smoke dope and do other stuff. The police only go down there when they know a lot of people will be there or before the prom or graduation. That's because they don't want anybody getting hurt or killed. It seems almost every year some seniors get killed or in a bad accident and the whole town gets upset and the description of the accident makes it into* The Sentinel *and there are the wakes and funerals.*

*It's sad. Two years ago, a week before he was to graduate, Vernon Tuttle was drunk and he raced out on the road toward Harmony. He lost control, flew off the road into the graveyard out past the Dean's dairy farm and got killed. He was tossed out of the truck and smashed his face on a gravestone. I have already mentioned the C & R word for this type of thing. My father wouldn't let me go to his funeral, even though I knew him and my family knew his family.*

*It's the bad stuff with Michelle that gets to me. The things she does might as well be flames because they engulf my feelings for her. They really devastate my heart. I kept this devastation a secret, of course. Maybe that's why I don't have any friends. I don't offer much up to anyone. I usually offer nothing about Michelle.*

*I want her to be close to me but she can't. She's too busy being who she is. I want to get close to her, but the way she lives doesn't allow me to do that, and I don't know what to do about it. Maybe if I tell about her, I won't be so confused, but I doubt it.*

*She's not a whore or a slut. I don't care what she's supposed to have done. And she's supposed to have done a lot. Not just with this Jack Tatum, either. She's done some stuff with guys at school. Not with Atwood and his friends though. That's good. But she hangs around with the tough kids. I mean they're eighteen goin' on thirty. Even Atwood and the athletes give these guys space. These guys have been arrested, in jail, and they do not care about what anyone thinks. You do not want to cross these kids. In school or out.*

*They break into summer homes, they break into the houses of locals. They get high. They're usually high in school. My sister, too. They beat people up...real badly. I don't know why everyone tries to keep them in school. They do no schoolwork at all. Sometimes they just get up from class and walk out. They could care less about any rules. Most teachers are afraid of them, except for Coccinella and Resnick, and the AD.*

*It's funny, these kids are the ones that spend time with the Army recruiters that come into our classes about every other week. I don't know why they want these kids. I don't think any of them could pass a test if their lives depended on it.*

*Which makes me wonder why Michelle hangs around with them. I think it's because she is smarter than they are, so she can boss them around, sort of, if you know what I mean. A better word is "manipulation." So, this means, basically, that the stuff she does, she does because she wants to do it.*

*So when she took Keith Stoughton to the back of the auditorium during the second lunch, she did it because she wanted to, not because Keith forced her. The rumor began first period, and it spread fast, so that by second lunch everyone looked around the cafeteria to see if they were at lunch. They weren't.*

*Keith started talking that afternoon. All kinds of guys gathered around him when he wasn't sharing what went on with his friends. Lots of laughter. Lots of rumors filled with details. I wanted to put my fingers in my ears, especially when Keith came over to me before my Earth Science class and whispered, "Beakface, your sister has big tits and a mouth that won't quit."*

*My heart raced. I started breathing fast. I thought I was going to faint. Mr. Sabine came to the doorway to bring me inside. Keith was laughing loudly, and Sabine told him to get to his class. I ran down the hallway toward the door to the auditorium balcony. I sat in a corner seat up there. I started crying.*

*As I sat up in the balcony, I asked myself why Michelle does these things. She must know what the town thinks of her, what my father thinks of her because of the way she acts, how she hurts Mom. I looked down at the stage, at the old curtains, and I realized that it was somewhere behind those curtains Michelle and Keith had been. Then the school, the whole world even, and everything in it seemed dirty to me. I wanted the school to go away. I wanted to forget about everything that happens in it.*

*I thought of the first time my father let me start the fire in the wood stove in the family room. I forgot how old I was, but the thrill of packing in the kindling over some old newspaper then placing one or two small logs on the kindling and lighting the paper gave me goose bumps. I watched the match flare into a little flame then, when I put the match next to the paper, how it jumped onto the paper's edge, then began to eat it deeper into the stove. The flames grew as they burned more of the paper, began to nibble on the kindling until there was a pop or a crack and they really came to life, feeding on the wood without any help.*

*The thought of the fire calmed me down. I stopped crying. I took a deep breath, got up and instead of going to class late, I headed to the library to see if Mr. Resnick needed any help. I didn't care if I got a detention for missing Sabine's class.*

❧

In Chaldea, as in most Maine towns, talk of snow pops up year round. There is a reason for this. Winter comes fast, comes hard, and when it comes early, one must be prepared. The year of the fires, snow came early. The talk of snow for the townspeople of Chaldea, tinged with the fear of fire, began immediately after the High School fire and built momentum along with the cold weather and the mysterious fires.

The early storm that had dropped almost a half-foot of snow two days after the High School blaze was a memory. By the time the Emerys lost their home to the warehouse fire, there was a foot of snow on the ground. That hadn't happened in years. The snow came as though it was intent on extinguishing the fires.

The Baptist preacher certainly believed that, and said so during his sermon on the Sunday after Thanksgiving, as the last flakes of a two-day blizzard danced in the air. With deer season ended and December about to begin, Chaldea had a good three feet on the ground.

The plows that rumbled around town throughout Saturday night had finished by sunrise on Sunday. Eben Titcomb sat in the family station wagon, waiting for his wife and son to come out. Church service began at nine o'clock, but he had deacon duties, so he dragged Peggy and Zeke along early.

"Come on you two. Hurry up, will ya?" he said to the dashboard. The car hadn't warmed up yet, so his breath hung in the air. He switched the defroster onto its highest setting. "What's going on with them?" he wondered aloud, this time to the steering wheel.

Peggy, followed by Zeke, came to the car. Before she had closed the door, Eben asked, "What took you so long?"

"Oh, there's plenty of time, Eben, don't worry."

"Ayuh, well, you know I like to have everything ready for Reverend Loveless."

"Stop fretting so much. How long have you been a deacon? God, Eben, it's a wonder you haven't driven me to drink." Eben stared straight ahead and smiled, but Zeke noticed it wasn't a very friendly smile.

Downtown Chaldea was quiet. Eben Titcomb stopped at the red light at the intersection of Main and River streets. A red Dodge pick-up rolled out of the Exxon station diagonally across from them and onto the intersection. It idled opposite the Titcomb family car. "That's Jack Tatum's truck," Eben said, "That guy wasn't at work last Friday. He's had a long weekend."

"Who's that woman with him?" Peggy asked.

Zeke stared from the back seat. He laughed quietly to himself.

The light turned and the truck came toward them. "Oh no, dear Lord, that's Michelle," blurted Peggy. Both he and his wife looked straight ahead when the truck passed them.

Zeke looked over. He thought he saw Michelle smile at him.

"Why that...that dirty little...," muttered Eben, teeth clenched. "I'd like to kill that..."

"Eben, please. It's Sunday. We'll talk to her later."

"Ayuh, it's Sunday. And we're just one big happy family."

In the backseat, Zeke was in his head, and he did not hear the end of the brief exchange between his father and his mother. He had put his face close to the passenger window. It was slightly frosted, and he felt the chill on his face. Zeke was thinking that if he lit a match and put it up against the frosted window, it would melt the frost into a liquid that would make some interesting designs. "Dad, when we get to church, can I light the candles for you?"

"Sure, Zeke."

# Hot Spot II

*Jimi Hendrix lit his guitar on fire in front of thousands of people. He did it like he was in church, like it was something religious, a ceremony that he was doing. I know how he felt. Lighting the match didn't mean much for him. But setting the match to the fluid that he had squirted on the guitar was serious. Look at the expression his face. You can see him staring down at the instrument like it was sacred.*

*I have no idea how he could set a fire, any fire, in public. And to his guitar, too. What's Hendrix without a guitar? Nothing, just another person. Which is how I feel most of the time. I am mostly invisible. Don't get me wrong I like it that way. Really, I do. No one sees me even when they are looking at me. Except when they want to make fun of me or tell me something about my sister.*

*I mean I can be in the library, standing by the magazine section and kids will walk up beside me with eyes all concentrated on finding their* Guns & Ammo *or* Seventeen *or* Hunting Life *and they do not even look at me. They reach for their magazine and then walk by without saying excuse me even if they bump my shoulder. Then, if one of their friends comes in and the friend is at the other end of the library, they blurt out "Hey" as though that person is a half-mile away and Mr. Resnick usually has to tell them to be quiet.*

*I am an accepted nobody. Even when I am being picked on, which I pretend doesn't bother me, I am really invisible. Like when Atwood and his crowd come around me. One of them will say something to a friend about me, but they will not even look at me. They talk about me right in front of me as though I am not there. Once, a group of guys from the football team surrounded me outside the cafeteria. This dumbass from over in Grimes, Rufus Mallard, said to Atwood, "Hey, the mung ain't wearing his grey sweater today." He was looking at Atwood even though he stood right in front of me. Atwood smirked. I guess he had other things on his mind that day. They left when they saw the Home Economics teacher, Mrs. Bouchard, come out of the Teacher's Room. Mallard said, "See ya, mung." and gave me a quick punch on the shoulder. It hurt. But he never looked at me.*

*At least my father, when he gets on my case, looks at me with that special look of disgust he saves for me. The C & R word would be "distain." Which is how I feel about school, the way my sister acts, and the way my father treats everyone, just about everything except making flames and watching fires. Flames do not show distain. Flames just are.*

*To finish the story, Mrs. Bouchard walked over and asked me if everything was alright. I didn't say anything. I didn't even look at her. I clamped my mouth shut so hard my teeth hurt. What did she think? She saw the guys around me before they left. She saw the punch. She heard him call me a mung, too. Everybody calls me that, or they call me "worm dirt."*

*I am the lowest of the low. The mung. Worm dirt. I have to laugh when I remember how Mr. Coccinella tried to cheer me up once after school when I was in his classroom hanging around. I was feeling like company and we started talking. We always talked about books and words and stuff and that always led to talks about life. Actually, he'd do the talking; I wouldn't say anything. But in a strange way his talking would calm me down enough so that I would let out something to him. I couldn't stop myself.*

*You know when a teacher always takes time to talk to you, you grow sort of used to him, and you begin to feel comfortable. So anyway, I told him a guy had called me "worm dirt." He laughed and said, "Zeke, you know, worm dirt is what soil is made out of. Without worms you wouldn't have any good soil. Without soil no life. So, he's saying you are important. Without you, there's nothing. He's calling you the essence of life. Consider it a compliment." He smiled a big smile. I didn't smile. I looked away from him out the window beside his desk. He was trying to be nice. I knew that. But there are times when someone being nice to you doesn't matter because you're so angry that you can't think.*

*There are times when I do feel very visible. When I really feel visible, when I set a fire, then I feel real powerful, like no one can move me. That must be how Hendrix felt when he lit his guitar on fire. But I never want to feel like that with anyone around. No, that feeling must be kept from everyone. It's my own private feeling, never to be shared.*

She cared about this kid. She felt in her bones that he was not an arsonist, but, rather, an adolescent pyromaniac. A big difference. But how, she wondered, could she convince the judge and prosecutors that an adolescent pyromaniac did not deserve to be judged as an adult? Could she?

As chief psychiatrist at the Portland Youth Center, Dr. Elizabeth Proctor balanced her administrative tasks with the more serious cases. She had been called in on Ezekiel Titcomb's right from the get-go, as the district attorney put it. The kid had been arrested in early December, the 13th it was, just before the big storm. She needed to work up a profile, then run tests on him, serious tests because the district attorney wanted to try Titcomb as an adult. Typical, she thought. If there ever was a juvenile, Ezekiel Titcomb filled the bill.

The charges against Zeke were all over the Maine papers, even in *The Boston Globe*, thanks to a special to the paper, Mr. Chip Arnold, who spent time up in Chaldea, just before and including the last fire. Dr. Proctor didn't really care about the charges or which of the several fires the authorities could prove Zeke had started.

These few journal entries that she had been reading were startling, but not very conclusive. It was this fourth one that troubled her. She picked the latest entry from last night. She reread it for the third time.

*When things burn, my mind clears up. As the flames grow, I can feel my mind taking control of me. I mean when the flames really begin to burn hot and high I see that things will be clean. No more house where my father rules the roost. No more sister giving it away to asshole guys. No more fear. No more helpless mother trying to make everything better. No more stomachache at school. No more school. All the dirt gone. Up in flames!*

*Yes, I can't tell you the power I felt when I set each fire. Even though some didn't work. All that stuff that makes me feel like crap the flames ate. Flames eat what hurts me. Plus, flames are beautiful. They are pure...a C & R word would be "pristine." The flames eat the crap that people throw at me and on me that I can't stop, the stuff that makes me so angry.*

*Anger feeds the flames. How would you feel if everyone talked about your sister, if everyone poked and pushed you because you're who you are, overweight, a bit pimply, wear sweaters and shirts that no one likes because it is you wearing them. Or your father has a big mouth and is a bully.*

*I can't fight back, so I just get real mad. Then the being mad turns into wanting to light a fire and the fire lets the flames loose. I like letting the flames loose because that is my secret, my secret defense against everything. Even now, staying in this place. No one knows my secrets. No one really knows what I did. They just know that I did something. Secrets, my secrets, go way deep down.*

*The flames burn away all the crap. They burn away Atwood and the cheerleaders, they burn away not having any friends, they burn away my father, they burn away my mother's hopeless hope that everything will be so damn okay when it never will be, they burn away Michelle's sorry life, hell, they burn away my life, even, because when I watch them I forget who I am. That's it, no more. Done.*

Dr. Proctor dropped Zeke's journal on her lap and sat back in her chair. She was tired. The case weighed on her. She was a small town girl once, from over in Livermore Falls. But she got out. To college in Boston, then to graduate school in New York, and some time on the West Coast with a guy who everybody, including herself, knew was bad news. She had come back to Portland, full circle so to speak. Yes, she knew the small town psyche.

# Chapter 21

*A low pilot flame burns deep inside all the time. I don't have to feed it; it feeds itself. Other things feed it, too. My father feeds it, my sister feeds it, my mother when she's helpless, which is most all of the time, feeds it. And the losers at school when they pick on me. But not the teachers. They don't feed it. In fact, I'll admit it, Coccinella and Resnick, they keep the flame low enough so that I can breathe. Most of the time, everything feeds the flame, and I can't catch my breath. Like it's stealing my oxygen. I have to concentrate on controlling the flame's heat; I have to control myself so that I can breathe.*

*The only peace I find is when I light a fire or when I plan to light one or when I imagine that I am lighting one. Then the flame inside me disappears. So when I light fires, or spend time planning them, I am free and I can breathe.*

*After I lit the warehouse on fire, I felt so free, so safe. I felt safe because I could breathe again. I think I have had this flame in me ever since I was a kid, which is not all that long ago, I know. Only the flame felt different back then. It felt like a friend. That's the only way to explain it. It felt like it wanted me to do something for it. The flame was like an urge.*

*I lit a fire in the backyard once. I think I was in the first grade. This new kid in my class came over one afternoon. When my mother went upstairs, I took some stove matches from the kitchen and we went out behind the shed. I found some sticks and then some dried grass and I started a fire. It took about four matches, I remember.*

*The kid, I forget his name, didn't stay in our class too long, maybe two months. He was scared and kept saying "You shouldn't do this. It's dangerous. My mother said never to play with matches." I laughed and told him not to worry, that I'd stamp it out before anything happened. Of course, something did happen.*

*After I lit the little fire, the breeze came up and spread the fire in two directions, in toward the shed and out toward the field. The kid started yelling and crying, which really ticked me off. My mother came out to see what the commotion was about before I could stomp out the grass fire, which was burning steadily. She screamed bloody murder, and put out the part of the fire that had just touched the shed enough to begin to singe a shingle by the back corner.*

*I put out the section of the fire that was heading toward the field. I had a smile on my face not because I was proud that I had put out the fire but because, inside, I was imagining how the fire would look once it spread to the field behind our yard.*

*My mother grabbed me and marched me into the house and told me to go to my room, said that my father would hear about this. The boy, who was standing by the backdoor to the house, had stopped crying. He just looked at me as my mother pulled me past him. She told him that he should go home now. He turned and ran down out of the yard.*

*You can imagine what happened when my father came home. I heard him drive up and then I heard him and my mother talking downstairs in the kitchen. The conversation was not pleasant, I know that. I could tell by the sounds of the voices of the two of them. My father's voice would rise up and then my mother's voice would respond, then the deep voice would get deeper only to be interrupted by the soft voice getting louder. Then the voices stopped and there was complete silence.*

*I had a dog then, Timmy. He was about five years old when I was in first grade. He was a mutt, mostly Retriever and German Shepherd. Timmy was my best friend. I used to tell him everything back then. When I felt bad, when I felt good, I would talk to Timmy.*

*I was sitting on the bed when the silence came. Timmy was on the bed with me, his head in my lap. The sound of my father's footsteps coming upstairs broke the silence. My father threw open the door, and, in his controlled, angry voice asked me, "What the hell were you thinking, Zeke? Are you stupid, or what?" I knew right then that I was not going to cry. I didn't say a word. I didn't say a word. I kept patting Timmy, who looked up at my father. My father stood in front of me and sort of yelled, "Say something, goddammit!" I continued patting Timmy, who now sat up beside me.*

*"Zeke," he yelled, "I'm talking to you! What do you have to say for yourself? Why on earth did you light a fire behind the shed?" I still didn't say anything. I didn't dare to even look at him. Timmy whined, then jumped off the bed and sat by the bedroom door where my mom was now leaning with her arms folded on her chest. She was pale. "Eben, stop it. Let him be for a while."*

*"I will like hell! He could've burned down the house. And the field. And who knows what else!" My father picked me up off the bed and shook me. Then he threw me on the floor. He raised his hand. My mother screamed, "Eben. Let him alone!" and quickly moved between us. "Don't you dare!" she said, looking him straight in the eye.*

*"Get out of my way!" he yelled, pushing my mother aside. She lost her balance and fell on the bed. My father slapped me twice in the face, even though I covered my head. I did not cry. "God damn you. What kind of son are you?" he said as he hit me the second time.*

*By this time my mother stood up from the bed and ran out of the room. I sat on the floor. I will always remember the look of total disgust my father had on his face when he looked down at me one last time before he turned to leave. And I will never forget what he did as he left the room. He yanked Timmy by the collar to pull him out of the way. Poor Timmy was doing nothing. He was just sitting in front of the door by that time, nervous about all the yelling. My father tugged him hard, dragged him inside the room. Timmy yelped.*

*I ran to Timmy. I petted him and he licked my face. Timmy's been dead for quite a while. I still can't talk about it. But maybe that's when the flame in me really began to burn. I wonder where my sister was when this happened. I don't remember her being around. Maybe it was one of the times that she had run away to her friend's house in Grimes.*

༻༺

"I like the poem, Morris...a lot," said David Coccinella. "I like the way you read it, too. Sounds good, and the ending works well." He downshifted his pick-up, put on his blinker, and slowed to make the left turn onto the Rome Road. Then he came to a full stop to wait for three cars coming the other way on Route 2. He noticed a fully loaded logging truck in his rear view mirror.

"Thanks. The questions you had about those lines in the last stanza got me to thinking again, so I reworked it last week." Morris Resnick put the poem back into his leather folder.

"It's a strong poem, for sure. You capture the essence of Aretha Franklin, her voice, her singing style, and the times." Coccinella saw the logging truck barreling toward his truck. It was headed toward the Livermore Falls mill. Every time one of these rigs passed him he wondered whether he would be hit. He gripped the steering wheel with both hands.

"Heaven knows; it's work," said Morris as the logging truck roared past his door. Looking up, Resnick watched the receding truck, the butt end of the logs that loaded it down.

"For sure and certain. Where will you send it?"

"I'm not sure. I'll wait until I can send it with several others. The galleys for the third book are coming this week, I think. They'll take some time."

"When's the volume supposed to come out?"

"In April, so they say."

"That's great, Morris. It's solid. I think you've read all of them aloud to me over the past year." Coccinella took a right off of the Rome Road onto Tucker Road. "We've certainly had some great talks about poetry in this truck, haven't we? "

"Ongoing truck cab poetics. It's fitting we talk about poetry in a truck traveling back roads. Poetry in America." Resnick looked out into the shadows slanting through the thick woods. "Janice said to stay for supper. She'll be back from Waterville in a hour or so."

"Yeah, thanks. Never pass up a Resnick meal. The best in the state."

He had the pickup in four-wheel drive now as he headed up the old, narrow logging road toward Morris's house. The snow, mounded high on both sides, seemed ominous in the afternoon light. The town plowed the road, making one trip up and back, and that was it. The driver, Buzz Hinckley, always cut a good swath as a turnaround just beyond where the Resnicks had shoveled a place for their two cars. The Resnicks house, the last of only two houses on the road, was a simply designed variation of a New England Cape.

"You got a pisser of a road here, Morris," laughed Coccinella. His pickup, a Ford F 150, slipped a little to the right as he passed over the culvert.

"Maine living, David, don't complain," Morris Resnick said dryly.

"It's always the same damn spot. That culvert is a problem in every season, it seems."

"Yeah, I once started a poem about it, but it never went anywhere."

"That's because the subject is so damn ornery. I thought Buzz Hinckley was going to fix it for you this fall."

"Well, he came up here in September, maybe two weeks before the fire, and poured some dirt around it and drove his truck back and forth over it to pack it down. Then we had that two-day rainstorm and it washed out again. There's no sense in trying to do anything until spring. We're lucky they can get the plow up over the culvert."

One of the unwritten upcountry rules is: check the stoves as soon as you get home. Regardless of the season, check the stoves. Stoke them if need be. Always keep the house warm. The last thing anyone would want is frozen pipes. Stoves were to be tended in any season. Up in Chaldea and environs, there easily could be frost in the middle of July, usually in the low-lying areas around rivers when the moon is full and the night clear. In winter, first allegiance is to heat and that means tending the wood stove.

The Resnick house was slightly chilled. Janice had left hours ago, and the fire in the Vermont Castings Defiant in the living room had burned down to embers, so Morris immediately fed it. Dave looked out the back window by the kitchen counter at the frozen path to the outhouse. The first few cracks and pops of the rekindled fire echoed in the living room.

He turned to watch his poet friend set some thin pine sticks on a few sheets of crumpled old *New York Times* in the side firebox of the vintage Victorian kitchen stove, a Franklin. The old cast iron and nickel-plated stove had cooked over twenty years of amazing meals to family, friends, and guests from New York City to Moscow. The snaps and crackling pops of the pine warmed David. He took a seat at the kitchen table as Morris shoved a few small poplar logs onto the kindling.

"We need a beer," Morris stated, setting the iron cook lid back on with the prong. He opened up the floor door to the root cellar and brought out two nicely chilled bottles of Cadillac Mountain Stout.

"Ah, yes, a clarifying ale. Thank you very much, Mr. Resnick."

"Gotta have glasses." Morris set down a tall one in front of David. "It's been a long day," he said, and sat down next to his friend. They were both quiet as they poured their beers.

David took a long swig, wiped his mouth of foam, and set his glass down. "I can't wait for Christmas break."

Morris took a swig. "It has been a rather interesting year so far, wouldn't you say, David," he noted. His high-pitched laugh and smile made David laugh softly to the floor.

When he looked back up at Morris, he said, "Yup, the fires

have taken their toll." The heat from the kitchen stove began to warm his face. He could see the bright orange glow of the living room stove through the tiny pie-shaped opening in the air vent on the door. The two-foot birch logs that Morris had stuffed in now threw some heat, though it hadn't reached the kitchen yet. "The kids are at wit's end, too," he added.

"Yeah. The whole affair disturbs."

"Zeke Titcomb came in after school today. He seemed more subdued than usual. That kid has something cooking inside, I'd say. Such a soft-spoken kid wound so tight."

"They grow them like that up here." Morris sipped his beer. "What did he want?" Morris asked.

"He came in and sat down in a front row desk without saying anything. I said hello, but remained sitting at the desk, grading some quizzes. After a few minutes, he asked me about, of all things, Ulysses and the other guy, if you can believe that. I mean he didn't name them directly, but he remembered me telling the class about them. He was fascinated about souls being flames. Odd."

"Nothing surprises up here anymore."

"No, I know. But you know how he is. He just appears sometimes, as though he just materialized. Then, after his visit, he quietly gets up and leaves without saying a word. Most of the time, that is. There is something very strange about him, when I think about him and how he acts." David fiddled with his beer glass, turning it with his left hand, all the while watching his hand.

"Well, today he came down to the library. He still visits two or three times a week, just like he used to do back at Chaldea. It must have been after he saw you. He walks over to my desk, self-contained and polite, and asks me if I need any help putting books away. I told him sure and gave him some magazines to sort and put back and a few books to shelve."

Morris stood and picked up two more small logs to fill the kitchen stove box, which burned hard and steady and wrapped the kitchen table area in a comfortable heat. "He's an odd duck, David.

How do you contend with a father like that, with a sister out of control?"

"I have no idea. I am fascinated by how he deals with the other kids. At times, he seems to inhale or ingest their teasing and their torment. It's as though he lets it pass through him, but it can't. No one, especially an adolescent, just accepts such hurt."

"Today, he mentioned that his sister loved all kinds of sixties music, and he wanted to know more about it. When I said that's interesting, how did she get involved with sixties music, he simply shrugged his shoulders and told me that his sister knew about a lot of different things. It was the expressionless look on his face that struck me. I have never seen him emotional about anything. And those eyes. Pure steel all the time. Has he ever said anything to you about his sister or father?"

"Once, before the fire I think, after school, Zeke said to me out of the blue, 'My father's an idiot.' I looked up from my desk and asked him why, and Zeke said, 'He's tries to push everybody around.' I asked him why he said that. He got up from the desk where he was sitting and said, 'Naw, never mind,' turned and walked out the room as quickly as he had walked in and sat down. He does that a lot."

"He's a peculiar kid. But I must say, David, he's one of many." Morris grinned.

"You can say that again," said Coccinella, "I've never seen him with a friend. I wonder who he hangs around with, if he hangs around." He stretched his legs out from under the kitchen table, holding his beer glass in his lap.

"He doesn't strike me as the hanging around type," said Resnick.

"Yup, he is definitely a loner," said Coccinella. "You wonder about kids like that." He surveyed the open floor space and fixed his eyes on the baby grand piano in the far corner of the living room. He noticed how the branch of the indoor orange tree stretched out beside the piano stool.

"I think I hear the Subaru coming up the road. Janice must be home."

# Chapter 22

*What are flames, really? Are they simply a fire? Then, what's a fire? I have no idea. Flames and fire are purely magic. There are a lot of songs about fire. The Doors song I've heard. My sister had me listen to it. The name of the song is "Light My Fire." Everyone has heard of it; it's an oldie. I like the line about setting the night on fire. That would be a real cool thing to do. Better than watching the northern lights, I bet. Can you imagine watching the night lit up in flames? Unbelievable. That would set me totally free. I would want to fly up and into the flaming night sky. I would catch fire, flames coming off my body, my arms and legs. I'd be like a fiery bird. I would swoop up and down and around like a fiery osprey above the river. A flying human flame.*

*I also like the line with the words love and funeral pyre. I had to look up the word "pyre" so I could try and make sense out of the line. It's a weird word because it means a fire to burn a dead body. I am still trying to figure out how love can be a funeral pyre. I mean, I don't know much about love.*

*In the sixth grade, Carrie Duchamp said she loved me. She used to send me notes all the time, in class, during lunch in the cafeteria, at recess, on the bus. She used to try and sit next to me all the time. Then one day, she said that she didn't love me anymore. I don't know what happened. She never told me.*

*I loved Timmy. I would have died for Timmy. He was always there for me, the way someone who loves you is supposed to be there for you. He was dependable. He accepted me just the way I was. He never made stupid demands on me. I know he was just a dog, but he was more than just a dog to me. That's why I can't talk about his death. That's why I wanted to...well, I won't say what I wanted to do to my father when he yanked Timmy way back when I was in the first grade. I know that I had no love for him when he did that.*

*I know this girl in my grade who I would like to like and then maybe, after a while, I could love her, but I'm not sure that love can happen like that. From what I can gather, love just happens. But if it just happens, then it can suddenly just not happen. Can't it? It makes sense that if you can fall "in" love, then you can fall "out" of love. I'm not sure that I could love anyone the way I loved poor Timmy. I've never stopped loving him even though he's dead. I wouldn't want to stop loving him. I mean I couldn't fall "out" of love with him. I don't know when I stopped loving my father, but I did.*

*Anyway, this funeral pyre idea is complicated, I think. For me, it's complicated. What does love have to do with burning a dead body? Love can burn you to death, I guess. It can consume you like a flame can consume something. That makes sense to me.*

*Love is a fire. Flames are love. I love flames and fires, does that mean that I love love? Okay, I'm getting weird. I have these ideas. But I do love fire and flames. Maybe I could love Charlie from Stephen King's* The Firestarter. *She was a pyrokinetic. Man, I wish that I could light fires with my mind. Even though she was a mutant – that would be okay because I feel like I'm a mutant, too. Only I don't have her power. My social studies teacher said that teenagers cannot love, that they are in love with the idea of being in love. This ticked a lot of kids off and the class went sort of crazy. The discussion carried over into Coccinella's class because we were reading* Romeo and Juliet *at the time. Coccinella didn't say much. He sort of monitored our discussion. He always asked questions like "What do you mean when you say 'you do not need to have experience to feel love'"? He always wants us to be precise, that's his word, to explain ourselves.*

*I wonder if Michelle loves that asshole Jack Tatum she's going around with now. I don't mean to swear, I don't like swearing, but some things just tick me off. And what she does with him ticks me off. My parents never talk about it, but they know, everyone knows. You hear everything about them everywhere, school, church, the grocery store, even at the gas station once I heard someone say to my father, "She was in here with him last night, Eben. That's all I know." My father came back into the car and shoved the car into first gear and took off real mad. I wonder if my father ever loved Michelle or loves her now...at all. I wonder if he loves anybody. He's hotheaded and has his own purpose, which is to be right all the time.*

*Anyway, I guess the line from the song means love can consume you and even kill you or maybe it means that love is a kind of killing in itself because it's such a strong emotion...I don't want to talk about it anymore. I keep my love about fires to myself. That is until I show my love of fires by lighting one. Lighting a fire is an act of love. You know, like Romeo willing to take poison for his love of Juliet.*

*Flames do not have any emotion. They simply exist. They do one thing: they burn things up. They do not think about whether what they are doing is good or bad. They just do what they do, which is burn. Fires do not think and they do not feel. They are perfect that way. I want to be like them and I try to be. I want to obliterate the world with fire. Without any feeling, any emotion whatsoever.*

The Chaldea town dump sat outside of town on the Grimes Road. A hand painted sign in black lettering that says "DUMP" loosely tacked to the trunk of a dead elm tree hangs eye level as a driver curves along the road with ole man Thompkins' cow pasture on his right. The gravel road into the dump is about a quarter of a mile long, severely rutted and where it is not rutted, its surface is like a giant washboard. Large intestines get quite a vibrating shake. The Chaldea joke is if you're constipated, then all you have to do is ride up and down the dump road for fifteen minutes and you'll be just fine.

The dump, a large open pit, has been scheduled for closing for three years, but the town cannot afford to close it and convert to the necessary means for sending all refuse to the new land fill site in Narratunk that is supposed to service the entire region. The Chaldea dump burns twenty-four hours a day in noncompliance with the new state regulations.

Several small flames flicker continually in various piles of trash. Narrow columns of black-and-white smoke rise from these smoldering piles. Old couches, recliners, shelves, beds, plastic bags of trash, heaped willy-nilly, lay off to the right of the drop off point. Old refrigerators, stoves, TV's, and aluminum vents, engines, and washing machines sit off to the left.

Where the dump road ends and widens into the drop off point sits a little shed shaped like an oversized telephone booth. There is one window in the shed that faces the dump, and a small potbellied Franklin stove whose chimney sticks out the backside of the shed. Inside, sitting in an old stuffed chair, Record Owens, the caretaker, watches the comings and goings. In all seasons, except in subzero weather with biting wind, the door to the shed is open so that when you drive into the dump, visitors can see Record sitting there in his chair, reading. He will look up from whatever magazine he has found in the trash to read, wave, and go back to his magazine.

A heavyset man, slow moving and slow to speak, Record wears black plastic glasses with thick lenses. Every so often, he will leave the shed and amble over to the drop off point to direct a vehicle if he thinks it needs to unload at a particular spot. Or he will pick over something that someone has left. Because of his job, he gets first dibs when dump picking. Record doesn't look for much, just magazines and a rare car part that he might need for his old truck.

Lots of kids, mostly boys, always show up at the dump. They want to shoot rats, mostly. They want to hone their rifle skills for hunting season. Record doesn't mind them doing that as long as they behave themselves and don't shoot when someone is unloading garbage. The older kids that come up there to drink and get loud don't do that until Record is gone. He leaves at five o'clock sharp and closes the dump entrance with a large chain that he connects between two posts.

On this cold December Saturday morning, Record poured a cup of coffee from his thermos and watched the Titcomb boy walk over to the fairly sizable fire burning at the rim of the pit off to the right. A small couch and some shelves burned heavily, and thick black smoke twisted up from the flames.

The boy stood close to the fire, watching it carefully. Every once and a while he would take a long stick he had found and poke a piece of wood. His poking stirred up sparks and created a sizzle in the flame. Record noticed the boy smiling at the sparks that the kid had prodded alive. The boy gazed deep into the flame, oblivious to fact that Record Owens was watching him as he sipped his coffee.

# Chapter 23

*I keep having strange dreams about fire. I don't really want to tell them because they're my secrets, but I keep thinking about this strange story that Coccinella told us one time. I think the story is Chinese, I can't really remember. It's about this boy who has a secret, and he wants to share the secret. He is bursting to tell it, but he promised not to tell anyone. He's upset because he doesn't know how to deal with his urge to tell the secret and with his promise to keep it. What's great is that the boy comes up with an answer.*

*He solves his problem...actually it's a "dilemma." What he does is he goes out into some deserted place and digs a deep hole. Then he whispers - I like that he whispers - his secret into the hole then shovels the dirt back into the hole and buries the secret forever. So he thinks.*

*The boy leaves his buried secret thinking well, that's that. But it isn't "that's that." Things are never "that's that," I guess...except maybe fires. But the boy thinks he has solved his problem. He thinks that he has satisfied his urge to tell his secret and that he has kept his secret buried so that no one can learn it.*

*But what happens next is really funny. Some reeds grow right on the refilled hole where the secret is buried. You know, those tall, long stalks that are hollow. I think that they were bamboo.*

*And then, guess what? Some other boy, who's a musician, comes along and cuts some reeds because he wants to make a flute from the reeds. Well, he cuts the reeds that grew on the soil that covered the hole with the secret in it and makes a flute. And, when he plays his new flute, the flute tells the secret in the musical notes that the musician makes when he blows a tune! That's so weird, I think. But it's a little scary, too. I mean it makes you stop and think. Which is what C & R would say is the only important part of learning.*

*The story makes me want to tell my dreams because it makes me feel that no one can really keep secrets. What I figure is this: I figure if I tell my dreams here, then no one will find out about them because I am really only telling them to myself, since I am my own story. And no bamboo reeds can grow out of my own story because I am only talking to myself.*

⁂

Sergeant Calvin Talbot, typing up a burglary report, picked up the phone. "Police, Talbot here."

"Get someone over here, quick. Someone tried to burn my house down. This is Naomi Crowell."

"What happened? Are you okay?"

"Oh, I'm fine. I put the fire out. No need for the fire department. But you need to take a look around. This is getting out of hand. If it keeps up like this the whole of this end of Blackstrap Road will be burned to cinders."

"I'd say. I'll tell Chief Avery immediately. We'll be out there as soon as we can. You sure the fire's out? We've got to inform the fire department in any case. So, someone from there will be out to your place, too."

"No sirens, Cal. I don't want sirens. The damn thing is out. I put it out with three buckets of water from the cellar. It's in the back corner. Someone tried to light me up around that punky sill."

"Ayuh, okay, we'll be over."

"Good. I'll put some coffee on."

࿐

"Not much damage. Randy is inspecting the site now. How'd you know there was a fire?" Chief Corson leaned against the kitchen counter and sipped his coffee. Naomi stood over her electric range.

"It was pure luck. I didn't have my back yard light on, and I usually do that. Tonight for some reason, I didn't get to it. I was in the den, but I came into the kitchen to heat up some water for tea." Naomi wiped her hands on her apron. She added, "I noticed an eerie, dull light rippling from the corner of the house into the dark. Well, given the state of things in this town, I ran outside and saw some flames just beginning to take hold of the corner of the house."

"Good thing you ran out outside," said Chief Avery as he set his down his coffee cup.

"I was terrified, Lionel. Without thinking, I ran back in here, almost tripped heading down cellar. Drew a bucket of water, opened the bulkhead and poured her on the flame. That about did it, but I added two more for good measure. I don't want to lose this house." She poured more coffee into Lionel's cup. "Poor Herbert and Dot. They stayed with me. They are real troopers. Now, they're in Portland. I wonder if they'll ever come back."

Randy Holmes knocked on the back door, opened it, leaned in, and said, "There's no hidden flames up in the wall. Everything is doused good. There's nothing of note around the area, but we should come back tomorrow, Chief, and have a good look around."

"Thanks, Randy," said Chief Corson. The chief sat down at the kitchen table. "Lionel, you've got to come over here with me. We've got to find something, some clue about who did this. When word of this gets out, and it's already out, no doubt, the town will be in complete panic mode."

Lionel picked up one of Naomi's famous tollhouse cookies and took a bite. "Ayuh, you got that right. Did I tell you that I saw Eben

Titcomb at Putnam's store the day before yesterday, and he was spouting off to some customers about his watch group and how they're patrolling town after their shift at the Mill."

Naomi piped in. "Land sakes alive. He's a piece of work. Mister Justice. Law and Order and that silly Lock and Load mentality."

"I hope to hell that he or one of his cronies don't shoot someone," added Renee. He stood away from the counter and added, "Well, Naomi, thanks for the coffee and those some fine cookies." He patted his belly. "I'm trying to lose some weight, but, by God, I can never pass up your cookies. Don't tell Hannah. God, she'll toss my beer out of the fridge." He chuckled.

"I'll be going too, Naomi. You're okay. Rest easy. I'll send Norman by in the cruiser in a few hours." Chief Avery picked up his hat and stood up.

"Thank you gentlemen. I'm sorry about all this bother. But I didn't want to be the next casualty on this end of Blackstrap Road. Isn't it peculiar that everything is happening down here? Except for the schools, of course."

"Ayuh, we've noticed that," said Lionel. "Naomi, if you need anything just call me at the office or at home. Don't fret."

"Well, I wonder if he won't come back and finish the job."

The two chiefs left. Naomi Crowell, smiling out at the men from the warm yellow light of her kitchen, shut and locked the back door behind them. Together they walked around to the front of the house. As they passed the front porch, both men caught sight of a dark figure, eerily illuminated by the streetlight across the street, standing beside Naomi's mailbox. It was Eben Titcomb.

Michelle Titcomb snuggled up against Jack Tatum, her right hand gently rubbing his right thigh. Tatum kept his eyes on the road despite the fact that Michelle began nibbling his ear. She cooed, "What ya thinkin', huh?"

"I was thinkin' about all these fires. Naomi Crowell's place is just three houses down from yours."

"I told you. That isn't my house any more. I'm never going near that friggin' hell again." Michelle sat up and put her seat belt on. "Besides I could care less about the fires."

"You could care less? Easy girl. Some friggin' idiot is setting fires, on your street for the most part, and you could give a sweet shit?"

"Awe come on. It's no big deal. Some fucked up freak is angry about his life or the world...or both."

"Hey, Shelly, people are scared. They're afraid they might be next."

"I'spose...I mean...I know that." She sighed. "I can't shake thinking about my family, that's all. It's clouding up my brain." Michelle lit a cigarette and blew her first drag against the windshield. The smoke bounced off and rolled around in the cab. "You're a good man, Jack."

"You're not so bad yourself...when you're not being so ornery."

"Ouch." She blew smoke in his face and grabbed his crotch. Jack flinched but continued to drive.

# Chapter 24

*I caught Atwood picking his nose once. It was right after Mr. James's math class, a class I truly dreaded. Not because of the math but because of the teacher and because of where I sat.*

*Another reason was that the teacher was a bully, and he played favorites. So, if you were a nobody, you were screwed to the wall. Aside from the fact that the guy was a Nazi in how he ran the class. He used to put little pieces of tape down on the floor and then put the leg of the desk on the tape to keep the desks spaced evenly between one another and between each row. How sick is that? He'd actually walk around and move your desk while you were working on a math problem if you had accidentally moved your seat.*

*He used to do the meanest things. He was careful about how he was mean, too. He was very subtle. He'd wear shoes with thick, wavy rubber souls that would squeak when he walked. So, during a test, he would walk by the desk of students that he wanted to bother and walk so that his shoes would squeak real loud. He would stand by my desk and just twist his shoes on the linoleum floor and make them really squeak. I'd look up at him and he would sort of grunt. Then he'd turn and walk away, pretending that he was only checking on my work.*

*Once, when Laverne Nichols pointed out that he had made a mistake on the board, he had a conniption. He got all red and stammered, and then he said that he had done that intentionally to see if we were paying attention. Yeah, right. I hated that guy. He reminded me of my father.*

*Anyway, I pretended that I didn't see Atwood picking his nose. And Atwood pretended that he hadn't picked his nose. But we both knew that I had seen him do it. It's funny when two people pretend that something hasn't happened when, in fact, that something has happened. It's embarrassing to ignore something that, inside yourself, you are not ignoring. It's like trying to ignore reality.*

*You can't really do it, even though I try all the time. I know because after Atwood and I had pretended nothing had happened, he came walking past me real fast and bumped into my shoulder hard, knocking me down in the hallway. We both knew what had happened. I picked up my books, thinking that I'd like him to feel as helpless as I did.*

*I remember the expression on his face the day the school burned down. A bunch of kids had gathered out on the street in front of the mess. He was there with his crowd and he was just shaking his head. He'd look down at the ground, then up at the devastation and then shake his head again. I wanted to smile, but I didn't dare. If someone saw me smile, I would've been killed. Really. But I was smiling to beat the band inside. There's nothing like a fire to shut everybody up.*

*The reason I mention this nose-picking incident is that I feel like this inside all the time, that I am ignoring reality, like I'm pretending that something hasn't happened when it has happened. I hate having this feeling. I wake up with it. I go to school with it. I have it when I am eating. I probably have it when I am sleeping, but I don't know it because I am asleep. There's one other time when this feeling goes away.*

*I don't have this feeling when I plan to light a fire or when I light one. I am totally free when I light fires. I feel light, like I can soar up in the sky and float, float away from Dad's moods, from Michelle's reputation, from helpless Mom, from Atwood's stares and comments, from everything that ties my stomach in knots every day of my life. It's like how a cloud must feel, maybe. Not that clouds feel. Like I've said before, I try not to feel a lot of the time. Feeling can get you into a whole lot of trouble.*

*There's only one feeling that I have when I light a fire. I feel excited. That's because I can't wait to see the flames start. It's great to feel that anticipation. I almost shake, I'm so happy to start a fire. Then I become calm and controlled, as though I was putting a small, important piece onto a model boat or plane. You know, one of those special pieces that make the model work and that tells whoever is looking at it that it was put together right.*

*I used to make models, planes and boats mostly, but I don't do that now. I stopped in the seventh grade. Once, when I was working on this big model, the World War II aircraft carrier* Yorktown, *my father came into my room. I was sitting at my desk, gluing some small guns onto special places on the side of the ship. It was taking a lot of time. I had my desk light shining on the model and I was looking real close at where the piece was supposed to be glued. Well, he barged in my room and said, "Zeke, you didn't put out the garbage. Go do it." I looked up, holding the model piece on the tip of my middle finger, and said, "In a minute Dad. Let me glue this one piece, okay? Please?" He walked over to me. "Now, son. The garbage is more important. Your models can wait. Besides, why you waste your time with that stuff, I'll never know. Don't you have homework?"*

*Anyway, lighting a fire is like planning to piece together a model once you read the directions. And, lighting a fire is a special secret. It's very personal. The word is "intimate." I remember Coccinella using that word about a poem he had us read. Maybe flames are like poetry in some way.*

"Are you ever coming back down here?" asked Susan Whitcomb. "What's going on up there, anyhow?"

Chip Arnold, with a dry mouth and a throbbing head from last night's meal with the President of Chaldea Paper Industries and its international contingent, took a few seconds to respond. The meal had turned into a late night of pleasantly rowdy conversation about capitalism, America, the consumption of paper and its necessity, none of which he could remember. Now, he had to explain the last several days to his editor. "Well, there's the weather. You've heard about the snow."

"Yeah, we got an inch of so down here, but then it turned to rain.

Lots of wind off the water."

"Then there were two other fires. The town is in a panic, actually. Guys are helping out the police by patrolling in their pickups. A lot is going on. So basically, I've got to interview some more people." Chip got up and walked to the window of the hotel and looked out across the road at the bleak, partially frozen Kennebec. The river wasn't completely iced over and river fog was rising from invisible open water off to the left. The sky was clear. The morning light made the scene look like a Hopper painting, he thought. Thank God there would be sun today.

"Okay, finish up. I know you like the human interest angle, so follow your nose."

"I usually do. But, listen, this whole thing is curious. Someone is lighting fires on a seemingly regular basis. I mean there's an odd pattern to it, the schools then the houses down on Blackstrap Road. Both the fire chief and the police chief are totally befuddled. I think they think it is someone from town. But they are holding their cards close to the vest."

"Well, small town police and fire work can't be all that difficult, I'd imagine."

"Susan, the town is strung out with fear. Everyone is on edge from the store owners to the diary farmers to the mill workers. There's something about fires. A fire is primeval."

"Well, stay for the week. Then phone me in the story."

"I hope to hell no snowstorm comes in. Old man Putnam, the grocery store owner, told me that usually there's a corker of a snowstorm around the middle of December, just before Christmas. I hope it doesn't come early."

"Good luck, Chip. Maybe something will break soon."

Chip peeked again out his hotel room window. A crow flew low across the river. "Bye, Susan. Have an espresso on me. It's not like I can order one at Putnam's Grocery Store." Arnold chuckled as he put down the receiver.

ஒ

"Well, city mouse, heard you tied one on with the big boys at the Mill over at Peltonen's house. His wife puts on quite a spread, doesn't she?" Chief Avery leaned back in his office chair and swiveled toward Chip Arnold. "Have a seat."

"Thanks, Chief," said Chip. He sat on the other side of Avery's desk, got out his notepad. "Tuula Peltonen can cook. She told me she wanted to serve reindeer meat but couldn't find any. She said that it's different from venison."

"Yeah, it is. She serves it raw. It's tasty, a lighter taste than regular deer meat. You eat deer meat?"

"I've had it up in Vermont when I was on a story about a supposed sea monster in Lake Champlain. Venison stew."

"It's gotta be cooked just right and the meat has to be cured properly." Avery reached for a report that his Lieutenant had left on his desk. "To what do I owe this visit?"

"The Crowell place. Did you find anything?"

"Not a blessed thing." Avery sighed. He looked at Arnold. "You know, I do not know how we are going to track this arsonist down."

"I'm going to talk to Chief Corson again this afternoon."

"Well, he'll tell you the same thing. This guy has no reason for what he's doing. We've said this time and again. There appears to be no revenge motive. There's nothing to be gained from any of the fires in terms of money or insurance or anything. We're stumped."

"The town seems pretty fearful."

"Oh, people are upset plenty. You know about the men that are patrolling."

"Yeah, why in the hell are you doing that? That seems like you are asking for trouble."

"No, not really. We've got people in this town that like to make a lot of noise."

"You mean Eben Titcomb," Chip added with a smile.

"Ayuh. And on top of that, I don't have enough men to patrol around the clock. So the few extra set of eyes keeps people quiet, and I suppose it helps people in town feel safer. There's not much else I can do, frankly."

"Everybody seems to know just about what you know, chief."

"That's right. It's the way it is up here. We help each other out. We know each other's business, but we pretend that we don't."

"People have talked to me."

"They have and they haven't. They've discussed the fire, sure, but they haven't told you anything about their suspicions and their fears." Chief Avery watched Arnold scratch some notes. "Fire is a special enemy of rural living. We're all scared to death of it. I mean, we use it to live; we burn fires in our stoves in our homes, many folks make a living from wood. But fire terrifies us."

"Pretty ironic."

"Well, we live so far away from things up here. Houses are made of wood. There's no real zoning up here, so people jury-rig everything from plumbing to electricity so that once in a while all hell can break loose."

"Maybe hell is breaking loose now."

"Maybe so, Mr. Arnold. Isolation can breed fear. You can get pretty unnerved in any season in these parts. Self-reliance is no joke up here. That's why we help each other out when we have to. Because we know our turn will come soon enough." Avery leaned back in his chair.

"How do you do it?"

"There's nothing to do, Mr. Arnold. You live where you live. You adjust. Country living is country living. I could never live in the city...the noise, the traffic, no woods, no hills, no stars, no sunrise, no sunset."

"Well, country mouse, I hope you find this arsonist. You can have this weather, Chief. It isn't even really winter yet."

Chief Avery laughed. "In some ways, it's always winter up in these parts. It's part of being up here. Part of the charm."

"Charm? Some charm." Chip Arnold put away his note pad into the breast pocket of his coat.

"Well, city mouse, you do what you do."

"I'm just a flatlander, an outsider. I come up here to vacation for a bit or to get a story." Arnold stood up.

"Ayuh, you won't even think about this town when you get back to the city." Avery came around from his desk.

"God no, Chief. Why would I do that?" Arnold smiled and turned to leave.

"Hey, city mouse, you gonna talk to Eben Titcomb?"

"You bet. After I talk to Chief Corson again."

"You're in for a real treat."

"So I've heard."

⁂

"Listen, Mr. Arnold, I've seen two-hundred-year-old houses burn down in less than an hour with a heat so strong that you couldn't get within fifty feet of the fire and with flames as tall as a full grown elm." Chief Corson leaned against the door of the station's rescue truck.

"I can imagine. I wasn't being disrespectful, Chief."

"No, I know. I'm just sore about this whole episode. Kenny Quinn and I have been racking our brains. We've been out to every site again and again. There's nothing."

"Quinn's the guy from the Maine Fire Marshall's Office, right?"

"Ayuh. He's back in Augusta at the moment. No need for him up here until...."

"Well, let's not be hasty, Chief, let's hope there won't be a next time," said Arnold.

"I have bad feelings," responded Chief Corson. He walked back through the door that connected the station garage with his office. Arnold followed, notepad in hand.

The Chief continued to reflect. "You know what fire does? It strips a person naked. Everything goes, everything dear to the family, to the individual. It's about power. A fire makes a person powerless. Having your house burned down is worse than having it broken into, I'd say. Everything is obliterated."

"It's so peculiar that you've found absolutely no clues."

"We've found nothing. We've combed every site. We've talked to people who we think might have seen something. The fire marshall's office knows what the hell they are doing. They haven't seen anything like it. We're stumped so far. It's frustrating as hell, I can tell you that." Chief Corson rubbed his forehead with his right hand.

"Well, I sincerely wish you good luck, for what it's worth."

The Fire Chief stood up, and so did Chip Arnold. "Thanks, Chief. I'm a bother, I know," the journalist said, suddenly feeling sorry for the town. How many days have I been here, he wondered. He drove up here just before Thanksgiving with the intention of doing a few interviews with the locals and then hightailing it out of town, back down to civilization. But things had changed when the snow came, and then more snow came and then he stayed and then the Emery place burned down. And now here he was in Chaldea, Maine, with Christmas on the horizon.

"Mr. Arnold, I know you're going to talk to Titcomb. Maybe you already have. I dunno. Let him blow steam, but I hope to hell he doesn't make much sense so that you want to quote the guy." Corson scratched his head. "Forget I said that. None of my business."

"Hey, Chief, I haven't spoke with him yet. But don't worry. I might be from away and seem like a fish out of water to you, but I'm not stupid and I am not up here to make you guys seem like complete idiots."

Chief Corson grinned. "Maybe you have some good in you."

"Besides, I like to save the best for last." Chip grinned back at the Chief.

"I didn't know flatlanders had a sense of humor, especially journalists."

# Chapter 25

*If I could have a girlfriend, it would be the kind of girlfriend who I could share secrets with. She would accept my secrets, keep them hidden from everyone. She wouldn't be bothered by my father and she'd like my sister. My sister would help her to understand me.*

*But if I had a girlfriend it would be nice to have her really love me. Once in math class, I daydreamed that Laverne Nichols and I were going to get married. The wedding was going to take place in a dormant volcano. Laverne had said to me, "Let's be married in fire!" Getting married in fire! That's what I imagined. There we were, inside this gigantic volcanic crater. Laverne was in a white wedding gown and I was in a tuxedo. I looked at her smiling face underneath her veil and then I looked above her head into the vastness of the crater and into the deepest part of it where the lava, ash, and gases come exploding out. I looked back at Laverne, feeling so peaceful and happy knowing that we were standing inside a volcano.*

*Then Atwood stuck me in the back with his pen and I let out a squeal. Everyone in the class turned and looked at me. I was embarrassed, naturally. Atwood laughed out loud. Mr. James rolled his eyes and said, "Zeke, what on earth are you doing? Sometimes I wonder what your purpose on this planet is." Can you believe that? I felt like disappearing. Really. That's when there's a real volcano inside me. I never let it erupt in school though. I wait until later when I can think more clearly. When I can conjure flames. Now there's a real C & R word. I never realized how many words that Coccinella and Resnick use have stayed with me. Very strange. Their words are little flames that keep me going.*

∽∽

"You know, Lionel, we're working this thing as hard as we can." Chief Corson took a slow sip of his coffee, adjusted himself on the wooden chair next to Police Chief Avery's large oak desk. "The fire marshall's office is on my case, big time. We're focusing on the Junior High School and on the Walloomsac High School attempt. There's gotta be something there."

"I'm pretty sure it's a lone arsonist. There's no group involved. My gut tells me that the fires are related, but I can't prove a thing."

"Ayuh, I agree. In a town like this you won't find a group inclined to do such mischief. Unless there's outsiders doin' it. But we'd a spotted any outsiders without much of a problem. You know, I keep thinking about the time of these fires." Corson looked up from his coffee. "They all occurred on Monday nights or on Tuesday mornings."

"Those Tuesday fires could have been started Monday nights, right?" Chief Avery leaned forward and put his elbows on his desk.

"I suppose. I wonder what's important about Monday nights or Tuesday mornings?"

"Beats me."

"But I agree that they are related. They've got to be. It's the time of the fires that connects them for me. It's got to be one person. This person got the bug after the High School fire. God knows what would've happened if the Junior High and the Walloomsac High attempts had succeeded. Jeez'um." Corson shook his head. He stood up. "I've got to get back to the station. See you at Walloomsac at five o'clock, right?" He nodded to Chief Avery.

"You bet. I'm hoping this time around that the fire marshall's inspection yields something. Maybe we can catch a break."

"Don't hold your breath, Lionel."

"The whole damn town has been holding its breath for too damn long, what with Christmas coming...what a mess." Chief Corson headed out the door.

Lionel Avery stood up and walked around from his desk, looked out the window to see the fire chief drive off. There was a mackerel sky. Weather was coming in. They'd be more snow though the weatherman said only light flurries. Hell, he thought, I really do need a new snow shovel.

# Chapter 26

*I love snowstorms. And not just because we get out of going to school. I like snowstorms because the world gets erased. There's nothing like a blizzard when the snow is blown around by the wind and it piles up and is hard to dig out because of the drifts. You can't see anything. You get blinded. You have whiteouts. When there's a blizzard, there's always a whiteout. But you've gotta be watching the storm so that you can see the whiteout. That's funny...you watch the storm so you can see the actual moment when the storm blows the snow around so hard that you're blind.*

*I've been out in the snow when there was a whiteout. I was lucky because I was just in the backyard. It was scary; I didn't know where I was. It seemed like forever, but it was probably not that long because I remember the wind letting up and then seeing the back porch and my mother hollering for me to come inside.*

*A really good snowstorm is like a fire. They both devour the world; they cover everything up. The snow covers the earth, and fires surround and cover what they're burning. It's like, though they are opposites, they do the same thing. The snow destroys by covering everything up in a blanket of ice crystals. Fire destroys by eating up what it burns.*

*One day, I was in the library, as usual, helping Resnick clean up. I was just lonely, but I never told him that. It was a safe place, the library after school, so I brought myself down there. You know, sort of to catch my breath, to feel I was safe from Atwood and his crowd.*

*Resnick always started the conversation. Sometimes he would just nod to my 'Hello' and wait a few minutes before he'd ask me if I wanted to help him. One day, after I had said hello and walked over to the newspapers and magazines, he said, "Zeke, it looks as though there's a snow storm coming. You must be excited about that, huh? No school." He was sitting at his desk reading a book. I said something like, "Yeah, I like it when it snows hard. I hope it's a real big storm."*

*Resnick said, "People used be afraid of big storms, you know. They caused all kinds of problems for people in towns like Chaldea, back before there were lots of cars." "Yeah, probably," I answered, not really interested in what he was saying. I was actually looking at a magazine, a stupid one, I remember, called* Country Living. *As if I needed to learn about how to live in the country. As if it even was living.*

*Then I said, and I don't know why I said this, but the words just came out of my mouth. I said, "I ain't afraid of a snow storm. Nothing's gonna happen. Maybe we'll lose electricity, but that can be fun because then we light candles and kerosene lamps. And we stoke up the wood stoves every hour. It's warm and quiet in the house during a storm."*

*"Well, you've got food, people near by, and access to help. Imagine when there were only farms up here in Chaldea and neighbors lived even farther away from each other than they do now. Imagine people only had horses and wagons to get to each other. Imagine how it would be to deal with a major snowstorm if you were totally isolated and couldn't easily get help." Resnick looked back down at his book.*

*I shrugged my shoulders. "What're reading, Mr. Resnick? You never stop. Every time I see you, you are reading." Resnick smiled and told me, "I'm reading a Frost poem called 'Storm Fear.' Would you like to hear it?" "Naw," I said. Resnick smiled at me and went back to his reading. I took some books from the book cart and started shelving them. The first one I picked up to put away was called* Winter in New England. *I had to laugh at that.*

*Coccinella taught us a poem by Frost called "Fire and Ice." Coccinella wanted us to memorize it. A few kids did. Most didn't do the whole poem, only a few lines. I memorized it. But I really like the opening.*

*Some say the world will end in fire,*
*Some say in ice.*
*From what I've tasted of desire*
*I hold with those who favor fire.*

*I love these lines because I want to world to end in flames. I can see flames a hundred times bigger than any dump fire, flames towering up and up and up into the sky, black smoke billowing and twisting up in the air like the smoke from a volcano. I saw pictures on TV of Vesuvius erupting. The show was about Pompeii and that other city with the long, strange name that sounded like Hercules. That's how I want the world to end. Lava, smoke, ashes falling down, explosions of flames and heavy fire.*

*Fire cleans up everything. You can start a fresh one. Everything is burned up, all the bad stuff especially. It all goes away, it just disappears, becomes incinerated.*

*Coccinella started talking about the connection between desire and fire. No one was really paying attention. Big deal, the words rhymed. Who cares? But now that I think about it, maybe there's something to it. He asked us, "How can desire destroy the world?" Everybody laughed at his question. Atwood mumbled to his friend, "This stuff sucks." Coccinella heard him, but ignored him as he usually did. No one said anything. Coccinella let it go. He could get a conversation if he wanted to, but this time he let things slide. He just said, "Okay, class is almost over. We'll tackle the idea tomorrow. Read silently for a few minutes until class ends." He usually never did that. Maybe he was tired.*

*English class can be so strange sometimes. I dunno. I don't like to think of it. I just remember the strange stuff. I like snow and fire. But fire is more interesting...C&R word "intriguing." Maybe fire does taste like desire, or does desire taste like fire? Does fire taste like anything, does desire? Poetry can drive you crazy, no kidding. I don't want to think about it.*

Eben Titcomb downshifted into second, slowing steadily as he passed the John Deere dealership. It was a little before five o'clock, dark as hell, and it had started spitting snow. He thought he saw a figure duck behind a backhoe that set back near the side door that led to the showroom and the service entrance. He drove into the driveway and up toward the door.

There was no one there. He drove around to the back of the building. Nothing. He drove out and back toward town. Wafts of snow began curling on the road. I'd better get home, he thought, it looks like we're going to get more than flurries.... Damn weathermen don't know whether they are afoot or horseback.

∽∾

"Get in here. It's starting to come down," Eben said. He knew it was her. He could tell by her gait, that easy movement of the hips even with a heavy winter coat covering her body. What in God's name was she doing walking down Main Street this time of night. Why does she do this to me? Peg will be glad that I brought her home, especially on a night like this. Eben Titcomb slowed down to give his daughter a ride home.

Michelle climbed into the truck without a word. She looked straight ahead as she shook the snow off her hair and rubbed her hands together to warm them. His eyes fixed on the road, Eben chewed the inside of his cheek. Every few seconds the swish of the windshield wipers interrupted the silence in the cab.

Finally, as Eben turned down the River Road, she spoke. "Why did you stop?"

"Because you're my daughter."

"Not hardly. Since when do you care that I'm your daughter?"

"Why don't you start behaving like a daughter?"

"All you care about is yourself and what this damn town thinks of you."

"How do you think I feel about you traipsing around town? How do you think your mother feels?"

"I don't care what either of you think. I'm eighteen. I can do what I want."

"Oh yeah, you can. You can take your drugs with those idiot friends of yours. You can hang out with men who work at the Mill, men that I have to see every day. Yeah, you're old enough to do all of that." Eben stared ahead at the road.

"What I do is none of your business."

"It is my business. You're living in my house." Eben gripped the steering wheel with both hands.

"Fine. I'll go stay with Jack. He said I could. He treats me right." She stared out the passenger window. The snow was falling steadily now. The flakes had become the size of dimes.

Eben slammed on the brakes and moved over on the shoulder of the road, the truck sliding a bit. "Jesus H. Christ! Think about your life, will you! Do you want to be a loser for the rest of your life! Huh?! Do you?"

Michelle continued to look out the passenger window. She bit a fingernail.

"Hell, Jack Tatum is about twice your age. He's a loser. He's lucky to be working at the Mill. He's not even divorced; he's separated. He's got two small kids, for God's sake. Do you think he's with you for a future?"

Michelle's jaw tightened. She shifted her weight.

"You don't know what you're doing. You are on the road to nowhere. What on earth did your mother and me do to deserve this from you? Tell me that!"

"You stupid asshole!" Michelle exploded. "You know nothing! You treat us all like pieces of shit! I'm sick of it! I'm sick of you!" Michelle began to cry. "Jack loves me. He treats me like a real person. Not like you."

"Goddamn it, Michelle! Everyone thinks you're a whore! Don't you care what people in this town think? Huh!?"

"I could care less! About them, about you. You're nothing. You work at the Mill. You think you're so important because you're a town moderator, because you're a deacon at the church, because you're a foreman at the Mill. Well, you're just another small town try-hard, no better than Jack or anyone else. You married mother when she was young, had us, and stayed put. What a great life you live!"

"We were both the same age, and times were different. Jesus, use your brain." Eben put the truck in gear and began driving again. "You're a selfish little bitch. Your brain's all gunked up! I've lost my patience with you."

"Who gives a shit! I'll move out for good this time." Michelle's crying died down into spurts of sobbing. Eben turned onto Blackstrap Road. The porch light was on and he could see Peg standing in the kitchen. He drove the truck into the driveway. Just as the truck came to a stop, Michelle pushed open her door and ran into the house. Eben turned off the lights and engine and sat for a moment in the truck. He wondered about the difference between Michelle and Zeke. The wild one versus the mild one, he mused. Life was filled with dichotomies. At least Zeke wouldn't hurt a flea and was under control. He stepped out of the truck and headed toward the house.

❧

"Mr. Titcomb, thanks for taking time to speak with me. I appreciate it." Chip Arnold, pen and notebook at the ready, put out his hand. Eben Titcomb shook his hand and offered the journalist a seat in the Selectman's Office, which sat on the first floor of the Chaldea Town Hall, another of the old brick and wood structures built during the early 20s.

"Well, Mr. Arnold, what would you like to know?" Eben had wondered when he was going to get his chance to talk to this fellow. He didn't especially want to talk to the guy, but he felt it was his duty to speak out for himself and for the town. He had seen the journalist skulking about town and sitting up in the back of the meeting the selectmen had with the police and fire departments.

"Why don't we begin with your take on what's happening in Chaldea."

"Sure, that's easy. Things like these fires don't happen in small towns like Chaldea. We all know each other. We take care of our own. So these fires have rattled us, for sure. We haven't had a major crime in Chaldea in over fifty years. So you can imagine how people feel, how I feel. We're real hurt. I take these fires personally."

"In what way?"

"I was born, raised, educated, married, and raised a family in Chaldea. It's my place, my home. We've gone through some tough times here. We don't have much, but what we have, we take care of."

"Have you traveled much outside of Chaldea?"

"I was in the Army, in the Nam. I came right home after, married after sowing a few oats, and eventually started a family, and never went anywhere, except to take the wife down to Portland shopping. No need to leave the state, really."

"So, what's your take on the fires?"

"I'll tell you something. Whoever is doing these fires will get caught. I have no doubt it's some damn kid. It's frustrating as hell."

"You started the community patrol, right?"

"Ayuh, me and a few others to help out Lionel. He's short of men, so we drive around and check out places. You know, we drive side roads and through parts of town that the officers can't get to because of other priorities. Everyone knows we are out there. It might help, but I dunno."

"You sound doubtful?"

"I'm not doubtful about catching the bastard. No. But if it's a kid, as I suspect, it's just that I know what will happen. They give the little baby a slap on the wrist, send him down to detention in Portland for awhile, and that'll be that. There's no real punishment anymore." Eben leaned forward, folded his hands together and rested his forearms on his thighs. He looked straight at Chip Arnold.

"Kids are getting away with murder and they're not being held responsible for their actions. Everybody can do what they want and then get out of it by saying that they're sorry, when really they're not sorry at all, they just want to get out of being punished.

I tell you, mister, if I get a hold of him, he won't be lighting no fires no more." Eben leaned back in his chair and stared at the journalist. He wasn't finished.

"I don't want to brag, but people know me in this town. I speak my mind. I think the townspeople respect that. We're good folk up here. We don't deserve this happening to us. We'll catch this guy, and we'll take care of the problem. We always take care of our problems. We don't need help from you or any other outsiders, people from away, if you know what I mean."

"Well, Mr. Titcomb, I sure do, especially after being up here since before Thanksgiving." Chip Arnold flipped his notebook closed and rose from his chair. "Thanks again for taking the time to speak with me," he added.

"No problem, Mr. Arnold. You make sure that you do us right and proper with your article. We're not often in the papers, and we're good people here, God-fearing people. We mind our own business."

"I get the feeling that you think I am not minding mine."

"Well, we don't need this kind of publicity, especially from a major paper. You city people think we're bumpkins, but we're not. We might not have much up here, as I said, but what we have we appreciate. We might live different than you city folk, but we like our way of life. These fires are disturbing all that."

"That's why I came up here, Mr. Titcomb. These mysterious fires are newsworthy. The disruption of a small town in Maine. In the short time that I have been here, I have learned a bit about life upcountry. I've observed a lot."

"Ayuh, no doubt, you have, but I won't be unhappy to see you leave."

# Chapter 27

*I'm gonna do it, for real. I am sick of all this crap. I am feelin' really strange inside. My stomach is tight and I'm not sleeping very well. I lay there in bed thinking about things. I think about what I want to do. I grind my teeth when I think about what I want to do.*

*I am sick of being invisible. I want to scream and yell at everybody. But I keep this inside, so my stomach is going crazy. It flutters every time my father tells me to take out the garbage. It flutters every time I see Michelle pouting in front of the TV or when I see her downtown with her stupid friends or with that Tatum. I want to crawl into a hole or disappear.*

*I remember when Michelle was into sixties music with some of her druggie friends from Piscata. You probably don't know this guy, but he was an original. Boy, the sixties had some serious music. She played this crazy record for me. It was an old 33 1/3 vinyl. She used to collect some of these albums and share them with her loser friends.*

*There's this guy that calls himself The Crazy World of Arthur Brown. Michelle told me, he puts on this show with a weird mask.*

*So this guy begins his song with all kinds of smoke on stage and he yells in this commanding voice, "I am the god of hell fire!" That's me. I am the god of hell fire. When I light fires, I am totally in command. Nothing can stop me. I really am God.*

*There's a brief pause after Crazy Arthur Brown says this first line. Then comes the rest, "and I bring you fire!" There are more good lines in the song, but I'm not going to say them now. I'll save the rest of the song for when I do what I plan to do. But right now, it's nobody's business. Secrets are for keeping.*

❧

Chief Corson sat straight up in his bed. He fumbled for the phone. The rings had startled him out of a deep sleep. "Ayuh," he mumbled.

"Renee?" It was Lieutenant Holmes. A deep panic spilled from his voice as it pronounced each syllable of the Chief's first name.

The chief's eyes widened when he heard his lieutenant's voice. He didn't want to hear Randy say another word, but he braced himself for them anyhow.

"The Titcomb place. It's roaring good. We're on our way."

Chief Corson hung up the phone, turned on the light, and started to dress. His wife, awake from the first phone ring, eyed him carefully. She did not speak.

"Milly, it's the Titcomb place."

"Oh, dear Lord. That poor woman. And the kids. I hope everyone is safe."

"Yeah, me too."

"Renee," his wife, out of bed now, said, sliding on her bathrobe, "be careful."

"Ayuh, I always am."

Out on the porch, the cold air bit his cheeks and nose. The sky was clear, the stars looked close enough to pluck. A heavy stillness lay like a quilt over the pre-dawn. The snowstorm had ended less than an hour ago. The plows had not begun their last go-around, so about six inches of the white gold covered the road. The storm had dropped close to two feet of new snow all told. And winter hadn't formally begun.

Corson jumped into his truck and backed it out of the

driveway without warming up the engine. A giant vapor cloud billowed out from the truck's exhaust as he disappeared down the town road, his truck engine a soft rumble echoing in the new fallen snow.

ཐ

The Titcomb place was aflame. The main house, the ell, which was loaded with a winter's worth of seasoned hardwood for the stoves, about five cord worth, and the barn attached to the ell where the cars, lawn mower, willy-whack, electric wood splitter, and old furniture were stored, and, above all, several large stacks of lumber for an addition to be started in the spring.

Flames shot out from all the windows in the house like tongues licking upper lips after a long drink. The ell was burning like a giant campfire. A single, large plume of white and black smoke rose from it. The flames rising from the barn were huge; they shot up twenty to thirty feet into the dark frigid air. They crackled loudly, an eerie sound that haunted anyone who heard it long after the fire. Sparks rose straight up into the air, dancing in plumes.

Pure unadulterated fire devoured the three old wooden structures that made up the Titcomb residence. Adding to the horror of the scene was the stark contrast of the wildly dizzying flames engulfing the buildings with the pristine snow covering of the early December snowstorm that had ended about three hours earlier. The flames twisting and winding up into the still, bone-chilling air. Fire and ice.

"Chief, we're not doin' so good!' yelled Lieutenant Holmes. "We've been putting the water everywhere, but the fire is hot and we can't get too close. All this old wood...it's like the place suddenly decided to come alive." Holmes took a breath. "We didn't get here in time to stop it. But it won't spread anywhere, that's for sure. But we never had a chance."

Chief Corson, his face lit orange from the fire's reflection, pushed his helmet back on his head. He scanned the scene, the heat stinging his nostrils. "All we can do is contain it. It'll burn itself out.... How's the water situation?"

"Fine. We're okay. Just helpless."

"Yeah, what else is new," said the Chief, spitting on the ground, a mixture of melting snow, mud, and ash. He turned to the water truck. "Larry, get Charlie to haul that other hose over onto the house, will ya?" Chief Corson shook his head.

The fire would consume everything. He watched the water from the large hose of the tank truck arch from the nozzle into the air and onto the roaring flames and disappear. The flames kept on growing. The Chief watched his men continue to douse the flames. The heat kept them from getting very close. One word of the Lieutenant's entered his mind: helpless.

"Why the hell aren't your men doing more?," shouted Eben Titcomb, his voice rising above the sound of flames, hoses, pumps, engines, and men yelling orders to one another, as he strode over to the Fire Chief. He looked like a zombie coming out of the darkness into the orange light that formed a circular globe in the pre-dawn dark.

"What else is there to do, Eben?" snapped Chief Corson. "We didn't get here until the place was roaring. Don't you see the water pouring on the fire?" He was not going to take much from Titcomb now. He had a rip-roaring fire to manage. Chief Corson contained his frustration.

But Eben Titcomb couldn't contain his anger. He rubbed his face with his left hand, took off his Boston Red Sox hat, slapped it against his thigh, and said, "You guys have all this damn equipment and what do you do? You spray a little stinkin' water on flames. Jesus! We've lost how many buildings, Chief? I mean, dammit, Renee, almost this entire end of Blackstrap Road is gone.

And you guys have saved what? Nothing at all. Ayuh, our fire department is a doosie. Our tax money at work. Between you and the police department, the whole town will be burned down by next spring. We can rename the town Arson's Delight." Titcomb spit down between his boots.

Chief Corson wanted to slug the man. Instead, he fired his own volley at the so-called moral bastion of the town. He bit his upper lip, turned to face Titcomb, and then said, "Let me get this straight. You think that we haven't been doing our job. And this is because...why?...exactly?"

A loud, creaking crash interrupted him. The barn had collapsed, some of the burning roof beams falling onto the ell. The walls caved inward, making an exaggerated pyramid of burning wood. It looked like a giant bonfire that the Chaldea seniors might have made for Homecoming. Sparks flew up, whirled in the air thicker than a flock of starlings. Smoke thickened the area, the acrid smell of melting metal permeating the air.

Lieutenant Holmes, standing with two men holding a hose on the flames roiling out of Zeke's bedroom window, hollered over to the Chief. "We're going to concentrate on the house and let the ell go! That's lost. It looks like the house is gonna fall soon. We can't get in there."

The Chief took a few steps toward his Lieutenant, yelling, "Don't worry, Randy. Do what you can. Get some foam on the ell." He stopped and walked back to Eben Titcomb who stood his ground. Chief Corson didn't give him a chance to say a word.

"You know, Eben, you are one sorry sonuvabitch. A real pain in the ass. You're quick to blame others. I've listened to you at meetings, shooting off your damn mouth, riling up people instead of trying to help us. You don't give a crap about anything but yourself." Chief Corson wanted to say more, but he didn't. He had too much on his mind. Another home lost in Chaldea. Another call to the Fire Marshall's office. Another search for evidence. More city reporter snooping, more newspaper articles. He felt like he had an uncontrolled fire burning within him that was being stoked by Eben Titcomb.

Eben Titcomb stared at him. "You're lucky, Renee. For now, that is." He scratched his forehead, and looked directly at the Chief. "One more thing, Chief. A reminder. The selectman are under no obligation to renew your contract. Remember that." He spit again, this time just missing the Chief's muddied boots, turned and walked hurriedly to his pickup.

Chief Corson gazed up at the angry flames devouring the Titcomb house. Divine retribution he wondered, just as he noticed his Lieutenant moving a hose closer to the front porch of the house. In a fast walk toward his Lieutenant yelled, "Randy, watch out over there! Looks like that porch is gonna collapse soon."

"All gone. Everything I ever owned. It was an inferno. Nothing at all. Nothing left. Black and gray piles of ashes, a few pieces of charred beams, and all that twisted metal sticking out in ugly shapes." Peggy Titcomb was still in a state of shock. She sat slumped in a chair at Doris Littleton's dining room table. "The remnants looked like the bottom of the woodstove at five in the morning after a long, hot hardwood fire burning all night."

"You really should drink your tea," Doris said, motioning to the steaming cup she had placed in front of Peggy. Doris and Peggy had been childhood friends. They both had married men from Chaldea, each had two kids, and had stayed in town their entire life except for their four-year stint in Orono and a few family vacation trips, including their honeymoons.

"Doris, you should've seen it. My God. It was a conflagration. It was biblical. It was terrifying. I couldn't even cry." Peggy let out a big sigh.

"Oh, you'll cry. That'll come later. Don't worry about that."

"You know, Doris," Peg said, blowing gently on her tea, "you never think it'll happen to you, but then it does. And then nothing is ever the same again."

"You're lucky you're alive, dear woman, very, very lucky. And your kids. And, your husband, too."

"Ayuh, my husband. Eben had a little spat with Renee at the scene. There he was, our place in flames, burning with such intensity, and he marches over to stand beside Renee and proceeds to give him a piece of his mind." Peggy took a sip of tea.

"I know how Eben likes to give someone a piece of his mind. I've been on the receiving end." Doris sat down at the table with her cup.

"Everyone in this town has, or so it seems." Peggy put a teaspoon more of sugar in her tea, stirring it slowly. She gazed into the swirling reddish-brown liquid.

"He has good intentions, but he's so high and mighty, so full of himself sometimes," said Doris.

"He's an angry, angry man, Doris. Heaven knows that," noted Peggy, who now stopped stirring her tea, set her spoon down on the saucer, and looked over at her friend. "We've been through this often, haven't we?"

"Ayuh, Peggy, we certainly have." Doris knew that was that, that it was best to change the subject. She asked Peggy, "How about the children? How are they dealing with the trauma?"

With a half smile, Peggy sardonically quipped, "Michelle...well, you know how emotional Michelle is. She thinks it's the end of the world. You'd think that she had never run away from the place, had never vowed to never come back to it, had never disowned it, us." She leaned forward and hunched herself over the table, placing her elbows and forearms on oak top. "You'd think that she loved the place the way she went on with her tears and her crying." Slowly, she wrapped her hands around the china teacup, and stared at it.

She looked back up at Doris and spoke softly, "It's Zeke that worries me. He is such a sensitive, quiet boy. He hasn't shown a bit of emotion. In fact, he hasn't said much at all. He seems to be very worried about Michelle and keeps asking her if she is okay. He tells her that it was just a house, that a new one can be built." Peggy stopped for a moment. Doris sipped her tea, waiting for Peggy, who added, "He's such a caring boy, Doris. He really is. He wouldn't harm a flea."

"I know. There's not a mean bone in that child's body," Doris said. She hesitated for a second, and then added, "But there's a terrible meanness in every bone of this person who likes to light these fires in our town. For the life of me I can't understand what compels such evil. Thank God no one's been hurt."

Peggy finished her tea. She put down her cup. "The fires make no sense," she added. "The mind of the person who lights them makes even less sense."

Doris gave a harrumph, then, as she reached over for the teapot, said, "I know one thing, Peggy. Fires don't have brains, and this guy that's lighting these fires has even less brains than any fire." She poured hot tea into her cup. Peggy Titcomb watched Doris pour the tea; the sound of it soothed her. She knew that she was safe.

⁂

"Hey, Michelle, are you okay?" Zeke peeked into his sister's bedroom, a spacious guest room on the third floor of the Reverend Loveless' Victorian home. The Reverend had taken in the Titcombs the night of the fire. He was alone and didn't even use the second floor, which is where the children's parents stayed.

Michelle's face was puffy from crying. She sat on her double bed with three pillows bunched behind her, legs tucked under her, reading a magazine. His sister looked younger than eighteen to Zeke and so helpless, sitting there in a cheap pair of new flannel pajamas, her hair hanging down covering most of her face, her slender shoulders hunched. "Of course, I'm okay, Zeke.

Come on in." She moved over so he could sit beside her.

"You were really upset about the fire."

"You're surprised by that? I don't believe you. What the hell did you expect?" She shifted herself on the small bed, closed the book.

"Michelle, you hate the house! You've taken off how many times in just this last year?"

"I know, I know, but it was our house. Everything that was us was in that house. Everything!"

"So? You hate Dad. You always argue with him. You lock yourself in the room all the time. You never wanted to be there." He couldn't believe how he was talking with his sister.

"But aren't you sad, Zeke? We've lost...we've lost everything, all our stuff. We only have what we were wearing when we got out." She brushed her hair back from her face so she could see Zeke better. "And you're wrong about not wanting to be in the house. I loved our house. It was like a member of the family."

"Then why were you always running away?"

"You know! Come on! It's Dad, that major asshole. I couldn't be around him when he'd get on my case. I still can't. But now with this fire what choice is there?"

"Aw, now you come on. You run over to Tatum's place when you're angry. That's stupid. Plus, he's a jerk. Everyone talks." Zeke decided to stop. He did not want to fight with his sister, but he thought it might be too late to stop one. He looked down at the floor and waited for Michelle to give him holy hell.

"Zeke, my business is my business. I'm not hurting you or anyone."

"That's not true. How do you think I feel when someone at school says something about you. You know what the guys say. It's dirty." He had dodged a bullet, so he felt free to say more.

Michelle laughed a little too forcefully. "Aw, Zeke, you poor baby. You sister's a slut and you can't deal with it."

Why does she say this, he thought. He was going to tell her. "Sis...."

"No, I'm not done yet." Michelle straightened her back. "I'll do what I want, when I want. Nobody can stop me...you, Mom or Dad, or those asshole guys that you let pick on you." She stared hard at her brother. "Don't worry about me, Zeke."

"But I do worry. I hate it when people talk about you, when Dad yells at you or hits you. I hate it. You don't know how it feels inside."

"No, I don't. But, listen, I know what I feel like inside, and I don't worry about other people."

"You don't care about me then? I care about you."

"Do you? Or do you just care about your feelings about me and the trouble they cause you because people in town think I'm the town pump?" Michelle pushed his shoulder.

Zeke felt strange. He felt like he should cry, but there were no tears, only a tightness in his stomach. "Well, no one will think that anymore. Everything's clean now. That's good."

"What on earth are you talking about?"

"I mean the fire took away everything. It erased all the bad stuff we went through. Maybe we will move outside of town and then we can start again." Oh no, he thought, why did I say that, why did I open my mouth. He bit his lower lip.

Michelle got up from the bed and looked very carefully at her brother, tilting her head slightly to one side as she did so. After a few seconds, she asked him, "What's wrong? You're not making any sense."

"Naw, nothing's wrong. I'm just being a jerk. Forget it." He looked down at the bed. "What book are you reading?"

"*Madame Bovary*."

"What's that?" he asked.

"Oh, I got it in the library. Mr. Resnick suggested it. It's book by a French guy about a woman who doesn't know how to deal with men too well."

Something you know all about, Zeke thought to himself. Instead, he said "Oh, sounds boring." He got up to leave. As he shut the door to his sister's room, he said to himself, I wonder when she's in the library. I never see her in there. He headed to his bedroom, equally spacious, down the hall.

# Chapter 28

*I'll whisper it to you, okay? I know that you want to know how I did it. You want to know everything. You want to hear my special secret. I'm just like the Chinese boy, I guess. Everyone must find a place to let their deepest secrets out.*

*I'll begin with the evening that I decided to burn our house down. It was snowing to beat the band. Wind and snow, a real surprise blizzard.*

*My father had brought Michelle home and was at it again with her and with my Mom, too. They started before supper, and they continued during it. As the storm built up, so did the argument. You can imagine. I stayed out of it. For me, it was the last straw. I was helpless. I'm a nobody to everyone in the family sometimes. At least that's how I feel. What do you expect when all I get is grief from Dad. I get "...the wood pile looks crooked, you'd better do it again..." or "I thought you said you cleaned up the garage," which leaves Mom left with nothing to do but pity me, though she thinks that's a form of support, which it isn't.*

*But I had already planned that the next day would be the day. So, at the dinner table, while Michelle told Dad "mind his own goddamn business" for about the millionth time, I sat at the table, slowly chewing a forkful of mashed potatoes. The wind howled and snow every now and again would tap against the kitchen windows. Dad said to Michelle, "What the hell did you think you were going to do, walking down Main Street at 5 o'clock?" "I told you. I was gonna visit some friends," she said in this real ticked off way that she has. Well, he got on her even more, saying, "You don't have any friends down town." You'd think he'd stop there, and maybe let things calm down, but not my father. No, he had to keep on dumping on Michelle.*

*He said, "I bet you were walking down to the Mill to see that no good loser. He's working the graveyard shift this month." He didn't stop there. Even when my mother interrupted saying, "Eben, don't start now. Let her eat and go to her room. Please." My father looked at my mother and snapped at her with a "Stay outta this, Peg." My mother just looked away. There was this faraway look in her eyes that made me hate her sometimes. And this was one of those times.*

*My father just barreled along straight into his rant. "Why on earth do you hang around scum like that? People see you with him, you know what they think? They think you're just a whore. Why else would an 18-year-old girl...a girl...plant herself next to that asshole? Tell me that."*

*Michelle, crying now, got up to leave, but my father reached over and grabbed her arm. He squeezed real hard. You could see how his fingers dented her upper arm. She screamed and fell to the floor. "Let me alone! All you care about is how people think. I don't. I told you, Jack is good to me." Michelle, a heap on the floor, struggled to get free from him. He dragged her away from the table over the linoleum to the sink. He was really, really angry. He leaned down toward her, getting real close to her face and said, "Ayuh, he's a real good guy, separated from his wife, with two kids, a drinking problem, and who knows what else. A real friggin' pillar of the community. Ayuh, you're a real good judge of character, you stupid bitch."*

*He stood up straight still holding Michelle by her arm. I thought he was going to hit her, but he didn't. Instead, he looked over at my mother, his eyes all wild and his face all distorted, and said, "Look at your goddamn daughter. She's a piece of work, she is."*

*Then, he shook her loose and sat back down at the dinner table.*

*Michelle sobbed quietly, rubbing her arm slowly. My mother stood up when my father dragged my sister away from the table, pushed her hands over her apron. Her face was blank. She didn't say anything, but she moved over to Michelle and reached down to help her up. Michelle yanked herself away without saying a word. Outside, the wind really blew and caked more snow on the windows. It was a wild night in and out of our house.*

*My throat was tighter than my stomach. I felt that my insides were curled into one of those knots that some loggers use to tie around tree trunks sometimes when they haul them out with a skidder. I couldn't swallow. I just sat there, looking at my unfinished dinner plate. I tried to be invisible like I do in class and in school. If you look away from what's going on and try to tuck yourself inside yourself, then you can make yourself invisible. That's what I tried to do. I had no choice.*

*But inside I started to light a fire. It was a small one at first. But I knew that it would grow and grow. At that moment, listening to the solitary sound of the buzz of the florescent light in the kitchen, trying to be invisible, trying not to let the tight ache inside me grow, I knew that that night was the night.*

*I knew that I had to clean up the mess. Fire cleanses everything. It gets rid of my feelings for everything that's bad. I told you this before, I know, but I've gotta say it again. I had to take control of things. I had to stop my father from being a stupid bully, I had to stop my mother from being helpless, and my sister from being outta control. Fire controls.*

*And you know what? Fire controls by being out of control. It devours everything. I love it. I control the uncontrollable when I light a fire. I control the cleaning up of the bad stuff in my life when I do it, too.*

*So. I cleaned up the family. It was real easy.*

*My father actually finished his meal, if you can believe that. My mother brought Michelle up to her room and stayed with her for a long while. I don't know how long. I was scared to death, sitting there alone with my father. He ate, and I didn't dare to move. No foolin'.*

*Finally, after what seemed like a day, he said, "Why aren't you eating? Finish up your food." I had trouble swallowing the cold mashed potatoes, but the pork chop wasn't a problem. I left the peas.*

*When I left my father at the table, he was staring straight ahead, chewing a piece of meat. The sound of his chewing made me want to vomit. I went upstairs to my room and I didn't even stop at Michelle's room though I heard my mother's voice softly talking behind the closed bedroom door as I passed by there. I threw myself on my bed, folded my hands behind my head, looked up at the ceiling and planned my fire, the fire that would burn away my aches. I knew that it would melt some of the snow.*

*The snow. The porch, the path to the shed, everything, buried in snow. There's nothing like the blanket of snow after a real serious dump, and we had been dumped on big time. The snow is pure and even, and it glistens with piercing, diamond-like dots of light in the bright sun. There were drifts everywhere because of the driving wind, and one drift had built up across the driveway to about four feet. So, I had tough work to do with the blower. Time I didn't want to spend but had to.*

*One of the ways I always tell if we've had a lot of snow is to check if it has accumulated even on small things, like the porch railings and the knobs on the banisters of the railings. That is if there wasn't a driving wind. I checked and the entire porch railing had a three-inch mound of snow on it, and the knobs even had about an inch on top, so the wind must've died at some point during the night and I knew that we had a real corker.*

*Dad had told me to shovel and do the driveway before school that afternoon, so I shoveled the porch and a path to the shed. The driveway needed the snow blower, so I had to crank that sucker up and do the driveway. That took some time. When I finished I went inside to warm up before I went back to the shed.*

*My father had kerosene and oil in the tool shed with the rakes and stuff. I soaked strips of a bed sheet that I tore up in the gas and oil. I soaked them up real good. I love the smell of kerosene on cloth.*

*The next morning after my father left for work and my mother left to help the ladies at the church. I had the house to myself, or so I thought. Michelle was still asleep, but she sleeps late because she's always up reading. Besides, after another catastrophe with my father I figured that she was up almost the whole night reading, trying to calm down. I took an old bed sheet for my bed, one that my mother never used unless the other sheets were not washed. It was folded and tucked way down under the pile of sheets in the linen closet. You couldn't even see it when you opened the closet to take something.*

*I took it out to the shed and ripped long strips. Then I took the gasoline can and the can that contained used oil from the lawnmower and willy-whack outside behind the shed. I had to smile because my father kept this stuff out of the barn to protect it since they are fire hazards. I remember thinking that this was irony, too. I remember thinking, Coccinella and Resnick, boy, those guys pop up everywhere in my life. They sure as hell wouldn't have liked what I was doing, what I had done. If they only knew.*

*Anyway. I had to be real careful out back because even though only Davis's pasture was out back, I was afraid someone driving by or maybe someone looking out of a window from a house a ways away might see me doing something. You never know. So I put the soaked strips in a plastic bag and lugged it into cellar.*

*Just as I closed the door to the cellar, I was scared out of my tree by a,"Hey, what'cha doin'?" I tried to contain my surprise when I saw my sister sitting at the kitchen table sipping a cup of tea. "Nothing much. I was putting some stuff away from the shed for Dad," I told her. "Oh," she said, immediately losing interest and looking out one of the snow covered windows. That's Michelle, or anybody, really, when it comes to me, they lose interest fast.*

*I'm boring, I guess. I was afraid she might smell gasoline or oil on me, but she didn't or if she did, she didn't care. Most people don't care about what I do. My parents don't, really. They only care when what I do affects them. Michelle, too, I think. So what, actually. It doesn't make any difference. If people find you boring or they don't care what you do, why should you care?*

*But lighting fires isn't boring. It's totally interesting because every time you light a fire, it's different. I had everything planned for this fire. Everything was in the cellar by the oil burner, which was never used much because we had a wood stove down there, too. And we had a lot of wood there, and the cellar ran under the ell where the rest of the wood was stacked.*

*Michelle finally dragged herself upstairs to get herself ready to do who knows what. Maybe she was going to school, maybe not. A horn beeped, and she ran downstairs and out the door. It was that tall, gawky kid from Skowhegan with the souped up Chevy, not you know who's truck, I know that. So maybe she was going to school that afternoon after all. But really you never really knew about Michelle.*

*I was free; I was alone. It was almost eleven o'clock. The kitchen clock ticked loudly. In fact, I remember that I looked up at it and noticed that the second hand was almost at the twelve, but it seemed like the thin black hand had stopped before it moved along again. You know how when you look at a clock, at the second hand real fast and it seems like it has stopped but then it moves suddenly? I mean, the hand is moving steadily, it hasn't gotten stuck; it's just what your eyes key on when you first look so quickly. At least that's what I think.*

*It was sometime in mid-morning, for sure. I really thought I was going to do it then, but I didn't. For some reason, I wanted everyone in the family to be in the house. I wasn't going to let anyone get hurt, no way, but I wanted them to be in the house. I wanted us to be together when the flames grew. I wanted us to help each other get out so we could watch the house burn down together. Together like that would be the best, almost like when we are together at church.*

*So I didn't do it in the morning. I did it that night, after supper.*

*Supper that night was low keyed. We had tuna casserole which I don't really like but I eat it. Mom likes to make casseroles, she really likes the tuna one. My father told my mother that the town was going to hire more police officers part-time to help investigate the fires. All of a sudden he said to me, "What are you smiling' about, Zeke?"*

*Man, that startled me. I was just about to take a bite. I almost dropped my fork. "What? I didn't mean to smile," I said.*

*"You don't find the fires funny, do you?"*

*"No, Dad, I was just thinking of something else."*

*"What were you thinking about?"*

*Why does he have to interrogate me like that? Can't he just leave me alone? Now I had to make something up. I couldn't tell him what I was thinking, that I was thinking of the expression on Brian Mulchahey's face the day after the police found the gasoline bomb I had hid in the ceiling of the library at Walloomsac High School.*

*A bunch of us kids were standing in front of our lockers before homeroom and someone, maybe it was The Weasel, yeah, I think it was*

*The Weasel, said, "Did ya hear? They found a gasoline bomb in the library somewhere. Man, this is weird, ain't it? Maybe this school is gonna burn down, too. Wow, that would be...amazing. I wonder where we'd go to school then?"*

*Jimmie smiled. "Maybe they'd cancel it. No place to put us. No buildings."*

*But Brian was upset, you could tell. His face got a bit wrinkled up while Weasel spoke and seemed to get tighter when Jimmie added his two cents. For a moment, I thought he might start crying. That's what it looked like. He shifted his weight from one leg to the other while he was standing there. He looked worried as hell.*

*I liked it that he was worried. I wanted The Weasel and Jimmie to be worried. I wanted everyone in that damn school to be worried...and scared. I wanted to keep things going, so I said, "Brian, what do you think about all the fires?"*

*"Me?" he said, "What do I think? I think it's stupid. Why burn down a school? Why set fire to people's homes? My parents say that whoever is setting these fires is sick, that he needs serious help, that he should be put away for life." Brian's face was getting all red.*

*I said nothing. I liked watching him get upset. I felt as though I had done something. People in town were paying attention to what I had done. Knowing that made me feel strong. I took my eyes off of Brian to see who was in the corridor. You never know about Atwood and those guys. You have to stay alert.*

Holy mackerel, Chief Avery thought, who in God's name is going to believe this. He stood up from his desk, walked to the window, gazed out at the main road where a logging truck was roaring past. Looks like Dan Turcotte's rig, probably overloaded as usual. The police chief turned, walked back to his desk, picked up the phone and called Renee Corson. The fire chief would help him decide how to handle this one, a real dousy. Not what he wanted, not what the town wanted. Hell, the town, just what they needed, a shit storm like this right before Christmas. Fa, la, la, la, friggin' la!

ం

"Augusta call this morning?" asked the fire chief. He shook his head. The half smile that curled his lips made his face look like he had seen a ghost but didn't believe it.

"The Sheriff's Office called at eight o'clock on the dot. I had just sat down to have my coffee. Sheriff Terry said the Fire Marshal's office and State Police found the prints from the Walloomsac site and from the Junior High School. Seems that the investigators went over some cartridges from the Xerox machine in the principal's office and found a set of prints that matched the Walloomsac prints dead on."

Avery stood up from his desk. He stretched his arms, looked down at his friend of over thirty years, and shrugged his shoulders. He took a long breath, then he said, "I've got to tell Eben. Any suggestions?"

Corson laughed, "Ayuh, tell him in church."

"Right. Thanks. In any case, the news is going to go over like a screen door on a submarine, that's for sure. You know Eben."

"Ayuh, we all know Eben," said Corson, adding "This'll knock him down, take the wind right out of his sails. He's a proud man, unprepared for this." He sucked on his teeth, letting out a mild wheeze through his lips.

"Yeah, well. I don't have much truck for or with that man. I keep thinking of Peggy. She's a good woman."

"Ayuh, she is. Good stock, that one. Her father, remember he'd pay us in quarters for baling and stacking his hay?"

"God yes, Renee." The police chief sighed. "We're a long way from that now, I'm afraid."

"Amen to that." The fire chief remained seated, leaning forward, forearms resting on his thighs, hands folded, as he stared at the floor.

"You know," Avery said to the fire chief, "all these other fires have to be connected, right? It only makes sense. This kid's a real pyromaniac. We're lucky no one was killed, kids especially."

"Lionel, we've found no evidence at any of the other sites that it was this kid lighting them fires. If we can't prove it, we don't have a leg to stand on, pure and simple."

"Well, we've got one troubled kid, absolutely." Chief Avery sat back down at his desk.

"Does that surprise you, Lionel?" asked the fire chief. "Look at the girl. A real wild one. Outta control. Bangin' every guy in town, it seems. Out all hours. Just lookin' to get hurt. Christ, I'm surprised it wasn't her that did it. I'm surprised she's not dead."

"Yeah," said Chief Avery, letting still another sigh. "She's a piece of work, that one. The boy, though, he seems like such a putz, a nobody, a little pudgy innocuous nerd."

"Ayuh, the kind you'd pick on in high school, right?"

Chief Avery chuckled. "Hey, Renee," he said, now sounding a bit defensive, "Those days are gone. I never hurt anyone."

"You remember Paul McKinnon?"

"Aw, come on, I never meant to hurt him.I didn't know he'd fall so hard. He was only sitting down, for God's sake."

"Lionel, he didn't know you had pulled the chair out. He really cracked that elbow on the fall. He shattered it, didn't he?"

"Ayuh, the whole arm was never right after that. Used to bend out to the side after that. I remember he couldn't get into the Army's OTS because of that elbow. He thanked me once for it, can you believe that? Said if he had gone into OTS, he would've ended up dead in Nam." Chief Avery's words were tinged with a sadness. "At his funeral, I stayed in the background; I didn't talk to the kids or wife."

"Darcy, his sister, slapped you across the face in the cafeteria, didn't she?"

"What's your goddamn point?"

"I don't have a real point. You know people. Your job is dealing with human nature; you're the cop. I don't have to tell you that troubled kids come in all sizes and shapes. Hell, we're all troubled, aren't we? It's that most of us can handle ours." Chief Corson got up off the chair. "The father's an asshole. The kid no doubt knows that. The kid's not stupid. People who light fires are not stupid, usually."

"Eben Titcomb thinks his shit don't stink and everyone else's does. That's his problem."

"Ayuh, well, he's got a great wife and two screwed up kids. That's the fact of the matter," said Chief Corson.

"Fact of the matter, Renee," answered Chief Avery, "is that I've got to tell this asshole that his kid's an arsonist and I will have to arrest him."

"Damn straight on that," the fire chief agreed. "I'll go with you, don't worry. When do you want to go?"

"He's at the Mill until 5 o'clock. Let him get home and relax. We'll have a visit at seven, when he digesting." Chief Avery sat down with a thud. "Let's hope he enjoys his evening meal."

Peggy Titcomb had tried to make the old Bean place like a new home, at least for the time being. She and her friends had cleaned the old house from top to bottom, and they had helped her organize the kitchen into some semblance of her old one, which she carried fondly in her mind and which appeared in sharp detail every time she cooked in this new environment with its musty smell still lingering in the pantry and the cabinets.

Peggy had scrubbed the last dish, was setting it in the dry rack, when she heard a knock on the back door. She wiped her hands on her apron as she walked over to see who could be coming round this time of night. She flipped on the porch light as she pushed aside the hand-made curtain covering the glass of the kitchen door window.

She smiled when she saw Lionel's face, tightly holding his police hat in from of him. Behind the Police Chief, she saw Renee Corson smile, his wide grin as friendly as ever. I wonder why they want to see Eben at this hour? Something's up, she thought, as she opened the door. "Gentlemen, come right in. You must be chilled to the bone. What brings you both out on a night like this?" she greeted them, "I'll put some coffee on right away."

"There's no need Peggy," said Lionel, "We've got to talk to Eben and you." The two men stood next to the kitchen stove, watching Peggy Titcomb make room for them at the table.

"Sit down, for heaven's sake," Peggy said. "Eben! You've got visitors!," she called into the living room.

Eben appeared in the entryway, newspaper tucked under his arm, and leaned against the wall, viewing the two men as they sat down. "Evenin' gentlemen," he said in a soft voice, "What can I do for you?" He walked over to his chair and sat down. Peggy busied herself at the stove, sponging around the already clean burners.

Chief Avery, fumbling with his hat, looked up at Titcomb. It's best to get right to it, he said to himself. "Hello Eben," he said, "Seems the Sheriff's Office in Augusta has found some prints from the Junior High fire attempt. And from the Walloomsac gasoline bomb. The prints match; it's the same person, for these two fires at least."

Eben, sitting down now, leaned toward the Chaldea police chief. "Well, that's damn fine. But what's this got to do with me?"

Chief Avery perched his hat on his right knee, rested his arms on the kitchen table, and looked straight at Eben Titcomb and came out with it. "Well, Eben, it seems that the prints are your boy Zeke's."

Renee Corson looked at Eben then back to Peggy Titcomb, who had stopped nervously wiping the stove to listen to Chief Avery. She slowly put her left hand to her mouth.

Eben shot a look at both Avery and Corson, then looked over to Peggy. Finally, he said, "I don't believe you're saying this. My Zeke lit two fires? Look at the kid for Chrissake's. He's a wuss. He's always in his room. He has no real friends. He's got no guts to do anything. I know my kid, and he's not capable of doing such a thing." Eben stood away from the wall and paced the kitchen.

Chief Avery glanced over to Chief Corson, who returned his glance. Neither knew what to expect next, and neither wanted to say anything. Instead, they sat and watched Eben continue his pacing. Finally, Peggy, who had been leaning against the kitchen sink, stood away from it, and said, "My boy did not light those fires. I know it. Prints be damned. That boy couldn't harm a fly. He's never done anything of the sort. This is impossible. You're both mistaken. Somethin' ain't right here."

"I wish it was, Peg," said Lionel, "but the prints don't lie. They're his. We've double-checked."

Suddenly, Eben Titcomb's anger spilled over. Pounding his fist on the table between the two chiefs, he leaned toward Chief Avery and bellowed, "You mean to tell me, Lionel, that my son lit all these damn fires in Chaldea! Knowing you, you probably flubbed the dub on the prints. You go recheck them before you come around accusing my son of being a pyro." Eben stood back up, exhaled and walked away from the kitchen table. "If this were my real house, I'd...."

"You'd what, Eben? Go on. Say it. If you do, though, you'd be a damn fool," said Chief Avery calmly, holding his hat in his lap. He paused a moment. "Well, Eben, you're not in your home. Your house was burned down. And I have an idea who did it. This is not a time to bloviate. Certainly not toward me."

Peggy moved toward her husband, who immediately walked away, turning his back to his wife and to the two town officials, men he had known since childhood."What should we do, Lionel? Renee, what do you think about this? What happens to Zeke?" she asked, her eyes clouding.

There was a long silence. Then, Police Chief Avery took a deep breath and began. "Well, Peg, we've got to take Zeke down to the station at some point. Not tonight, obviously. But we've got...."

"You're not doing a goddamn thing until I talk to Ron Rust. Not a blessed thing, you understand," chimed Eben Titcomb. "My lawyer first, then you, Lionel." Eben spat out the words. Again, silence.

Lionel Avery stood up. Renee Corson watched his friend. The man is a pillar of this town, he thought. He's spent his adult life trying to keep the emotions and the desires of Chaldea in balance through every season for many, many years. He knew everyone in town; everyone in town knew him. He'd been cursed, depended upon, and thanked profusely time and time again in his career. Perhaps this moment was as little different, or maybe it was as unique, as every traumatic event suffered in Chaldea. Perhaps this moment was more significant than either of them could ever know. Perhaps not. But this moment was, as sure as the early, heavy winter that had fallen upon the town, singularly important, something that had to be reckoned with no matter what the outcome.

"Peg, we're sorry. Truly," Chief Corson said softly.

"Ditto, Peg," said Chief Avery.

Peg moved to open the back door for them, brushing her hands on her apron, as always. She flipped on the porch light. She shook their hands. "I suppose I'll hear from you boys tomorrow," she added as they walked out the door. "Good night now," she said without a smile.

Lionel turned on the porch steps, put his right hand to the rim of his hat, and said, "Night, Peg. I am truly sorry about all of this." Peggy Titcomb closed the door slowly.

As Renee Corson opened the passenger sidecar door on the cruiser, he saw Eben Titcomb standing in the living room of the old Bean house, built in 1790 by all accounts, the third oldest place in the town. He was on the phone.

# Chapter 29

*The night of the fire, the night when I burned my family's house down, has to be the best night of my life. It was...pivotal, that's the word, for me. I'm smiling just thinking about telling you, you know? That's how exciting the moment was.*

*It's so easy to fake out parents. They really don't know anything. Mine keep on making these dumb assumptions, ones like I sit up in my room all the time. How can they think that when Michelle is in and out continually and they don't even know it.*

*I'll tell you why they make such stupid assumptions. They think because I am who I am that I don't do anything. They think I am this little quiet do-bee sitting alone in my room happy as a pig in manure playing with models or reading or listening to music. Yeah, right. What a joke parents are, especially mine. They had to pay a price for being the way they are. I couldn't take it any more. And Michelle had to pay a price, too.*

*I wish that the guy Michelle goes with whose name I will not mention, I wish that Atwood and his cronies...another C & R word...I wish the stupid principal who actually thinks there is no drug problem in our school, I wish the numb nut of a football coach, I wish I could burn all their houses down to the ground. But the night I burned down my house with my family snug inside was a great, great moment. It was heroic...yes, if there ever was a word for the occasion, it was this one.*

*So. Here it is; here's how, when...all that stuff. I'm smiling' when I say it.*

*It was about nine o'clock. Michelle was giggling to herself in her room. She was probably high on something. Who knows. She was listening to some old stuff, some Led Zeppelin or something...maybe she was just dancing and stuff, like girls do when they are alone and want to let loose.*

*My parents had come upstairs early. That usually means that my father is real tired from work at the Mill. Usually my mother is either upstairs before him or else she comes up after he does. But tonight was my lucky night because I heard them both come up together, talking about some meeting that my father had attended and spoke up at. By the tone of their voices, I could tell that they were disagreeing about what he had said.*

*I waited about a half hour just to make sure. I heard my father snoring. The light was out so I knew my mother had gone to sleep as well. Michelle was oblivious so I didn't have too much to worry about with her. I waited an extra fifteen minutes until I felt safe.*

*This is the cool part. I took some of the soaked strips out to the barn and to the ell so the fire would begin almost at the same time in three places. In the barn, I put the strips with the wood my father had stored. I lit several strips and hurried to the ell and lit some strips under the stove wood that I had so neatly stacked last August, a chore that I loved to do. There is nothing quite like stacking stove wood that is all split and ready to burn. I love to stack wood. Then I put some real juicy strips, the ones that were at the bottom of the pile, in the cellar by the tool bench and the oil burner, which we used when the dry blows in January made us use the extra heat, which my father hated to do and only did because my mother would hound him.*

*Once, on a Christmas day, it was only zero at noon time, and the wind picked up so that by four o'clock when the sun was just about down, it was blowing close to sixty miles an hour, no kidding, and my mother asked my father to stoke up the stove down cellar and turn on the furnace so that the upstairs would get warmer. He said, "Peg, don't worry. The house is warm enough. It's banked with those oak straw bales, there's snow on top of them, and nothing's going to happen." He continued to read the paper, but Mom said, "Eben those kitchen sink pipes by the sills face west and that's where the wind is coming from." My father looked up from his paper and snapped, "Peg, I know the direction of the wind and I know where the damn water pipes are in the kitchen. Believe me, the cellar is warm enough and the wind isn't going to touch them." My mom tried to argue, ever so gently with a, "But, Eben, the kitchen window over the sink is icing on the inside." Mistake, big mistake. My father shook his paper hard, looked over at her and snapped, "God, Peggy, don't you ever stop? That window has a leaky storm on it that I forgot to fix. The cold is seeping in and icing the inside pane. And, you are an inside pain as well." My father, a real funny guy.*

*Yup, you guessed it, the pipes were frozen solid by the time my mother tried to wash the carrots. Boy, was my father ticked off. It was the kind of ticked off that went in all directions and hit everything in its path, as usual. Needless to say, Christmas Day night was not a barrel of laughs, though Michelle had a good guffaw at the whole show. I just went up to my room.*

*I haven't forgotten about what you want to know. I lit the strips in the barn and the ell rather quickly, then snuck down cellar and lit the last strips. It's funny, but as I lit them, I started muttering to myself some words to that song "Fire" by Arthur Brown that I told you about. As I crept up the stairs to my room, I was reciting to myself the words, "Fire, I'll take you to burn, Fire, I'll take you to learn, I'll see you burn."*

*Now, just so you know that I am not stupid, I knew that I was starting a fire underneath where my family and I were sleeping. We have these chain ladders that attach to all the windows. All you have to do open the window and toss them down the side of the house. We have an emergency door and stairwell at the end of the hallway by my parents' room for just such an occasion. My mother made my father install it.*

*Well, I settled back in my room, lying on my bed looking up at the ceiling, waiting to smell smoke, muttering softly, "You fought hard and you saved and earned, But all of it's going to burn, And your mind, your tiny mind, You know you've really been so blind, Now's your time, burn your mind, Oh no, oh no, oh no, you're gonna burn."*

*Then, just as I was trying to picture this guy Arthur Brown doing his dance and singing the words, I heard my mother scream, "Oh, no!" Then,*

*I heard her yell, "Kids, get up! Fire! There's a fire!"*

*I jumped up, ran out of my room, to see my father pulling open the emergency door then rushing downstairs. My mother screamed. "Michelle, Michelle! There's a fire! Get up!" as she raced past me and flung open my sister's bedroom door. She dragged a drowsy Michelle, who had been actually sound asleep, from her room in her pajamas and pushed her toward the emergency door. My father came back up the stairs coughing with a bandana over his nose and mouth. "Everyone, get out right now, the whole house is in flames.... Move it!" he yelled. And we did.*

*We slipped down the snow-crusted steps, pushed through the powdery snow and made it around the house and into the driveway. You could see a yellow glow in the living room and weird shadows rippling in orange light from the den. I could barely contain myself. I wanted to laugh and jump up and down and dance. The only dancing were words in my head as I watched the flames grow to gigantic size in the barn and ell, way before the house finally gave in to them. "Fire, to destroy all you've done, Fire, to end all you've become, I'll feel you burn...." I did feel the deep heat of the flames that night, and I felt so light, like I could float to the moon, which looked so cold and distant, like a white marble.*

*My father was yelling in a way that was almost crying. "There's no phone. Peggy, I'm going up to the Trasks." But he never went. He simply paced back and forth in front of the house. Every minute or so he would say, "I can't believe this is happening. No! This can't be real." Or something like that.*

*My mother cried. She stood there, rigid. I almost felt sorry for her, to see her so upset hurt me. I almost told her, "Don't cry, mom. Everything will be fine." But I never said a word. Nothing. I just watched my flames grow. It was a sight to behold. I stood there stupefied and I stared intensely as Godzilla-like flames roiled up from the barn and ell and house.*

*Poor Michelle, she was hysterical. She was screaming, "Our house, our house! Mom, what'll we do? Everything's gone! All our stuff. My room is gone!" Mom held her close, each crying into each other's hug.*

*Who would've thought that Michelle would've cared two cents about a house that she had always snuck out of and that she had always hated to come home to.*

*By the time the fire trucks showed up, all hell was breaking loose. The flames were immense. The sound of the fire was ferocious, like a crazy mountain lion was snarling. One was spotted in Chaldea a few years ago by Nathan Wilton, a Viet Nam veteran from Plymouth, Massachusetts, who had been living way out in the woods near Cambridge Plantation, but no one believed him. People in town used his claim to make even more fun of him and how he lived. That's what people do up here - they make fun of everyone and use what people say against them to make even more fun of them.*

*Then the county forest ranger with his camera got a real picture of one outside of town. Nathan Wilton didn't care what people thought. He knew what he knew, is what he told my father. No one got very close to Nathan Wilton. He'd come out once in a while on a Friday night and drink at the bar up in Solomon, at the Solomon Hotel. He'd tell stories about Nam and then he'd get mad and mean. Then he would go back into the woods. He'd always show up at town meeting time, though.*

*I saw him once. He was walking down Main Street past the hardware store toward where I was. He was wearing his army fatigues including his medals. It was in June and school had been out for a week or two. I was in Putnam's store and he walked past. Mrs. Liston said to old man Putnam, something like, "He's a queer bird, eh, Jed?" Old man Putnam never got overly excited about much of anything, and he seemed to know everything that went on in Chaldea. Anyway, he responded with, "Well, it's the anniversary of his Army discharge, Mrs. Liston." She answered, "What kind of people wear their uniform to celebrate their discharge?" Old man Putnam, quick as a martin, said, "A man who wants to remember what he escaped." Us kids were all afraid of Nathan Wilton, though I never heard of him hurting anyone. People are funny.*

*There wasn't a thing the firefighters could do. No way. And I couldn't even smile. I had to look all teary-eyed and upset. But I was laughing inside. I was king, as though I had knocked down my whole world and was now standing with one foot on its chest. Me, the conquering hero. And, I was singing a hero's song, to everyone in this damn town and to my family, "You've been living...in the middle of your little world, And your mind, your tiny mind, You know you've really been so blind, Now's your time, burn your mind...ohhh."*

*As I watched the firefighters creep around the inferno that once was where I lived, I began mouthing the word fire. I began quietly then I remember that I began to recite the last lines to that stupid Brown song. Standing there, watching a wooden house be absolutely and entirely engulfed in roaring flames, I said aloud, "Fire, I'll take you to burn, Fire, I'll take you to learn, You're gonna burn, you're gonna burn, You're gonna burn, burn, burn, burn, burn, burn, burn, burn, burn, burn, burn...."*

*That's when the fire chief came up to me and hollered, "Hey, Zeke, get the hell away from there. The wall is going to cave. Get over there with your mother." And he pulled me by the arm away from my flames. They were mine. I made them.*

Even though it had been over a week since bringing in Zeke, Lionel Avery braced himself. He was tired. He rubbed his face. He looked toward the outer office and said, "Marsha, can I have some coffee, please?"

"Coming up, Chief. It's almost done perking."

Lost in thought, he finally offered up a "Thank you." Marsha entered his office on the heels of his words.

"Here you go, Mr. Man. I hope you have a great day," she said with a devilish grin as the chief was about to take a sip.

Lionel hesitated, looked up at the only secretary he'd ever worked with in Chaldea, and smiled wickedly at her. "You are a real peach, Marsha, why thank you." She laughed and then left as quickly as she came.

It was eight-thirty, and everyone would be arriving by nine o'clock sharp. He sure as hell did not look forward to questioning and holding Zeke. But he must. There was no doubt about that. There was no question that he and Gardiner had to interrogate the boy. He knew that Dr. Proctor's presence would be invaluable, too. He knew Ron Rust, the Titcombs counsel, knew his wife and kids. They had moved to Chaldea over twenty-five years ago from down on the coast near Kittery. He was a fair man. Rumor had it that he had come from old money, money long gone before his arrival in Chaldea.

Eben was another matter. Avery had decided that should Eben lose control, he would escort him to a cell. That would cool the bastard down. He chuckled to himself thinking of Eben's expression once the cell door closed. Lionel knew that that wouldn't happen though. But it was fun thinking that it would, an oddly pleasant distraction from the sad circumstances.

Chaldea, after the initial shock of Zeke's identification, settled into a relieved calm. The authorities had connected Zeke to only two fires, the Chaldea Junior High attempts and the attempted fire at Walloomsac High School. There was no case against Zeke for the houses, the warehouse, or even his own house. But suspicions ran rampant.

Gossip generated in small towns like Chaldea is legendary. This special type of after-the-fact gossip allowed the town to steady itself from the blow of the trauma. The suspicions, and the talk about such suspicions, quieted Chaldea in a subtle way. Such gossip allowed Chaldea to get back to normal, to settle back into its routine of commenting on itself. It was a soothing type of gossip that brought closure to the horror of the fires. Add to the talk of the fires the talk of the serious winter that had descended on the town and you had some solid, homegrown commentary. Thus, it might be said that such gossip warmed citizens of Chaldea in ways that their wood stoves could not.

What the authorities actually could trace to Zeke was the topic of this morning's meeting. The main characters had all arrived on time; everyone dressed appropriately.

Zeke dressed in khakis, a button-down, long sleeve shirt, and a grey sweater vest. His love handles caused the sweater to bunch up a bit around the beltline of his trousers. His thighs filled the upper pant legs fully, the tightness causing the legs to stop an inch too short above his loafers. His hair was slicked back. He wore black, plastic framed glasses. His moon shaped face was stolid. His small, grey-blue eyes, sharp and piercing, looked squarely at the tabletop. Chief Avery noticed that everything was soft about the boy except those eyes. Those eyes sent a cold streak down his back.

Ron Rust sat with his hands folded on the table. Zeke sat beside him. Beside Zeke sat his parents. Across from them sat Police Chief Avery, the state District Attorney from Augusta, Silas Gardiner, and adolescent psychologist Dr. Elizabeth Proctor. When she had walked into the meeting room, the Chief had noticed Elizabeth Proctor's dark blue wool skirt, how it held close to her hips and flared ever so slightly out and down to just a tad below her knee.

With both parties seated, Lionel Avery gazed outside and noticed a mackerel sky fanning out from the west. Another storm was supposed to hit in a day or two, the weathermen weren't quite sure yet. He turned back to the meeting, slowly eyeing each person.

A formal man, Rust spoke first. He spoke in a clipped Maine accent with certitude and assurance. "We can't stop you from holding the boy, of course. We're glad that he will be held at the Portland Youth Center. The facilities are commodious, and Dr. Proctor has been more than cooperative with Zeke's family."

Gardiner, a bit of a renegade and freewheeling with his words, smiled. He responded with an upcountry ease and a matter of factness that was as smooth and sweet as newly made maple syrup. "Well, Mr. Rust, everything is in order. We thank you for your work on behalf of your client as your cooperation is paramount. Proceedings should move smoothly once we enter the court phase. No court date has been set yet. I expect we'll hear from the judge soon. We want to keep this thing as low-key as possible so that we can move Zeke's case along smoothly. We do not need a circus atmosphere." Gardiner smiled widely.

Chief Avery leaned forward, his forearms resting solidly on the table, his hands neatly folded. "If there are no questions, then I'll review the actions to be taken." Eben Titcomb, who sat as stiff as an old solitary oak, looked to Avery and asked, "I would like to know this. I would like to know...." Eben Titcomb suddenly stopped talking. He looked over at his wife, then to his son. Then he looked down at his lap.

Chief Avery broke the silence. "After this meeting, Zeke will be remanded to the Portland Youth Center where he will be confined indefinitely. As you know, the facility holds those minors who have been accused of committing a felony. While at the facility he will be given psychological tests administered by Dr. Proctor and her associates. In addition to the psychological tests, Zeke will be interviewed and assessed by Dr. Proctor. The tests and her report after several weeks of working with Zeke will help determine if he is to be tried as a juvenile or as an adult."

Peggy Titcomb began to sob. Eben Titcomb sat up straight and stared past Chief Avery, his eyes fixed on some invisible horizon. Ron Rust leaned forward and, looking at Gardiner, added, "Of course the Titcombs will have their entitled visitation rights to Zeke as we have discussed."

Gardiner nodded. "Absolutely, Mr. Rust."

"And they will be informed immediately of the test findings and the recommendations based on those findings prior to the court proceedings."

"Positively, counselor."

"Okay, then. I believe that the proceedings speak for themselves." He looked around the table. "I think we have finished up here."

"Excuse me, Mr. Rust, I have something to add." Elizabeth

Proctor opened her notebook. "I would like to have a talk with Zeke before he is taken down to Portland...with parental permission, of course. I would like to..."

"You've talked to him enough, haven't you?" blurted Eben Titcomb. "It seems as if you've been trying to pry open the boy ever since he was taken in custody. You shrinks think you can split open a person's brain like a melon and then suck it dry, don't you? He's been with you for over a week now in Augusta, ever since the Chief brought him in here." Eben twisted in his chair, then straightened himself upright again.

"Mr. Titcomb, all I want to do is talk to Zeke about how he feels about all of this. I'll be talking to him a lot in the next several weeks, you know that. By talking to him today, before he heads down to Portland, maybe I can help him, assure him, that what he talks about with me today can lead to further solid discussions when he arrives in Portland."

"Zeke doesn't need your kind of help, doctor."

"I'm afraid that he most certainly does, Mr. Titcomb."

"You're calling my son crazy, is that it?"

"No, I am not. I am saying that the boy needs to talk, and he needs to talk a lot." Dr. Proctor looked over at Zeke. He sat, like his father, rigid, staring at the table.

"Talk doesn't do much around here, Ma'am. You shrinks think that talk can clear up a person's life. What a joke." Chief Avery, with a blank stare, watched Eben very carefully.

"Mr. Titcomb, you and I have been through this before. Your son needs help, and I am the one to provide it."

Elizabeth Proctor officially had her dander up, and Lionel Avery saw it, as did everyone else. Lionel let go a smile, but then quickly caught and stifled it completely. Dr. Proctor pushed further. "Listen, legally, I can talk to Zeke today, before he leaves, whether you give me permission or not. I wanted to include you so that Zeke sees that you are supporting the process and thus supporting him." She leaned back in her chair and folded her arms on her chest.

"I have always supported my son. Who are you to imply otherwise? You do not have the slightest...."

"Oh Eben!" sighed Peggy Titcomb. Tears welled up again. She blew her nose.

"Excuse me. This discussion will not take us in any favorable direction," added Ron Rust. He pulled the cuff of his left shirtsleeve out from under sport jacket. "I think that it would be most prudent for Dr. Proctor to talk with Zeke before he leaves for Portland. In this way, she can explain the details of the process to him, and she can allay any fears that the boy might have regarding his stay at the Youth Center."

Zeke might as well have been a statue made of granite. He never moved, only stared down at the tabletop. Words swirled around his head and he would catch one, or a phrase, every once and a while, but it made no sense and no difference to him. "Juvenile instead of an adult," "process of confinement," "psychological test series," none of this registered with Zeke because he didn't hear it.

He was thinking about how he had never had the chance to watch the strips flare up and burn the wood, how he never had the time to observe the incendiary nature of the oil and gasoline soaked strips. Those flames must've been something, he thought, blocking out his father's words. They must've started so small then suddenly ignited the wood, the logs ever so gently, a steady burn to total conflagration, total annihilation. He had missed all of that because he had had to move quickly to complete his overall plan. The house had to burn down, completely. Nothing could be left. And nothing was left. And he still felt so clean and empty and relieved after it.

"Well," said Chief Avery, "I think we've covered everything. I thank you all for coming over. I'll keep everyone abreast of what is happening on our end."

Eben Titcomb reached over to lift his son from his seat. Zeke pulled his arm away and lifted himself from the chair. He accompanied his father out of the meeting room. Outside the room two Maine State Police officers stood chatting with Marsha. When the meeting room door opened, they turned from Marsha and walked toward the group.

"Good Lord, does it have to be like this?" asked Eben Titcomb.

"I am afraid it does," answered Ron Bush. "This is state law. It is real and it is binding."

Eben was beside himself. He wondered, how will I look the congregation in the eye? What will the men at the Mill say behind my back during coffee break? Then, once again, he grabbed his son's arm. "Zeke, I can't believe this; I can't believe you'd ever do such a thing. We'll get you out of this, I know."

Zeke stood still. He did not blink once. His eyes focused on the two state patrolmen. And he thought to himself, "Yeah, sure dad, you're gonna fix everything, like you always do. Yeah, everything will be fine. You know, Dad? In case you do not know it yet, you're an idiot, a complete idiot. No foolin'."

Eben let go of his son's arm as they walked into the common area of the Chaldea Police Station. The two troopers stood, waiting for instructions. Chief Avery walked over to them and whispered a few words. The men turned back to chatting with Marsha. Chief Avery stepped over to Ron Rush and said, "I've got to speak with Zeke, so Eben and Peggy and Ron would you, please, bring Zeke over here for a minute?" The chief ushered the four into a side room to his office.

Chief Avery offered the boy a chair. "Zeke, why don't you sit down? I want to go over a few things. Okay?" Zeke stared at the tabletop.

"He can stand. There's no need for him to sit," Eben said, his lower jaw muscles pulsing.

"I have to talk to your son, Eben. Let me do it." Avery took a deep breath. "Ron, will you tell Eben to be quiet for once?"

Rush put his hand gently on Eben's shoulder. "Let's stand over there, away a bit, and let the man do his job," he said quietly.

"That'll be the day. I'm going to stand right beside my boy. So will Peg. Get over here Peg." Eben strode to where Zeke sat, which was directly across from Chief Avery. Eben put both hands in his pants pockets and leaned back on his heels. Peg, the good soldier, stood a little behind and beside him, one of her hands on her boy's shoulder.

This should go well, Lionel thought as he leaned toward Zeke, trying his best to ignore the two parents standing guard over him. He took a breath, and then spoke. "Zeke, you know what's going on, so I'm not going to bother with every detail," he began, "but I want you to tell me what's going to happen this afternoon, after you speak with Dr. Proctor, okay?"

Zeke stared at the tabletop. His hands, clenched fists on his lap, tightened. "Why should I care?" he mumbled. He looked up from the table and stared at Chief Avery. Zeke's grey-blue eyes burned with a deep hatred. Chief Avery returned the stare.

# Hot Spot III

*I hate my body, okay? And I know that you probably know why. I'm a pudgy, doughy kid. I am made of silly putty. My face is round – featureless. It's a good thing I have an okay nose otherwise I'd be so picked on that I'd be dead by now. In other words, I'm just dumb enough looking that I make others feel good about themselves because they're not me. I'm also built in such a way that there's nothing to remember about me....I'm nondescript...thank you Coccinella and Resnick...I'm almost fat but not quite. My gut doesn't hang over my belt except on the sides. And I waddle when I walk. I can't help it. But I am not uncoordinated. I just look like I am.*

*I'm deceptive that way. I can move much faster than you'd think. That's me. What I am on the outside I am not on the inside. I've always felt there was a different me inside, one that was lean and mean and very strong. I like my inside self, and I hate my outside self. And, I hate those that hate my outside self...which is just about everyone, including you know who....*

*It's my inside self that lights the fires, that burns like the flames it starts. I wish that I could move like a flame, snake, twist and turn around things. Get up close to things as I devour them. That would be pretty special, I think.*

*My inside self is clean as a whistle. It is in fighting shape. It could be a Marine, this self inside me, no foolin'. Yeah, I know, my outside self is the worst kind of wuss. But the flames, making them, kicks this self outta the way. My Marine inner self kicks butt, any time and any place. Nothin' stops the guy.*

*I just wish that my inside was my outside. Then, boy, watch out. Because Atwood, my father, everybody wouldn't bother me. They would actually see me.*

*There's a big ole space where our house used to be. And the space where Chaldea High School used to be is really big, and it's still there. Nothing's been done to it. None of the spaces that I made when I burned down the places have been touched. I wonder why. But I like to look at the space in the places where the fires were whenever I go by them. They are mine, in a way. I made them. They're my marks. They're proof I am who I am. They are my inside self, showing through. Because when I light fires, it's my inside self using my outside self so that it can become visible. That's me; that's who I am. And I don't care much if anyone gets it or not. I get it. That's all that matters.*

*I try not to look in the mirror, but I can't stop myself, usually. I have to look at myself when I wash my face, brush my teeth and comb my hair. I really do not like what I see, which is the outside me. Sometimes I stand there and I can see my inside me, which is very different from my real face. My inside me is tough looking. It has a square jaw, a regular GI Joe face. I call it a shovel face, angular and tight. Not like what I really am, which is loose and soft and squishy. My squishy looks make even me want to punch myself sometimes.*

*I know what you want to know, but it's none of your business. Maybe I'll tell you later. Maybe I won't. My secrets are special. Sometimes I feel like telling them. Sometimes I actually ache to tell them. Really. But then the ache disappears. The inside me tells me to grow up, to keep the secrets to myself that only squishy people, like my outside self, cave in to such stuff and spill their guts to other people. You know who I'm talking about....*

~

Dr. Proctor expected Zeke any minute. His latest journal entries were wearing thin; they skimmed the surface of his feelings. She knew Zeke wasn't revealing much more about himself. At this point, he was pretending to please her, coating his real feelings about his family and himself in subterfuge. An adolescent's game. This was typical, but it wouldn't help her in terms of the upcoming court proceedings about what to do with this boy. She glanced back down at Zeke's latest entry, rereading the entire one paragraph entry. Zeke would be brought in shortly.

The phone rang. "Elizabeth, did I catch you at a bad time?" It was Lionel Avery.

"I was about to get a hot cup of coffee."

"Oops. Sorry. I can call back."

"No, Lionel. Now's as good a time as any."

"Boy, you sound peeved, doctor. Maybe I should go."

"Oh Lionel. I'm just tired is all. This boy is a hard nut. He's playing games with me. I meet with him soon, in fact."

"He scares me. You know, when we brought him into the station to interview him I watched him carefully. He's not living in the same world we are. He's far, far away. That's my impression. His eyes unsettle the hell out of me. He's a dite off that one. But that's your domain, Dr. Proctor."

"Thanks for bucking me up, Chief."

"I aim to please, ma'am," Lionel chuckled into the phone. "Hey, go get your coffee. I'll call you before you leave the office. Good luck with the kid."

⁂

"I'm writing in my journal. That's what you wanted, wasn't it?" Zeke made a pouty face.

"Zeke, do you remember what the purpose of the journal was?" Dr. Proctor sat back in her desk chair, staring at the adolescent, who now was looking out her office window.

Zeke looked down at his shoes. "I'm supposed to tell you what I feel about all this stuff. And I have. So, why are you getting on my case now?"

"Come on, Zeke. Your writing is much different from when you first started, you know that. When did you begin writing for me? It was before Christmas, wasn't it, a little after that storm hit when you first arrived in Portland."

"Yeah, it seems like a long time ago. I was scared coming down here. I was more afraid of..." Zeke stopped talking and looked back down at the floor.

"Afraid of what?"

"Nothing. Never mind."

"Come on. Are we going to have another one of those sessions?"

"I dunno."

"Zeke, we've discussed your tests. The judge is going make some important decisions about you next week. I am going to be giving my professional opinion about you on the stand, so I need to talk straightforwardly with you."

"We have been talking seriously. You just don't like what I say. You're like my father; you're never satisfied. You can tell them that I am a pyro, that I'm whacko. Say what you want. Nothing makes any difference anyway."

Dr. Proctor took a deep breath. "Zeke, I don't call writing in your journal a sentence such as 'I lit the junior high school on fire because it was a stupid building' exactly getting to the heart of the matter, do you?"Dr. Proctor regretted the sarcasm immediately.

What was it about adolescence, she wondered. The raging hormones coupled with the urge to be independent, to be an adult, to live and work and be free. Little did they know what they were growing into, what adulthood meant. But she knew it wasn't for any adolescent to know what was happening to him, let alone Ezekiel Daniel Titcomb. It's a wonder we survive as a species, given how long it takes for us to mature, for our brains to develop. She looked at Zeke, who was fidgeting with his wristwatch.

"Zeke, a lot of things are bothering you. You know that. It's best we talk about them in some way. If you are sick of the journal, fine. We can simply talk; we can have as many conversations as you want."

"I told you already. Nothing makes any difference. Why don't you just leave me alone now? All we do is talk about why I lit the fires."

"Yes, we do. That's because it is not normal for someone to go around lighting fires. Setting schools on fire is destructive. It is not the average thing to do...for anyone. I thought you got that part." Shit, Dr. Proctor thought, I can't do this anymore.

"Look, Zeke. I'm sorry. I am not your enemy here. I do not want to see you tried as an adult. That means jail. And you have no idea about what it means to be in jail, believe me."

"I feel like I'm in jail now."

"This is not a jail. It's a detention center for adolescents. You are being held over pending your trial. And at this trial, a lot of adults are going to be saying stuff about you and what you did. Some of them want you to go to jail. If you're lucky, you'll get to remain here."

"I don't care." Zeke stared hard at his sneakers. He moved his feet up and down. "Why should you care? I got caught. So what?"

"So what? You do not mean that, Zeke. I know that." Dr. Proctor put down her notepad. "Here's the deal. I thought we were making some progress. I thought that you were starting to reveal you true feelings about a whole lot of things, things that were relevant to why you lit those two fires. I want to make more progress with you, but I can't do that unless you help me. If we explore what's inside you together then we can make plans for improvement to your behavior. See?"

Zeke smiled at Dr. Proctor. She thought he was going to laugh. Instead, he said, "What do you write in that notebook? Can I see it?"

"I keep notes about our conversations. It's privileged

information. No one can see it."

"I show you my journal. Why can't I see your notes? That's not fair." Zeke's eyes hardened.

# Chapter 30

*I would've liked to work for ole man Putnam. I never stole gum or candy from him like Jimmy and Bernie. I could've stacked cans and food, helped bag groceries for everybody. I really would've liked to unpack the wooden crates that the vegetables and fruit came in. Ole man Putnam had them delivered down in the basement of his store. I loved the smell of that basement filled with all kinds of stuff. There were thousands of canned goods from soup to vegetables to seafood. There were packages of rice, beans, and wheat. There were bags of potatoes and onions. But the crates of fresh produce made that cellar smell like it was a garden, like it was alive and growing. It smelled like fresh loam.*

*I know because he showed me the cellar once. He even said that if I helped him, I could work down there rearranging stuff because it had gotten too much for him to tend to. I raced home to ask my father if I could work at the store. I was so excited. I told mom, but she said wait for your father to come home, which I did. I sat at the kitchen table waiting for his truck to drive in the driveway. I wiggled in my seat so much that mom had to tell me at least three times to be still. She was cooking and I was wiggling.*

*Finally, my father came home. When he walked in the back door, I just about leapt on him. He didn't even have a chance get his coat off or put his lunch pail on the kitchen counter. I just about attacked him, saying, "Dad, Mr. Putnam asked me to work for him. Isn't that great? I can work after school and on the weekends. I can help him rearrange his cellar and put all his stuff in order, then I can sweep and help bag. Won't that be great?"*

*My father never said a word. While I was talking, he placed his lunch pail by the bread bin and he took off his jacket and hung it on the clothes rack by the door. Then he said hello to mom. Then, he looked straight at me.*

*"No boy of mine is going to work for that old coot. He's losing it. He'd probably forget to pay you. Half the people in town owe him money because he lets them put their food bill on credit every week and they never pay him because he never thinks to send them bills at the end of the month. I'm surprised he's still in business, if you ask me. Besides, you don't need to work. Titcombs don't have to work. You get an allowance."*

*My father in all his glory. I ran up to my room. I refused to cry. But I really felt like it. I wanted to hide so I buried my head in my pillow. I might have even screamed into it. I did not come down for supper until my father made me come down.*

*That's the one time I remember that Michelle showed real concern for me. She came in my room. She was high. A happy high. She pranced around my room, telling me that father was a flaming asshole, that when I had the chance I should get out of the house. She babbled away all happy and floaty. It was kind of sad.*

*But at the time, she made me forget him, and I even laughed because she had been getting ready to go out when she came into my room, and she didn't have a bra on and her breasts were bouncing in her low cut slip. So, while she was parading around my room, talking to me, she was bouncing and all happy.*

*She's talking and bouncing and all excited and one of her breasts popped out of her blouse. She stopped bouncing immediately, stood perfectly still, tucked her breast back in her blouse very formally and then said, "Besides, Zeke, the man is a cretin. Ignore him. Live your life. You'll survive this." With those words, she left my room, closing the door quietly behind her. Two days later, she ran away from home for about the zillionth time. I loved it that she said, "He knows not whereof he speaks." She gets that stuff from reading.*

ஒ

It's the damn skiers, Marcie Phillips said to herself, they get all riled up after a snow storm. She poured three more mugs of coffee. Every booth and counter stool at the A & C diner was filled. She was nonstop. This last storm had dropped another foot and Christmas more than two weeks away. Unbelievable. "Hey, Ethan, those two orders of scrambled with sausages ready yet?" she yelled into the kitchen as she set the filled mugs in front of Lionel Avery and that city journalist who never seemed to leave.

"So, Chief, how'd you like my piece in the *Globe*?" Chip Arnold asked Lionel Avery.

"Fair enough, I'd say. Got a lot in a few columns. Didn't badmouth anyone and gave the facts straight forward. No hoopla." Avery sipped his coffee.

Chip took a sip from his mug, too. "Well, I just sent in a small follow-up about holding the youth. You know, town captures youth, youth being held for x and y, Police Chief Z says such and such."

Chief Avery looked over at Chip. He swiveled slightly in his stool toward the journalist. "When's the piece appearing?"

"Tomorrow, I hope. The sooner the better. It'll be a good filler in Sunday's regional section."

"Well, Mr. Arnold, I'll say one thing. You didn't put too much bother into us. How long you been up here now, city mouse?" Avery smiled and chuckled once.

"Too damned long. Since before Turkey Day. The new fires. The damn snow."

"You leaving soon, I suppose."

"You bet. I'm going to pack, check in with my boss. Then head down early this afternoon. This place is far away." Chip Arnold stood up, tossed three dollars on the counter.

"If it don't snow." The Chief smiled up at the journalist. "You drive careful now."

ꕥ

Doris Littleton poured Peggy Titcomb a cup of real King Cole tea made from the package of bags that her daughter had sent her from Nova Scotia. Doris figured that the poor woman needed time away from Eben and the family, so she invited her over for Saturday lunch. She was afraid that Peggy might be under too much stress since Zeke had been held and then sent down to Portland. She knew that Eben and Michelle were not going to show her much support, and Doris suspected that's what the woman needed now. "Here you go. You want some sugar? I have real cream, too."

"My, my, look at the color of that tea. Beautiful. I'll take a spot of cream, though I really shouldn't."

"Oh nonsense. Here you go. This tea was made for some fresh cream." Doris passed the porcelain cream holder.

"You know, I can't believe all of this is happening. I don't even know my own children. Between Eben's furor and Zeke's silence I'm at a loss." She sipped from the bone china cup. "I swear I don't know whether I'm head or hind quarters." She gazed out at the snow twinkling on the branches of the blue spruce in Doris's back yard. "My son lights fires. Can you imagine? Quiet, inconspicuous Zeke is a lighter of fires. He's an arsonist. He's read about in the newspaper. Everyone has seen *The Sentinel* article and God knows what that city journalist is doing. I haven't read the Boston paper. I can't bear to."

Doris listened. She poured herself and her childhood friend more of the perfectly brewed tea.

"Everyone thinks...no, everyone knows that he lit all the other fires, too. The police can't prove them, but the fires have stopped." Peggy finished her tea and looked directly at Doris. "My son burned our house down...with all of us in it. How could he have? He was in his room! I swear."

Doris wanted to say, "We all have our crosses to bear," but

she thought better of it. Instead, she said, "We get hit with so much we do not expect."

"Blindsided is a better word," Peg added. "I'm devastated, Doris. I have no idea how I'll pick up the pieces on this one."

Doris reached over from her chair and grabbed Peggy's hand. "But you will, dear. That's what we do. We tidy up the house...and the family. We pick up the pieces. Every woman I know in Chaldea has done her share of picking up the pieces."

Peggy Titcomb sighed. "Lord knows that's true," she said, raising her cup. "Land sake's alive, Doris, this tea tastes mighty fine, even if I'm not."

Jedediah Putnam was up especially early Saturday morning. He hadn't slept well. All the talk about the Titcomb boy didn't sit well with him. Besides, there was work to do at the store. He always opened at eight sharp; no exceptions. He was always at the store by 6:30, just in case there was an emergency and someone needed something. Today, he decided to skip the diner and to make himself some coffee at the store in the little back room where he kept his books, records, and receipts in an old oak rolltop, a desk that a rich skier coming back from The Loaf offered him five hundred cash for.

As he pushed open the cash register, he noticed Nathan Wilton standing out front, slapping his sides and lightly dancing up and down. Tying his apron as he walked past the candy counter, he unlocked the door, flipping the closed sign to open. "Morning, Nathan, what brings you to town on this cold morning? Come in, come in, get outta the cold."

"Morning, Jed. Up early, that's all. I figured I'd check on you. I'll shovel some snow for you. I'll clear the storefront nice and neat. Also, I need to pay you for last month's food. I got cash. I went to the bank in Skowhegan yesterday."

Putnam laughed. "I never seen the like's of you, Nathan. You can't owe someone something for more than a minute, it seems. Anyway. Come to the back room. Have some coffee with me."

Putnam took the pot off the hot plate and poured two cups into the chipped mugs that he had taken from the A & C. "Sit down, young man. You want something to eat?"

"No, no. Coffee's fine. I'll shovel a bit and be going."

"For Chrissake's Nathan, relax. It's Saturday. What've you got to do? Stay with me. Help me with the store. You know I'm gonna leave this place to you."

"Jed, don't say shit like that. I'm not your son."

"You might as well be. How long have we known each other?"

"Since I came up here...when I was discharged."

"Ayuh. That was quite a while ago."

"Besides, Jed, you ain't going nowhere for a while." Nathan laughed.

Jed Putnam did, too. "Didn't say I was."

"What about your kids?"

"My kids? They're out on the West Coast. Do they ever come out here? I got a Christmas card from one of them yesterday...a tad early, I'd say, but at least I got one. The other's in Alaska. Last I heard she had tracked down a fourth husband. Good hunting up there." Jed Putnam smiled.

"Well, when there's property at stake, family comes out of the woodwork...like carpenter ants. Don't you think they'll swarm over this store before you're cold?"

"Nathan, I lost them long ago, when their mother died. They never forgave me. They know that she was the one that was drunk that night, not me. Kids are tough."

"I'll say. What's the scoop with the Titcomb boy?"

Putnam put down his coffee mug. "That's a classic, that one," he said.

"Well, his father is one s.o.b."

"Sure enough. He's a bully. I imagine the boy has had it

tough...and the sister."

"His sister is a beaut, that's for sure. I seen her many a Friday night up at the Solomon Hotel with Tatum. There's a guy on the fast track to nowhere."

"This town's got its share of bad seeds. They come in all shapes and sizes."

"Well, this kid appears to be one of them. Damn shame. He's so dumpy looking that you'd think he couldn't hurt a flea, but I know from hard experience kids can never be taken at face value." Nathan gulped the rest of his coffee. "I suppose I should shovel."

"Hell no, sit down, have some more coffee." Putnam poured more into his mug before Nathan could argue. "Let me tell you something about that boy."

"I'm all ears."

"Well, his father scolded him once, right here. It was in the last aisle, where the dry goods are. I can't remember why the father was so irate, but he was. I tell you that boy shot him a look that could've stopped a tank. Didn't faze the father. He grabbed him and ran him out of the store. It must've been him that tried to set this place on fire. Odd, too, because he liked this place. I once asked him to work for me, about a year or two or so ago it was. Never heard from him."

"No one in Chaldea will be hearing from him for a while."

Chip Arnold took a deep breath outside the Birchwood Motel. The air, crisp and fresh, tickled the insides of his nostrils. He gazed out at the Kennebec, its swift current black, snake-like. More ice formed in the still areas where the river dug itself into the shore. He was happy to be leaving. Chaldea was no place for him. The people unnerved him, the early, harsh winter weather unsettled him, and the place itself, the natural setting, scared him. He felt in the middle of a Marsden Hartley painting. The nights were too dark, too quiet, and he felt his stomach tense every time the sun set. A sense of foreboding here had wrapped itself around him. He did not like the feeling.

He tossed his travel bag and briefcase into a back seat of the rented Jeep. Wisps of mare's tails lined in the west, dainty and bright white against the blue sky.

There was some local traffic as Arnold cruised along Route 2, especially from Narratunk to Waterville. People traveling to do their Christmas shopping, food shopping, and laundry, maybe grab a bite to eat, maybe take in a holiday movie, if they could afford it. The fir trees along the road seemed to taunt him. Up ahead he saw a hitchhiker with a backpack standing on the gravel shoulder. An arm was stuck out.

He slowed down and pulled the jeep over on the shoulder. When the hitcher walked up to the passenger side, he put down the window. "Hop in," he said. Only after the person chucked the pack into the back seat and opened the front passenger door did he realize that the hitchhiker was female.

"Hi," she said, climbing in the Jeep and shaking her hair. "I'm Michelle. Where you headed?"

# Chapter 31

*I got close to having a girlfriend once in junior high school. She was a new girl from outside of Boston. Everyone up here hated her immediately because she was from away. She was in all of my classes in the 7th and 8th grade. Her name was Shirley Kirkum. She was tall, thin, and wore her hair straight down, sometimes in a ponytail and sometimes with pigtails.*

*Once, a day or two after she had been here and people were gossiping about her, in English class, we ended up sitting next to each other in the front of the class. Everything weird that happens seems to happen in English class. So, "T" got to sit in the front seat of the fourth row beside "K" in the front seat of the third row. Coccinella would say we sat together through a stroke of "alphabetical luck."*

*Anyway, Shirley and I got to talking one day before class. She was petrified of being up in Chaldea. She was from the suburbs of Boston, Arlington I think. I never heard of the place. Her parents dragged her up here. Both her parents were writers, and she told me that they had had enough of Boston and the suburbs. They wanted to have some peace and quiet. I told her that her parents would have enough of that up here. Her laugh was a short, uncomfortable one.*

*At first, I felt mushy around Shirley most of the time, but she either didn't care or didn't seem to notice. She was so quiet. That gradually made me feel calm when I was with her. Just when I felt good about being around her was when the trouble started.*

*I had to be careful with the fact that I liked her. In junior high school, secrets must be kept, especially if you are a person like me. I did not want to get picked on and embarrassed because I liked Shirley Kirkum. Schools are lethal.*

*It took all the courage I had one day just to say hello. I walked into English class, sat down, and Shirley was already seated with her book out. I snuck a look at her and saw her playing with her pencil, so I took a chance and turned to her and said, "Did you read the assignment?"*

*She actually answered me. Then, like an idiot, my mind went blank and I couldn't think of anything to say. I barely managed to tell her my name. "I know who you are," she said. I must've turned beet red because my face felt really warm. I felt about as big as an ant, but she was sort of smiling when she said it, so I figured I could say something else to her. So I said, "How do you like Chaldea?" My mouth felt like it had about three cotton balls in it.*

*Just when Shirley was about to answer me, the teacher came into the room. It was Mr. O'Reilly. I hated him. He was always hung over, and he never really cared about much of anything, except for Friday's when he and a bunch of teachers from the school would head down to The Anchor and drink. Us kids heard all kinds of rumors about him, especially about him sneaking around with the wife of his best friend, Mr. Randall, the phys. ed. teacher. There was always something in Chaldea that was supposed to be a secret but never really was. One day, when he didn't show up for work, we found out that he had run away with Mr. Randall's wife to Florida. No one was really surprised. I remember my parents had quite a talk about it in the kitchen one evening soon after the incident. I could hear them plain as day from the living room. I had the feeling that they wanted me to hear it.*

*That's why with Shirley I should have expected something to happen. And it did...unfortunately for me...and for her.*

*The day after my sorry attempt to talk to her in class, I was walking home from school and I saw her walking up ahead of me, so I caught up with her. We walked along Main Street since she was going to the town library to meet her mother. That's when we talked about her being up here in Chaldea, her parents, where she was from, and all that stuff.*

*Luckily, all the school buses had left so no one saw us from a bus. But I am not a very lucky person, and as we turned to walk into the library, who should drive by with his mother but Atwood. He stared at us with this dumb smirk on his face.*

*My stomach sank. I could've vomited right there on the library steps. Instead, I sort of panicked, almost dropping my books. Shirley didn't notice anything. At the library door, I told her I had to go. She looked at me funny. I said, "I'll talk to you tomorrow, okay?" Shirley said, "Sure. Maybe we can have lunch together. We have the same lunch." "Yeah, okay," I said, "I'll see you tomorrow."*

*When I walked away, I have never felt so excited and so scared. I was going to see Shirley tomorrow for lunch, which meant in public in the school cafeteria. And that meant in front of Billy Atwood.*

*Did I say that Shirley was real good-looking? She wasn't as good-looking as Michelle. Shirley's good looks were my downfall. And there's Atwood. I get sick just thinking about him. Not anymore though. I often wonder why I never got to do his house. I know why. It's because he lived way out toward Grimes. That was like light years away if you lived in Chaldea.*

*I didn't know that Shirley had talked with some of the popular kids and knew some of them already, including Atwood, because she lived out on the Grimes Road. Just my luck. I never saw her talk with those kids. I thought that I was her first friend. I thought that she really liked me because she asked me to sit with her at lunch. I was wrong.*

*I wasn't so pudgy in 7th grade. I got pudgy in the 8th grade. I started eating a lot. Potato chips, ice cream, all that stuff, cookies by the barrel full. My parents didn't seem to mind. Michelle would say something to me now and again and then shake her head. Me? I ate and watched TV after school, on weekends. I didn't have friends, except for the two weirdos, Jimmy and Bernie. They weren't exactly the kind of guys you wanted to hang around with or who wanted to even hang around.*

*The point is that I wasn't the Pillsbury doughboy – not yet. I didn't look all that strange to myself, so I assumed that I didn't look all that strange to other kids. But it wasn't looks that mattered. Once you've been labeled, it's all over. I was a loner. I was weak, so I didn't play sports. I didn't join clubs. I had no special talent for anything.*

*The nobodies in this world never, ever get the girl. If they somehow manage to get a girl, they definitely don't get the pretty girls. So you can imagine the lunchroom scene.*

*I was so embarrassed. The thought of it still makes me angry. It "rankles." What happened close to three years ago still rankles me.*

*So, I enter into the ridiculous cafeteria, which is a real joke because it is in the painted-over cellar of the school. The kitchen, crammed in a small space, is stuck over on the side of the room, which only holds about seventy people, but over hundred are squeezed into it. There are those stupid cafeteria tables, those fold outs that hold about eight people on each side. I'll never forget the lunch that day. We had peas, mashed potatoes, and what they called a Salisbury steak with some gravy on it.*

*I come in and there's kids eating at all the tables, and I look around to find Shirley and she's sitting with three girls who are real popular. My heart sinks. I panic quietly, inside. My inside self began to get angry. I began to 'seethe.' I had to look that word up for Coccinella one day.*

*I don't know how I did it in front of everyone in the cafeteria, but I walked over to where Shirley was sitting. My legs felt like they weighed a ton and I was sure that everyone was staring at me. I kept my eyes on Shirley, who was leaning her head over her food tray to get closer to her friends, and whispering to them. She looked quickly back at me then bent toward her friends who were giggling and sneaking looks at me. When I was finally standing next to where Shirley was sitting, I felt like dying, but I stood there, waiting. One of the popular girls who sat next to Shirley, Nora Johnson, stood up with her tray and walked past me. She never looked at me and never said a word. Me, the Invisible Man.*

*I sat down beside Shirley. I managed to eke out a "Hi, Shirley." I could barely breathe. Shirley glanced quickly over at the two girls sitting across from her, Rosemary St. Pierre and Sandy Ouellette. Rosemary had this long black hair and these deep green eyes. She was bright and she was very developed for a seventh grader. She dated a high school guy, so no guys in junior high school tried to mess around with her, not even Atwood and his friends. Sandy was blonde and she was great looking, too. She was always dressed so nice. She liked to wear short skirts. She had a great body. Neither of them were as good looking as Shirley though.*

*They looked away from me and her and down at their half-eaten meals. They barely ate. They pushed the peas and potatoes around, mixing them, dabbed at a pea. The steak had a few pieces cut off.*

*Finally, Shirley said, "Hey Zeke. You know Rose and Sandy, right?"*

*"I've seen them around," I said, as I opened my milk carton, "Hi."*

*They both said hello to me in a very negative way. They shot the word "Hi" out of their mouths as though the word was a bullet aimed at my face. The sound of the "Hi" was sarcastic. Then, they got up quickly and said good-bye to Shirley. They paraded in front of the whole cafeteria as they brought their trays to the drop-off area. They knew every guy in the cafeteria was checking them out. They liked and expected to be checked out. They were very visible and they enjoyed it.*

*That left me and Shirley sitting side by side at that end of the table. I can see now that this moment had disaster written all over it and deep down I knew it, I suppose, but I never realized it. There I was with Shirley in the school cafeteria, and that made all the difference. I was caught in a moment that I had never dreamed could happen to me. I had "succumbed" to my desire for this moment. I was where I had always wanted to be. I was with a very pretty girl who wanted to be with me. Or so I thought.*

*I was about to cut a piece of steak when the bomb dropped. Shirley said, "Zeke, you know Billy Atwood, right? He says that he knows you. Well, he's taking me to the movies, Friday, and he said that you could come along, too, if you wanted, but you should probably bring somebody cuz everyone else will be coupled up."*

*I put the piece of steak slowly in my mouth, and I chewed it carefully. I never looked at Shirley. After I swallowed my piece of steak, I got up and hurriedly took my tray to the drop-off area. I never said another word to Shirley. In the eighth grade, her parents divorced. Her father had an affair with a student from the local state university over in Farmington where he was teaching some kind of writing course. Shirley went with her mother back to the Arlington area outside Boston. Good riddance.*

*Chaldea is full of stories of people who come up here from away and then leave after a few years because of divorce, the long winters, the lack of work, even loneliness. The rich people who come up here to live, the trust-funders, as my parents call them, they stay the longest, some of them even stay forever, but not many. I could never light any of their places on fire because they usually owned a lot of land and lived far outside of town, deep in the woods.*

*Besides, I didn't know those people. They never bothered me, though their presence seemed to bother some locals, especially the likes of my father, who was always complaining about how these people from away wanted Chaldea to be like the cities and towns they came from, how they were trying to change Chaldea's identity. He said they wanted their garbage picked up, they wanted town sewage, and they wanted to change the town budget, or something like that. Me, I could care less.*

*I remember Mr. Resnick saying that a person's really got to be at ease with himself if he's to come to terms with living upcountry. He should know. He's been here for over thirty years, for so long that he's not even looked upon as being from away. He had been talking to his assistant, Mary Ellen Robideaux from Athens, who would come and work for him all day every Wednesday. I overheard them. I always overhear stuff.*

"Sergeant Whitten, thanks for seeing us at such short notice," said Mr. Sampson, nudging his son Jimmy into the Police Station's meeting room.

"Have a seat," said the Sergeant, "What can I do for you?"

The father and son sat down at the meeting table and faced Whitten, who sat across from them. Mr. Sampson spoke slowly and easily. "My son has something to say. With everything that's been going on, I thought that the police should be notified as soon as possible." Mr. Sampson turned to his son, "Go on, Jimmy, tell the sergeant what you know."

Jimmy sat slouched in his chair. He looked at the sergeant, but his eyes quickly drifted away from him and toward his father. He squirmed in his seat. "Sit up, son. Look at the sergeant. Go on and tell him what you told me."

Jimmy stopped moving and looked at the sergeant then back at his father then at the sergeant again. In a low, matter of fact voice, he told the police officer, "Zeke Titcomb told me a while back that he set the high school on fire. He said he lit the auditorium curtains. That's how he said he did it. I thought he was joking."

~

"Eben, why do you say such things?" Peggy crossed her legs and turned away from the table and from her husband. Eben leaned over his apple pie. She tapped her fingers on the kitchen table, snuck a glance at her husband, and saw that he wasn't looking directly at her. She turned slightly toward back toward him. "You know that Dr. Proctor has his best interests at heart."

"She's full of herself. She could care less about Zeke. She cares about her reputation in court and in the papers."

"Eben, why is it that you never trust anyone? You always assume the worst about people. Don't you see that?" Peggy sat up, a little surprised at herself.

"What do you know? It's best not to worry about what I think. You think everyone is a goody two shoes. You think people care about us, about Zeke, about what we think?" He stuffed a large piece of pie in his mouth and chewed loudly. He knew his wife hated when he did that.

"I know that our boy is in trouble."

"He was in his bedroom when we went to bed the night of the high school fire and he was in his bed when we woke up the morning of the junior high school fire, and that is what I am telling the judge. That's all I know."

"I'm tired. I'm going up to bed. Put the plate in the sink, please."

She stood up and wiped her hands on her apron before she untied it and placed it on the hook in the pantry. When she came out, she said, "This old house served the Beans well. It's serving us now." She sighed. "What are we going to do?"

Eben was silent, chewing the last piece of his pie and staring at nothing in particular. Finally, he answered his wife. "We'll do something. Let's get this damn trial out of the way first. We can stay here as long as we want."

Peggy Titcomb walked over to the oven. She wiped a spot of the door. "I haven't seen Michelle today. Have you seen her?"

"You're asking me? It's Saturday night. Do you want me to tell you where she is? If I had the guts, I'd shoot that bastard Tatum."

"She'll get this out of her system. We've just got to give the girl a chance."

Eben turned from his seat and looked at his wife with the wide-eyed look of having smelled a skunk. "You're not serious, are you, Peg? All we've done is give that kid a chance. Your daughter's not going to be saved. You're daughter's a whore. Once a whore, always a whore."

# Chapter 32

*There's supposed to be vampires up here in this neck of the woods. Ole Nellie Branch is buried up in one of those really old cemeteries that you see driving the back roads like the one that goes from Chaldea up toward Harmony. There's this old cemetery out toward Cambridge Plantation enclosed by an old iron and stone fence. The Branch family, the Tuttle family, and Avery families are buried there. It's off the road by about fifty yards, but you can see it when you drive past. The cemetery was on Branch property. How the Avery's and Tuttle's are related, I don't know.*

*New Yorkers own the land. They wanted to stop people from visiting it, so they posted their property, but, by law, they couldn't stop people from going to the cemetery. People ignored the signs anyway. Teachers take kids there to rub gravestones, and out-of-staters just driving by stop to take pictures or to picnic, if you can imagine that. I know that the older kids go up there on Halloween to get scared, drink and party.*

*Ole Nellie Branch's gravestone sits alone, moss covered. They say she was a vampire. The townspeople steered clear of her. She was supposed to have turned cow's milk sour and tried to eat small children in the community. She lived alone and was seen on some summer nights flying above the roof of her barn. No one would go near her homestead, except one old timer, an Avery, and he was supposed to have gone crazy and had a fit while haying up there. Someone saw him lying out in the field beside his scythe two days later.*

*Nellie Branch died alone. When she didn't come into town for her monthly groceries, someone went out to her place and found her sitting in a rocking chair. The chair supposedly was rocking back and forth. They say she bought the farm. Very funny. The story is a whole bunch of bats were seen in town the night she died. She had family in town and some more family came up from the coast, Vinalhaven Island, I think it was, and they buried her out in the family cemetery. Since everyone in Chaldea thought she was a vampire, a short time after she was buried, the town fathers went out there with the family and unburied her, took her out of her coffin and turned her face down. Then they reburied her. That's supposed to keep a vampire dead.*

*That wasn't enough. A few years later, she was dug up again and her body was burned. That's because people in the town began calling the family members who lived in Chaldea vampires, so just to make sure that they weren't, the family went out to the cemetery, unburied ole Nellie again, burned the body and smelled the smoke from the fire so they could be cured.*

*The kids love to rub her gravestone and bring their rubbing home to scare their parents. I did it with my third grade class. My father got ticked off and said, "Don't bring that stuff into the house. Why'd Mrs. Brewer take you up to that place, anyway? I don't like her. I should talk to her principal about taking kids up there. Waste of a bus and gas. That's not education."*

*The gravestone has her name and dates on it. That isn't so special. It's what the other words say. The words say, "My eyes are watching for you and I am waiting, waiting." And if that isn't strange enough. No grass grows on her grave.*

*That's why Stephen King's* Salem's Lot *is one of his best books. I love that book. I even liked the TV movie version. Stephen King knows these old stories. Weird stuff can end up being so true. If it wasn't, then why would my father get so angry with Mrs. Brewer when she took our class out to the cemetery? I don't have the rubbing anymore. It was in my closet.*

*I've not seen a vampire up here, but there are people who claim that they live up off the grid. A few years ago someone said they found a guy who had lived way out on Diamond International land, a Viet Nam vet like Nathan Whitten, with no blood in his body. Some hunters found him while they were hunting moose. There are so many stories up here. This is why I love Stephen King. He grew up in Maine, and he still lives up here.*

*It takes a special person to live off the grid. The real poor people up here have to, but there are people who come up here, not just the trust-funders, but people from the 60s who wanted to live off the land, who wanted to be honest...the C & R word is "genuine."*

*There's a whole bunch of people that settled over in this town called Temple. It's a town that has only one road that leads into it. Then you have to turn around on it to leave. The people who live over there are writers, translators, and old protesters from the 60s. In Social Studies, we studied these types who came up here to live. Mr. C gave us some poems about being in Maine while we studied these people.*

*Mr. C even gave us a poem about a local, at least he said the speaker of the poem was local, who visited a couple one day. We had to copy it down while he recited it. It was written by a friend of his from Portland who lived there, then moved to Australia. That's amazing. I can understand going to Australia, but I can't understand why he would come up here to live. He should've stayed in Portland. The poem he wrote that Mr. C dictated to us is called "The Visit."*

*The Visit*
        *took a young wife*
*plucked her from the countryside*
        *she snaps beans*
*in the kitchen – his student*
        *green with his attention*
*and baby-proud , she is shy*
        *with me, a visitor*
*from the next town*
        *in silence we sit*
*awaiting his return from the fields*
        *in the slow-burning*

*stove shifting logs settle*
*into an easy chair of ashes*
*twilight crouches outside the window*
*dry, coiled, and the sound*
*of the snapping of beans*

*she is my age*
*yet older and I rock*
*into some quiet corner*
*where books climb the bared wall*
*my polite questions falter across the room*
*her answers falter back*
*our talk sticks*
*to dried bean branches, beans*
*until the man enters*
*flushed boyish from farmwork*
*trailing the cold*

*Mr. C started talking about how people choose to live. Then he started asking the class about the point of view of the speaker of the poem. Everyone didn't really care about the poem. One girl, who lived way out in Athens on a dairy farm, Myrna Dowd, said, "Those people are strange, Mr. C. They come up here and buy land then they need all kinds of help. My father says, "'Let'em all freeze to death.'" But Mr. C said decisions about how to live life were very important, that people such as these we were studying in Social Studies and the people in the poem were serious people. He said that they have tried to fit in up here that living off the grid takes real effort and a lot of courage.*

*Mr. Resnick does. He built his own house, raised two kids with his wife, cuts his own wood, uses well water, has a two-seater for an outhouse, and uses kerosene for lamps instead of electricity. He's lived there for over twenty years. He tells me things about plants and animals that no one else knows. He is definitely a cool guy. He's a real poet. Poets are strange. They do things like live off the grid. I get sad when I think of him...I don't want to talk about it now.*

ঔ

The guitar player let go a subtle, jazzy riff that stopped Elizabeth Proctor in mid-sentence. She turned toward the trio, tucked away in the corner of the dining room. Lionel watched her. "He's from Machias, I think," he told her.

"It's fine music," she said as she turned back to the table and her plate of antipasto. "I've needed a pleasant meal with you, some real down time," she added, stabbing a sun-dried tomato and a small chunk of prosciutto. Elizabeth grinned and ate. The blue, green, and red Christmas lights from the fake pine tree in the corner opposite the trio reflected in her silver necklace.

"It's a nice evening. I think we both needed a break." Lionel took a strong sip of his Wild Turkey. He swallowed slowly. The liquor warmed his throat, his heart, his entire being. The booze plus the heat from the steady burn of the fireplace beside the couple's table comforted him. An easy blush covered his face. It didn't get any better than this, he thought, well, maybe a little better. He chuckled softly.

"What's so funny?"

"I was thinking how content I am. Plus, the fire is warming me nicely."

"Yes, me too." Elizabeth smiled.

"What? The fire or you're content?"

"Both." She nudged his calf with her boot. "And, Chief Avery, I suspect that you were most definitely not chuckling at how warm you felt." She took a sip of her vodka martini. Lionel smiled and took a piece of bread.

The waiter, a young man from the artist collaborative in downtown Augusta, came to the table with their entrees. Elizabeth dived into her scrod with gusto. "I love fresh fish. I haven't had any in a while."

"Take some chewing time to enjoy it." Lionel cut into his lasagna slowly. "You've a busy day tomorrow."

"You needn't remind me. There's Zeke on Monday and then my prep for the sentencing on Tuesday morning. Fortunately, the hearing isn't until late morning. God, I just want this to be over. I am afraid for the boy. He's in no position to handle the Youth Center. That place is no joke."

"It all will be over by Tuesday afternoon. Then all of us can get back to some semblance of a routine. You've spoken with Judge Shibles."

"Yes. I've spoken with him, the District Attorney, defense counsel, the Titcombs, and Zeke. Everyone's up to speed on my position." Elizabeth toyed with the last of her entree.

"The trial was smooth enough, so the sentencing hearing is pro forma, I'd suspect. It's up to Shibles. He's fair. But the kid did some substantial damage, and he has several major screws loose." Lionel reached for what was left of his wine.

"I wouldn't quite put it that way. He's a kid, an adolescent. Their brains aren't fully wired. Their moral reasoning short circuits. The cognitive research is strong."

Lionel wiped his mouth with his napkin. "Ah, the research," he said. "It doesn't quantify the devastation to the town or the little Stuckey children now homeless for all practical purposes."

The waiter appeared suddenly. "How is everything?" Elizabeth and Lionel nodded. "Great." The young man smiled and left.

"All I am saying is that adolescents are biologically not all there yet."

The Chief sat back in his chair. "That's why almost every year some kid gets drunk, crashes a pick-up, maybe kills himself and several of his friends. I see the delinquents. I see the ones whose wires are really crossed, the real troublemakers, young rural losers who grow up to be old rural losers. I see these punks every day."

Elizabeth sipped her water. "Adolescents are by nature

recalcitrant. Zeke is fifteen years old! What's that in terms of a life?" She finished the last bite of a stalk of asparagus. "I have been trying to get him to reflect on his choices, his feelings, on school, peers, family, you name it. The kid's wound tight, and I have been trying to get him to pick his brain. It's not an easy task."

"He's an arsonist, pure and simple. He looks mean, so angry. That stare of his. I think of what he might become. Even if Shibles gives him the maximum time for a juvenile, he'll only be eighteen when he gets out. I wonder how developed he'll be by then, given the Youth Center experience." Lionel caught the waiter's attention.

"I worry about that, too. I've not come across the likes of him. He's closed. I wonder what he thinks about the world. I'll be spending a lot of time with that boy in the next few years." Elizabeth gazed at the Christmas tree and at the elderly couple laughing and holding hands at the table next to it.

Lionel reached for his wallet and slipped his credit card into the bill. "In any case, Dr. Proctor, the night is young. Let's head over to The Pier for a night cap and some dancin' to the Blues. The Landfill Blues Dilemma are playing. We'll catch the second set. Remember the last time we heard them?"

They skirted past the crowd at the long wooden bar. A couple, covered in snow, entered, innocently blocking their exit. They shook themselves off in front of Lionel and Elizabeth. The man, smiling, said, "It's startin' to come down."

"An Alberta Clipper," commented Lionel. "Fast moving. Thankfully."

"We won't have to worry about a white Christmas," said Elizabeth.

"Or a white May, if this weather continues," said the other woman. Elizabeth laughed.

# Chapter 33

*I've got to tell why I tried to burn down ole man Putnam's store. I can't really say why, but I can describe what I was feeling when I decided to try and do it.*

*I really wanted to work there. I felt all scrunched up inside about not being able to. I wanted so much to help him. That's why I tried to light up the place. My flames would give the store to me. So, one night I snuck out back where Mr. Putnam keeps the empty crates and cardboard boxes and I set them on fire.*

*I lit one of the boxes and poured some kerosene on it. I giggled with delight. I felt like this sometimes when I would play alone with my models. Except when I played with my models, sometimes my feelings about my family, about school, about everything would enter my head and mess up my pretending that the aircraft carrier was being attacked. When I lit a fire, nothing entered my mind except a feeling of happiness.*

*I stood watching the boxes catch fire, and I was looking forward to watching the fire for a few minutes, but then the strangest thing happened. I heard someone coming out back of the store. It was old man Putnam. I ran outta there so fast. Next thing I know I was sneaking along Main Street toward home when a siren wailed and a fire truck whizzed past.*

*It's a funny thing about lighting fires. After I do it, I feel a release, as though I no longer was carrying something heavy, as though I lost a lot of weight.*

*I remember Ms. Brown in Social Studies class last year told the class about these martyrs that were burned at the stake. I sat there totally interested... She started talking about medieval times, about martyrs and stuff. It was weirder than a Stephen King novel. There was this guy Bruno, an Italian guy that was burned in the middle of a courtyard or something. The statue is famous and its still there in Rome, Italy. At least that what Ms. Brown told us. She showed us the statue of the guy. The statue was pretty scary...I'd say that it was 'foreboding.' The statue has a cloak with a hood draped over his face and the statue is tall so he looks down on the square with a big black shadow covering his face.*

*She had told us about Joan of Arc. A sad story. They burned her when she was still young. Older than me, almost my sister's age.*

*She told us about this weird book which Mr. Resnick had in his library by this writer Aldous Huxley called* The Devils of Loudon. *It was about this medieval church priest that the nuns all loved since he was really nice and also good-looking. The nuns talked about him so much and he became so popular that the church had to burn him.*

*I saw the book in the library. I even took it off the shelf and flipped through it. It had small print and was pretty long with lots of long sentences. I can't remember if there were any pictures. Anyway, I put the book back.*

*Ms. Brown also told us that a movie had been made from the book, and it ended with the priest getting burned at the stake. Kids in the class looked at each other and smiled. I tried to find the movie at Blockbusters. It was in the classic movie section. Someone had taken it out.*

*A kid asked Mr. Coccinella about this movie. To test him. Kids were always trying to test Mr. C. to see what he knew and didn't know. He had seen the movie. Coccinella seldom used the word "movie"; he'd use the word "film." He told us that there were some juicy parts in the movie. The class egged him on to tell us stuff, but he wouldn't. I guess back then priests could have sex, if they wanted to. He said the nuns suffered from a "sexual hysteria." No one cared. Then he started talking about* Brave New World. *No one was listening by that time.*

*Those martyrs seemed like pretty serious, somber people. I'd like to see that movie to watch the priest getting burned, to watch how the flames devour him.*

*Witches get burned at the stake. There were all these books in the library about witches in New England, especially during Pilgrim times and just after that. Everyone in school has had the Salem witch trials drilled into them. To top it off, we had to read* The Crucible *so teachers can make sure that we get why they burned witches. I haven't read that book yet. I wondered why Mr. Resnick had those books about witches in New England. There were three of them. I saw him looking through one once. I don't think there was a book in that library that he hadn't either read or looked through. "Perused" is the word he would most use.*

*Mr. Resnick always had the right book. I never knew how he did it. His library was special. I call it "his" library because it really was his. He cared for that library and those books as though the library was a place separate and far away from the rest of the school, as though the books were alive. Every book had its place, the same place, as though that space was its home. All those books sitting there, waiting to be read. It's amazing when you think about it.*

*Coccinella called the Chaldean High School library a "sanctum." He would give a pass to the library as a prize for good writing or special participation in a class discussion. He was always taking his classes down there to find information.*

*No one really used the library. Except for Coccinella. A few teachers did for their classes once in a while. Some teachers used the library to dump their tough students, the ones they couldn't handle. Funny thing though, no kid who was ever sent down there gave Mr. Resnick any crap. If they tried, he'd just send them out and back to their class. No one wanted to be kicked out of the library, ever. Isn't that weird? That students who really didn't care about books, didn't want to get kicked out of the library?*

ஒ

Dr. Proctor pulled off her new winter boots, already rimed with sand, salt, and water marks from the snow, and slipped on her flats. She glanced at her watch. One hour until Zeke Time, the final pre-sentencing meeting. The sentencing hearing with Judge Shibles tomorrow would take place back in Skowhegan at eleven o'clock.

From her chair, Dr. Proctor gazed out her office window at the Maine Statehouse, state flag flying almost straight out from the pole. She realized, observing a cloud of blowing snow as it swam across the courtyard, that Christmas was a little more than two weeks away. She definitely was not in the holiday spirit. Dr. Proctor turned back to her work. She picked up Zeke's ever thickening file and flipped to a colleague's report. Taking a deep breath, she exhaled and began to read.

ஒ

"I don't care what you tell me. Nothing makes any difference." Zeke slouched in the office chair. He wanted to put his feet on the coffee table, but he knew that Dr. Proctor would have a conniption if he did. He'd tried it a few sessions ago and she told him to sit up and pay attention. He was sick of talk, sick of adults, and sick of being stuck in a room here in Augusta while waiting for decisions to be made.

"Zeke. Listen. Tomorrow's the hearing. We've got to go over everything today so that after the hearing, when you know definitely what's going to happen to you, you and I can begin to talk more extensively. You and I are going to be talking for a long, long while. You know that."

"I'm gonna go to jail. Big deal."

"You're not going to jail. You'll go to the Youth Center in South Portland. There are all kinds of kids your age there."

"I don't care."

"Zeke, look at me. Let's just talk. Okay?" Dr. Proctor took out her notes from his file.

"Don't you want to talk about my journal?" Zeke asked.

Proctor skimmed the notes. "Nope, I want to talk about you and what I and other doctors think about you, about your diagnosis."

Zeke shrugged his shoulders and slouched a bit in his chair. He looked down at the rug and then up at Dr. Proctor. "I know...I'm a pyromaniac."

"Yes, you light fires. Remember the definition?"

"It's a person that likes to light fires. You got it out of that big, thick book in your bookcase. One that Mr. Resnick would probably have in his library."

"Yes, I got the definition from the manual. It's a clinical definition of pyromania. It's a special type of disorder, remember? You have a problem with impulse control. Remember we talked about this?"

"I can't stop myself from lighting fires. I like to light them, so I do."

"Yes, you light them when you get the urge to do it. And, you seem to obsess about the fires."

"Because I like to think about the fires that I light? I like to think about fire, too, not just the fires that I light."

"Yes. But there are all kinds of fire setters, right? Remember?"

"You and everyone else thinks that I'm crazy, that's all I know."

"That's not true. We think...."

"It is true! Everyone in town thinks it. Why shouldn't they? But they know who I am now, don't they?"

"Your troubles, and they're serious, can be resolved over time. I've told you this over and over."

"My father doesn't think so. He thinks I'm as messed up as Michelle. She hasn't come to see me, either."

Dr. Proctor looked at the pudgy, meek-looking boy sitting across from her. Zeke Titcomb, a boy without power, without hope of ever being accepted, without a natural way to satisfy his latent sexual urges. He was, Proctor thought, one of Peter Pan's lost boys. "You continually mention your father, but you never talk about him. Why?" she asked the boy.

"There's nothing to talk about."

"That's not true and you know it."

Zeke sat up. His shoulders tightened. "I'm not talking any more. I'm done now."

# Chapter 34

*Books. I know. I'll talk about him and his books. The poet and his library. Yes, I burned his library when I burned down the school. Nobody can prove it, but everybody knows I did it because of douche bag Jimmy. I've never talked about the books. Coccinella called him the guardian of the written word.*

*Mr. C. loved it when I began helping Mr. Resnick. He thought that it was just the right thing for me to do. I know he was pleased with Mr. Resnick for getting me involved, because one day when I was stacking books, he made a comment to Mr. Resnick, asking how I was doing and saying how perfect a job it was for a closet reader like myself.*

*I never figured myself for a closet reader, but I was. Now that I think about it, I was like my sister in that way. We both liked reading. Life is weird, I swear it. I know that I'm weird. But so is everyone.*

*I'm avoiding talking about burning books. One basic question, if you haven't figured it out by now, is this: how can a kid who really likes words and likes to read and helps the librarian in his school who happens to be a poet burn down the library and then burn up his own books, and my sisters' and parents' books, when he burns his house down? Honestly, I don't know. And maybe that's not the point.*

*I mean I'm not stupid. I know how important books are. We read* Fahrenheit 451 *in the ninth grade. In the book, there's this fireman who loved fires like I did. He got his pleasure from watching the flames devour things. If I remember, he used the word "eat." For him, the flames were alive like animals. He burned books; he burned anything he was told to burn. That would be an ideal job for me.*

*I don't feel scared when flames rage. I love that they grow. I remember in* Fantasia, *when Mickey Mouse played the sorcerer's apprentice and got all scared and hectic when the broom kept on splitting into more brooms and they kept carrying all those pails of water. When I light a fire, which I guess is like a magic spell, I love it when the flames multiply and grow. I want there to be so many of them that they engulf everything.*

*Anyway, I thought the fireman in the book was cool. He loved the smell of kerosene, too, like I do. I wanted to give the world what he gave the world: ashes. And I did. I mean, Resnick loved books. He cherished them. So did Coccinella. But at school Resnick lived with them, tended them as though he was tending a garden or herding them like animals. Coccinella would tell me to use the word "nurture" here, that it's more precise. Resnick nurtured the books.*

*Resnick loved words the way I loved flames. I imagine that my feeling of what I had done was just like his feeling for his books. I got excited knowing the school was going to burn to the ground, that all that would be left would be ashes and bricks. I was never thinking of Resnick. It's only now that I think of him, of Coccinella. The feeling leaves as quickly as it comes. I really don't care what anyone thinks about the fires that I lit. It's too bad that I hurt C & R, but flames do not care. They have no emotions.*

*Books are "incidental." Today, a general would call the books in the library collateral damage. I don't care. As if anyone really cared about the books. No one used the library practically.*

*Poor Resnick, the Guardian of the Books. When I think of him now, he was like that old man character in one of the original* Star Trek *episodes. This old man was like a librarian, who remained behind to organize the records since his world is about to be destroyed. He was the only one left after sending everyone off into another dimensional world where they could live out their lives. Only Resnick didn't have another dimension to escape to. He had to deal with the loss of his library.*

*Books kept me in my own mind, allowed my outside self to create flames. Books fed my inside self. I escaped into them. The author of* Fahrenheit 451, *I forget his name, has a character say something about books, that people are afraid of books because they show you the face of the world. I'm not afraid of books, but I'm afraid of the world.*

*When I lit a fire, I was doing something. I wasn't thinking about words, how special they might be to Resnick or to Coccinella, how they could help people. I didn't care about that.*

*The Stephen King books got burned, twice in fact, mine at home and the ones in the Chaldea High School library. Resnick had the whole lot of them. Every one. Paperback and hardbound. There were a group of kids who read them besides me. Even some girls.*

*I don't even want to think about C & R and what they might be thinking about me. I mean they were nice to me. They never bothered me in a bad way. I like Dr. Proctor, though she doesn't know that.*

*I never let them or anyone know me, really. I guess that's why bad things happen to people. It's because people never really try and get to know one another.*

*Maybe that's true, maybe it isn't. Maybe it makes no difference.*

The sweet smell of homemade bread hit Coccinella as soon as he walked in the door. It made his mouth water. "God, the snows piling up along your pathway. It looks like February out there."

Coccinella loved visiting the Resnick household. The warmth of the fires coupled with the soft gentle glow of the kerosene lamps. The substantial vegetarian food served on hand-made plates anchored the feeling. The house was solid, firm oak, maple, and pine. To gaze up at the wooden ceiling after taking a bite of a spicy rice pilaf or a scalloped potato was as close to heaven as it could get, Coccinella thought.

Janice Resnick, at the stove stirring some peppers and mushrooms in a fry pan, smiled. "Hi, David. Yeah, I was shoveling all morning to clean up a bit. The kids helped, too. So, how are you doing?"

A painter, Janice Resnick was a walking recipe book. She knew more ways to cook more vegetables than anyone Coccinella had ever known. Janice's encyclopedic knowledge and expertise came from years of rural living and growing her own vegetables and most of her herbs. Coccinella loved the Resnick's because, while steeped in rural life, they maintained their aesthetic eye. It was a consummate blend that he adored and fed off of, literally, as he came over for dinner at least once a week.

"I'm as fine as can be expected, given the situation. This afternoon session stuff has me, along with everyone else, a little screwy. This coming home after dark crap is for the birds, for sure."

"It's got us all messed up, though Morris can help a bit with the kids in the morning. But his writing time has been altered."

Just then Morris came through the back door with an armload of wood. "Hi David," he said, dumping the load in the kitchen wood box. "Janice, I'm going to get one more load."

"Morris," Janice asked, "should I put more than two cloves of garlic in the veggies? What do you think?"

"Two should be fine, dear," he added as he opened the back door again.

"Morris, want some help?" asked David.

"No need." Resnick shut the door and walked out to the woodpile behind the house. Resnick's woodpile was neat and tight. Up here, the woodpile a man kept measured his character, and Coccinella considered Morris's woodpile a manifestation of his poetry. The logs were split evenly, piled neatly in square rows, oak with oak, maple with maple, ash with ash. The woodpile stood conveniently located between the back of the house and the outhouse. One could not afford to waste time once winter had begun, and it certainly had begun before its time this strange year.

ঌ

The Resnick kids had gone into their rooms to do homework and to read.

"Another fine meal at Trattoria Resnick." David smiled as he sipped his green tea. "A refreshing stay against the prevailing turmoil."

"Oh David, you're such a pleasure," smiled Janice as she planted a big, friendly kiss on his forehead. "I'm heading upstairs to read. You guys can talk. I'll eavesdrop. Good night. Morris, there's lots more tea in the pot if you guys want any."

"Good night, Janice," said David.

Morris took a sip of his tea and looked over at David. "Thanks for driving tomorrow. What time do you want to pick me up?"

"I'll pick you up at ten o'clock sharp. That should get us to Skowhegan in time to get a seat." David stood up. "I've got to go. My stove is probably down to embers, and I'd like to read a bit before bed, if I can. Thanks for everything, as usual, Morris. Tell Janice, good night and thanks."

"Good night, David," yelled Janice from the upstairs bedroom.

"Night again, Janice." David headed out into the cold December night. His old friend, Orion, commanded the clear deep sky. The enormous pines around the Resnick home swayed and sang a soft elegy in the wind, which had suddenly picked up. Yes, Coccinella thought, the Resnick place was a home, not simply a house.

He jumped in his Ford 150 and started her up. The cab was biting cold. It's not even winter, he thought. He glided down the old logging road. The truck would just be getting warm when he pulled into his driveway. Once on the gravel town road, Coccinella wondered whether Zeke might be awake. If he were, he wondered what the boy might be thinking.

# Chapter 35

*I've only seen the ocean once. My parents never took me down to the coast. I never understood why. It's not that far, I don't think. An hour and a half, max. A lot of kids up in Chaldea have never been to the ocean. Kids like Atwood. Michelle has been down to Portland. She went there with you know who. More than once.*

*My father said the coast has too many out-of-staters and too much traffic, that people on the coast, flatlanders he called them, aren't like us in Western Maine, that they deal with the summer people, even though some work as fishermen and some even log. A few have farms, too, but that's all changing. He said that lots of people on the coast have sold their land to people from away and made their money, so they aren't real Mainers any more. He said that they call the coastal area around Portland and south the Gold Coast.*

*I would like to see the ocean again, but I won't be able to for quite a while. They've put me down here in South Portland. It's strange. I can smell the ocean, even in my room sometimes. The smell of the sea is different than the smell of the woods and farms, of pine trees and freshwater lakes. It smells of old boats, engine oil, fish guts, seaweed, and salt.*

*Living in Chaldea is different.*

*And I've never been skiing. I had snowshoes but I hardly used them. Lots of kids can snowshoe in Chaldea because they use them for hunting or trapping. Some people go snowshoeing for pleasure, but mostly people cross-country ski. Not many up here can afford to ski at The Loaf, which is what they call the Sugarloaf Mountain Ski Area.*

*I've never been up to Sugarloaf Mountain to watch the skiers. My father said skiing was frivolous, for the idle rich from the cities, people who like to waste their money and time on extravagances. Those were the specific words that he used. But I know some teachers like to ski. Coccinella skis at Sugarloaf sometimes. He also cross-country skis. Resnick cross-country skis. He would talk to Mr. C about it in the library.*

*I never did any of that outdoor stuff. I stayed inside mostly. I had models, I read, and I planned fires. I don't remember exactly when I began thinking about setting fires. I think it was in junior high school. I know that the thing with Shirley really upset me. But I can't remember about wanting to burn her house down or anything like that. I don't think that I ever thought that, maybe I did though, come to think of it.*

*I did go home that day and spend a lot of time lighting the stove in the cellar, which my mom asked me to do. I crumpled up a lot newspaper and stuffed it in the big old barrel along with some kindling. Then I lit an edge of a piece of newspaper. I loved to watch the flame crawl along the edge of the piece of paper then eat the words. Then it licked a stick of kindling slowly until that began burning. I would light several edges of the crumpled newspaper so that several flames would grow simultaneously. I would just kneel on the cellar floor and watch the flames. Watching the fire start, watching those little flames grow took me far away, as though I had left my body.*

*It's funny, but there's this poem I remember from Coccinella's class. It's a poem about this kid named Hazen who likes to go what we call "muckin" out in the woods. You know, he just likes to go walking, or as C & R would say "traipsing," through fields and woods. Some people might call it bushwhacking, but it isn't really that intense.*

*"Muckin'" is a kind of exploring without a plan. I have no idea where the word came from. Maybe it came from the name for the shoes that L.L. Bean invented way back. They're called "mukluks" and they're very popular. They're in every Bean catalog, especially the fall season.*

*I remember that the poem had the phrase "them Maine smugs" in it.*

*Some kids in class got real mad about that, saying that people in Maine were not smug at all. Mr. C had someone go to the library with pen and paper and copy word for word the definition. When the kid came back, we talked about why the poet used that word. Some kids didn't care. They hated the poem because they thought the poet was calling them smug.*

*I thought the poem was good. I liked it because the kid wasn't in his body really, even though his body was in the English class. He was far, far away, there but not there, like I am when I light a fire. I muck around with flames, go muckin' with fire.*

*I have the poem tucked away inside a book I have here in this room.*

*Down in Maine*

*them muckers*
*them Maine smugs,*

*s'all in their boots*

*they always know*
*where they can go*
*and you can't*

*know the swampy wood*
*the moss*
*-which side the tree*
*it grows –*

*they know terrain,*
*can smell their way*
*back home from miles*
*in rain or sun*

*and even if they can't*
*they know damn well*
*they can*

*not one don't know the color*
*of the sky*
*any day*
*got it figgered*
                    *snow*
*tomorrah sure*

*know where you can't go*
*and they can*

*s'all in their blasted boots*

*them muckers*
*them Maine smugs*

*had a boy once*
*in a high-school class*
        *in Maine*

*named Hazen*
*sat in class*
*and looked straight through you*
                                *and the wall*
        *at the sky*
        *all day*

*and couldn't say*
*what he didn't see*
*or saw*

*just smile*
*when you'd ask him*
*to decline a verb*
*decline*

*and look right through you*
*at the sky again*

*you knew then*
*he was miles away*
*muckin'*
*through places I could*
*never know*
*with them blasted boots*

*jest muckin'*

*and even when he was wearing shoes*
*you could tell he had boots*
*on his mind*

*like all them muckers*
*them Maine smugs*

*I keep a lot of poems from Coccinella's class. He liked to give us poems about Maine. He was always trying to get us to see that Maine was a good place, that it had beauty and deserved respect. It wasn't a major cause with him, but he would every once and a while give us poems, paintings, and articles about Maine hoping to excite us.*

*I know why he did this. All the kids knew. Once, last year, when Mr. C and some other teachers took us on an outing to Small's Falls over off of Route 4 toward Rangeley for a school picnic on a beautiful late September day he got really mad.*

*First, if you have never been upcountry on a beautiful September day with the peak foliage coloring the landscape and fresh, clean air that has a special warmth from the sun then I feel sorry for you. To experience a day like we experienced that day up at the Falls is even better than reading Keats's 'Ode to Autumn.' Mr. C read that poem to us out there in the woods with the sound of the falls in the background. I must admit it was kind of cool hearing a poem in the woods. He read Frost, too, naturally. "After*

*Apple Picking." We've got apple orchards in Chaldea. Lots of kids know about apples, cows, corn, and wood.*

*We just wanted to swim, to slide down the rocks and off the waterfall into the deep pool below. Even I relaxed a bit since no one was picking on me. That's because there was more than one class so everyone was kind of happy to be with people they normally don't get to be with. There were kids from every class, so you could stay away from kids that you knew would bother you.*

*We were picnicking and talking, swimming and splashing. Finally, Mr. C says it's time to go, to gather up our stuff carefully and head out down the trail toward the busses parked off the road about a mile from where we were. Everyone was picking up their clothes, towels, and blankets and their picnic stuff like plastic utensils, Tupperware, potato chip bags, and paper bags with left over submarine sandwiches. Stuff like that.*

*While we were all packing, kids were laughing and joking. It was a friendly, safe sound in the late afternoon light. Mr. C. yelled above the voices, "Hey, gang, don't forget to pack out what you packed in. This is a beautiful spot and we want to keep it as pristine as possible." I remember that word, pristine. His words echoed gently then fell below the sounds of all of us getting ready to leave.*

*As we were about to leave, Atwood tossed a Styrofoam cup down into the pool from the bank. Mr. C. saw him do it. He watched him carefully and did not stop him. After Atwood threw the cup, Mr. C walked over to him and confronted him. "Atwood, why on earth did you do that?" Mr. C. asked. "Hey, Mr. C.," Atwood answered, "it doesn't make any difference. It's only Maine. So who cares?"*

*As soon as Atwood said it, he regretted it. There was complete silence in those woods. I mean, there were forty kids, six teachers, and all I heard were two crows, a blue jay, and the cry of a distant hawk. Time stood still.*

*Mr. C walked over to Atwood and whispered something in his ear. Atwood's whole body tightened up after Mr. C. had whispered to him. We all saw Atwood make a fist. Mr. C. stood tall, stepped toward Atwood, and said calmly, but loud enough for several kids and teachers to hear, "Go ahead, Billy. If you do, you and your parents will lose your farm and you'll be in the hospital." That's what he said.*

*Mr. C walked Atwood down to the pool. Neither looked at the other. Atwood took a branch and fished out the cup. Mr. C asked for it. They walked back up from the pool to the riverbank. Mr. C took the cup and shoved it in Atwood's bag. "Now, Mr. Atwood, you can go and get on the bus."*

*Coccinella didn't let him off the hook, either. He followed him onto the bus and sat down next to him. I wasn't on that bus, but I saw them laughing together on the way into the school when we got back.*

*I wonder what Mr. C would say to me about the fires. I mean I know why he ripped into Atwood. It was about having respect for place, especially for the place where you lived.*

*I have no respect for Chaldea. I hope the place falls into hell. It sucks living up here. At least I never threw a Styrofoam cup or any garbage on Main Street.*

*Atwood never told anyone what Coccinella had whispered to him on that day. I wonder what Mr. C, if he could, would whisper in my ear now.*

⁂

"I remind you that you are under oath from yesterday, Dr. Proctor," Judge Elihu Shibles told her as Elizabeth Proctor took the stand. Today was her day.

"Dr. Proctor, you have worked with Zeke since he was brought into custody, is that correct?" Counselor Gardiner looked forward to Proctor's testimony. Clean and efficient. There would be no objections from Mr. Rust. He and Rust had spoken with the judge after the second day of the trial, and Mr. Rust had made it known that Mr. and Mrs. Titcomb only wanted their chance to testify that Zeke was in his room prior to the fires and in the morning of the fires, that as the attorney for the defense, he was seeking to minimize Zeke's incarceration at the Youth Center.

"Yes."

' how long has that been?"

Approximately four months. He was arrested before Christmas. It's April, so I have seen him that long."

"Thank you. And, Dr. Proctor, during this time you had the opportunity to diagnose the defendant. Is that true?"

"Yes, I collaborated with my colleagues regarding his diagnosis." Dr. Proctor looked over at the boy, but Zeke had his head down.

"Would you please share with the court your findings?" Judge Shibles, though he had read a brief from Dr. Proctor, turned to listen to her testimony.

"Zeke has a disorder called pyromania."

"Will you explain to the court exactly what pyromania is?"

"Pyromania is an impulse-control disorder, though some in the field disagree. Basically, this means a person diagnosed with pyromania fails to resist the impulsive desire to set fires, as opposed to the organized planning of an arsonist or terrorist."

"Zeke has been arrested for arson, Dr. Proctor."

"I realize that. There is no doubt that Zeke planned these fires, but I believe he couldn't control himself. I believe that he had to light them. His emotional state dictated it."

"Foggy territory, Dr. Proctor, wouldn't you say?"

"In one sense; in another, not really."

"Please explain."

"This is what we know about pyromania. Adolescent fire setting is a growing social and economic problem. It poses major risks to the health and safety of people and to the protection of their property, as the town of Chaldea can attest to. According to recent statistics, children and adolescents who light fires cause more deaths than any other type of household disaster. Chaldea was lucky."

Mr. Rust shot out of his seat. "Objection, your honor!"

"Sustained," Judge Shibles said calmly. He pushed his glasses up onto the bridge of his nose, sat up, and turned toward the witness. "Dr. Proctor, try to keep the opinions to yourself."

"Zeke's problem is repeated fire setting. It may be that there is less an impulse control problem than a manifestation of psycho-infantilism." Dr. Proctor looked at Mr. and Mrs. Titcomb. They sat in the first row behind Zeke like two statues. They stared ahead, avoiding eye contact with Dr. Proctor.

"With adolescents the fire setting might be more of a conduct disorder than actual pyromania as it is defined by the DSM."

"The DSM?" Gardiner asked.

"Yes, the *Diagnostic and Statistical Handbook of Mental Disorders*, the clinician's handbook."

"So, Zeke is, in your mind, a fire setter and not a pyromaniac?"

"I believe so."

"Explain this distinction."

"Most of the psychiatric literature views adolescents as fire setters and not pyromaniacs. One type of fire setting is a cry for help. The fire calls attention to an intra-psychic problem. Maybe it's depression, an interpersonal problem, parental divorce or separation, even sexual or physical abuse. The delinquent fire setter is someone usually between the ages of eleven and fifteen. For them, setting a fire is part of a larger pattern of aggression. They usually want to destroy property, not injure people." Dr. Proctor cleared her throat and took a drink from the glass of water. She shifted to a more comfortable sitting position, adjusted her skirt, and folded her hands on her lap. "The causes of fire setting among adolescents are complex and, truth be told, not very well understood. Still, there are individual and environmental factors that contribute to adolescent fire setting."

Zeke stared at Dr. Proctor. She smiled back. Then he leaned over to Attorney Rust and whispered to him. Eben watched his son and turned to his wife but said nothing. Attorney Rust stood and asked Judge Shibles, "Your honor, it's close to lunch time. I would like to suggest a recess until this afternoon. Dr. Proctor has more to say, obviously, and we should hear it on a full stomach."

"Agreed, counselor. Court recessed until two o'clock. Step down, Dr. Proctor." The judge softly banged the gavel.

Dr. Proctor stood down from the stand and walked toward Zeke, who stood behind the defense table with his lawyer and his parents now pressing against the three-foot high, varnished oak barrier that separated them from their boy. Dr. Proctor leaned slightly over the table to speak to Zeke.

"Doctor, don't speak to my son," snapped Eben Titcomb. Peggy, staring at the floor and holding her handbag with both hands in front of her, had stepped away. Dr. Proctor stood straight up, staring into Eben Titcomb's eyes. "I only wanted to see how your son was holding up, Mr. Titcomb." She turned to Zeke. "Hang in there, young man. Remember what we talked about last week," she said and strode out of the courtroom.

# Chapter 36

*I'm not suicidal or anything. That would be stupid. I don't regret a thing. I'm simply a messed up kid. Everybody says so.*

*I've been talking to Dr. P for how long? She talks and talks to me. We do okay. It gets tiring, and I sometimes screw around in my journal and don't really say anything much. She knows what I'm doing. I don't have the nerve to tell her what's really on my mind. I don't want to know what she has to say about my feelings and thoughts.*

*Sometimes I tell her things, but I'm pretty careful. She's like a drill. She bores right down on me. She tries to get to the serious stuff in a way that doesn't bother me.*

*I really don't want to talk about what we say in our sessions. It's private. I'm pretty messed up. I close up with her a lot more now. I don't know why. I don't trust her. I want to trust her. I thought I could trust her at the beginning. But I can't.*

*She talks about me. She talks to my parents. Or tries. My father gets furious. He's still mad at me. But he was always mad at me. Mom, geez, I end up feeling bad for her. She's a sorry case. She's as sorry a case as I am. I wish she was here, even though I wouldn't say much to her except stupid stuff. She would probably say stupid stuff like am I eating enough or am I doing my therapy as I'm told, or am I wearing clean underwear, stuff like that. What is it about mothers and clean underwear?*

*I don't talk much. There's no reason to. It's not like I have friends here.*

*Dr. P would like to be my friend, and she is friendly to me, but she isn't a friend. How can she be? She's like a teacher. Good teachers are friendly but they can never be friends. I'm stuck, alone. I have to be my own friend. Which is good, in a way. I don't have to worry about how other people feel all the time.*

*I'm sick of things. This makes me angry. Anger makes me feel powerful. Not as powerful as when I light a fire. I feel my old inside self. I need to get that inside self to stay on the outside. My inside self could handle this place, but I can't get it to come out. My outside self gets shoved around, picked on, the same old stuff. I spend time thinking how I could burn this place down. I would never tell Dr. P that I think that.*

*She'd have a conniption. They'd probably put me on some kind of medication. There's lots of kids down here on medication. Or she'd make me talk to her for about twenty hours a day. Or write in my journal for ten hours a day. She would be all over me like flies on manure. Several kids used that phrase at school. I like it. I've heard it down here. In Chaldea you smell a lot of cow manure and chicken manure, especially in the spring. It's getting to be spring now, but I only smell the ocean. It's tangy, not musky.*

*Ever since I was arrested, things have seemed like a dream only the dream has been a nightmare, especially when it comes to my father and even my mother. Before Christmas seems like another life.*

*There was no Christmas at home. Michelle wasn't there. Who knows where she is. She left one Saturday and she hasn't been heard from since. I would've given anything to see the look on my father's face on Christmas Day. I bet his nose scrunched up. His dear family no longer together. God, what would the neighbors think?*

*I shut down with my father. I don't look at him any more. I sneak looks when I know he's looking at my mother or when he's taking a breath, pausing before he continues his mission to scold me into submission.*

*He's been doing that since I was put down here. I have spent my life dealing with my parents. It's like trying to find your way down a road that has been booby trapped with land mines. You never know if you're going to be blown up when you take your next step. It was like my experience in school. I am sick of being afraid. I miss lighting fires.*

*School was worse than this place. It's more of a jail. Do this, do that. Go to the guidance counselor, get a pass to go to the bathroom. Asking permission to go to the bathroom. Is that for real? You get stuck with kids and teachers that you could care less about. I mean there's some good teachers, like Coccinella, teachers that treat you like a human being, but they are very rare. Besides, you don't get to see them all the time. They can't be there to help you most of the time and you can't talk to them when you need to. By the time you do get to talk to them, you don't feel the same way or you've gone on to worry about something totally different.*

*I have not met a kid who really likes school. Kids say they like school, but they don't. They do the right thing to get good grades so they can get out without any hassles. No one learns anything in school. They memorize stuff for a few hours then forget it. It's easy to make teachers think you're learning something.*

*I remember the class talking about learning and education in Mr. C's class, and I started to thinking about how you really learn. That afternoon, I went down to the library to help Mr. Resnick. I happened to mention to him what we were talking about in Mr. C's class. Mr. Resnick said, "Here, read this." It was another poem, naturally. It was by that Maine guy now in Australia. That's where they have all kinds of amazing, huge brush fires. I read about them. Awesome, gigantic fires.*

*I have the poem in my poetry journal, which I brought down here. Don't ask me why. I just did. I needed something. Mr. C made us keep one all the time. He used the poem in class so we had to put it in.*

*Possibility of a Hand-Hewn Education*

*They brought down these three French-Canadian fellers*
*and they cleaned up them birdseye poplar in no time*

*With five-foot handles and 14-inch blades*
*they scored them trees, they hewed them trees*

*Hand-hewn because they were*

*too big for the mill.*

*And I said how long does it take*
*to learn to hew like that?*

*And he said oh you may improve a little*
*but you don't learn*

*You get up there with an ax*
*and in five minutes I'll tell you*

*Whether you can hew*
*or not*

*The class liked the poem because it was about logging. Mr. C said it wasn't only about logging. We talked about the poem. Class was fun for a while. That was until Mr. C started talking about how poetry usually was about more than its subject. Sometimes he just goes off to places we don't follow. He goes muckin'.*

*The best way to get out of school without hassles is to be invisible. But here's the problem for me. I draw attention to myself. Ironic. It's good to be invisible in school if you're not strange like me. I mean why else would I be so picked on when I am trying to be invisible? I know plenty of kids who can be invisible and they don't get picked on. It's because they are basically normal. They can have a girlfriend even if they are ugly or their girlfriend is ugly or they can climb the ropes in gym to the ceiling or they can be the manager of the basketball team. They can be invisible because they can connect to other kids.*

*If you're like me, trying to become invisible only pisses off the popular kids. I piss everyone off, even my parents. That's when the land mines go off.*

*I can't help screwing up in school. It's a hazard. I step directly onto one of the land mines planted there. Billy Atwood, for instance. But there are others. Other kids can escape real damage but I can't. I ask myself why all the time. Who the hell are they to escape danger and I can't? That ticks me off. I think about it when I am alone.*

ஒ

"Hungry?" asked Lionel Avery as Elizabeth Proctor stuffed a forkful of spinach and mushroom slices into her mouth. She chewed greedily with a smile.

"Famished," she blurted after an exaggerated swallow. "I feel as though I've been lecturing all morning."

"You have."

"Very funny, mister." She gobbled another forkful of her salad. "Ummm. I love balsamic vinegar."

"Lemme ask you something."

"Go ahead. Shoot."

Lionel leaned forward. "What's the story with this pyromania?"

Elizabeth put her fork down. She smiled at Lionel. "You know what Freud says?"

"Absolutely not, but I think I'm going to."

"Freud thought fire setting represented a regression to a primitive desire to demonstrate power over nature." She stabbed a slice of mushroom and a chunk of goat cheese, and put the forkful in her mouth.

"I get that."

The doctor poured a little more salad dressing on the remaining spinach. "Researchers try to theorize fire setting as a primarily male disorder by connecting to Freud's belief that fire setting has a symbolic connection to the male's sexual urge. There was a study way back, I forget when, that attributed fire setting to fear of castration in young males and speculated that adolescents who set fires do so to gain power over adults." She smiled and lazily mixed her salad.

Chief Avery smiled. "Enough of the psychology. What type of environment do these kids live in to do this?"

"Could be a number of factors." She circled her fork over a large spinach leaf.

"Like what?"

"Poor parental supervision, neglect, and emotional uninvolvement. Attention seeking. Peer pressure, stressful life events. The whole parental psychopathology idea, that adolescent fire setters are more likely to have been physically or emotionally abused, seen their parents abuse drugs or act violently. That's about it."

Lionel took a sip of water. His eyes stared at the glass.

"Fire setting among adolescents can be chronic or episodic. If fires are set frequently, it's seen as a way to relieve tension during unusually stressful periods." Elizabeth wiped her mouth with her napkin. "You thinking about the Titcomb family?"

"Ayuh." He smiled at her. "Finish up your rabbit food. We should be getting back."

"Relax, Mister Man, we've got time." Elizabeth took another forkful of her salad and teasingly pushed it toward Lionel's mouth. "Here, have some."

Lionel turned his head away. Turning back with a smile, he asked, "How many salads do you eat in a week?"

"Not enough. Got to stay lean and mean. Hey, I forgot to mention something. A number of serial killers, including 'Son of Sam,' turned out to be fire setters in their adolescence."

"Great. Nice tidbit."

"You need more greens in your diet."

Spring comes late up-country, even when it comes early. In Maine, April is a cruel month, crueler than poets imagine. It arrives, though it never stays long. Summer hounds its heals, anxious to get its turn before autumn pushes it away unexpectedly after August. April in Chaldea continued wet and cold, then grudgingly gave way to warm day temperatures and nights above freezing.

The maples showed signs of budding, so a soft, reddish tinge blanketed the distant landscape. Morning air filled with a cacophony of birdsong, cardinals, blue jays, red-wing blackbirds, peppered by the notorious song of the white-throated sparrow. The stale, cold smell from blackened piles of winter snow lingered in backyards and in parking lots. Ice on the Kennebec had all but broken up, and the river flowed fast with mountain snowmelt, just below flood stage.

The four-day trial had ended the previous week, the testimony finished. The jury's decision took less than an hour. The judge, accepting the verdict, declared a sentencing session the following week. Peggy Titcomb softly sobbed. Lionel Avery noticed that Eben Titcomb sat bolt upright and stared at the jury foreman.

Judge Shibles, after two hours of deliberation in his chambers, surveyed his courtroom from the bench. He looked at Ezekiel Daniel Titcomb, guilty of arson and attempted arson. The boy sat stiffly at the defendant's table in a wool sport coat, off the rack from Arsenault's, the local clothing store in Skowhegan, keenly pressed khaki chino pants, white socks, and loafers. He looked down toward the tabletop. Judge Shibles wondered whether this boy, who had caused over a million dollars' worth of damage from the fires in Chaldea, was, in some remote way, cognizant of what he had done to his town and its inhabitants. He wondered about pyromania, the human brain and its complexity.

"The defendant will please stand," ordered the judge. Mr. Rust whispered into Zeke's ear. Then, Zeke and Mr. Rust stood up behind their table and faced the judge. Zeke looked at the judge, his eyes focused on the judge's hands, which held several typed pages.

Judge Shibles perused the pages, cleared his throat, sipped from his water glass, and prepared to speak. "On the sentencing of

Ezekiel Daniel Titcomb, there has been much to consider, given the fact that he has been tried as a juvenile. I have a few comments to make prior to sentencing." Judge Shibles shuffled the pages, glancing at paragraphs on two specific pages of the text.

"I have met with Dr. Proctor prior to and throughout the trial. Her expertise has been invaluable in my sentencing decision." Judge Shibles looked at Mr. Rust and Zeke while speaking.

"Ezekiel Titcomb is properly diagnosed with the disorder of pyromania. Ezekiel Titcomb meets the six criteria to be so diagnosed. He has set a fire deliberately and purposefully on more than one occasion. And while evidence wasn't admitted on several fires in Chaldea, he did set two fires. According to Dr. Proctor, Ezekiel experienced feelings of tension and emotional arousal before setting those fires. Additionally, he exhibits a release, a pleasure, and a satisfaction after the lighting of fires. Ezekiel does not light fires for money or due to delusions, brain damage, substance abuse, and the like. Lastly, his lighting of fires cannot be better explained than by a conduct disorder, an anti-social personality disorder.

"The court subscribes to a case-management approach for Ezekiel. This has been the court's approach since the defendant has been held, arraigned, and tried. He has been interviewed, with and without his parents, to assess family stress, family patterns, and supervision procedures. This evaluation has been ongoing. Individual treatment has begun. I expect Dr. Proctor to continue treatment with Ezekiel. It is my understanding this treatment will include problem-solving skills, anger management, communication skills, and cognitive restructuring. Any treatment by Dr. Proctor necessary for Ezekiel will be conducted with the notification of the parents. If the parents disagree with the proposed treatment, other than those aforementioned by the court, they may petition the court for a review.

"Given this information and given the measures agreed to by this court since Ezekiel's arrest and confinement, the court hereby sentences Ezekiel Daniel Titcomb to confinement in the South Portland Youth Center until the age of eighteen years, with the possibility of an extension until he is twenty-one years old. An extension depends upon Dr. Proctor's complete psychological evaluation of the defendant prior to his eighteenth birthday."

# Hot Spot IV

*Flames are the stuff of the universe. Think of it. The sun is composed of gases, those gases burn and you've got flames. Solar flares are the ultimate flames that reach out into the cosmos. You have all of those supernova explosions and all of those gaseous nebulae. Fire rules.*

*Since I've been down here, I've been wondering about explosions in space. If there is no air in space, how can flames exist? They must create their own air. They're nuclear explosions. Flames are that strong, that smart, that creative. They create their own space. That's what I would like to be able to do. To have my inside self make its own atmosphere.*

*I feel a lot of different things down here on the coast, away from Chaldea. I've always wanted to escape Chaldea. I don't know a kid that doesn't want to leave that place. Staying there is a fast ticket to nowhere. Most kids end up staying there or near there. They are nowhere.*

*I'm not there. I'm here. I have no plans of going back. I can't. They'd kill me. Maybe I'll try and find my sister. My mother told me that they got a postcard from her with a picture of the Boston Aquarium. Why would she go look at fish? She knows nothing about fish or the ocean. I've never seen her eat fish of any kind. My mother told me that my father called the Boston Police and had my sister declared a missing person. They told him that she was an adult, so they couldn't do anything. My father started yelling on the phone, then slammed it down. He then informed my mother, that's her word, "informed," that she was not to mention Michelle's name in the house again, that she was never to be allowed home, that as far as he was concerned he had no daughter. Way to go, Mr. Titcomb.*

*I've turned more sarcastic while down here. I've had to do it so that I don't get bothered. I use words to keep the idiots at a distance. And believe me, there are some definite idiots down here. I don't want to get into that. This place makes school look like a picnic. You learn here very fast. Like that poem I mentioned. You know in five minutes whether you'll survive here.*

*The first time I was punched in here I had to figure out how to get along. This place isn't a jail, but it might as well be. We're guarded and fed like it is. That's all I'll say about that.*

*I imagine myself carried on a flame so high that I dance among the stars. I remember Mr. C's description of heaven. Dante was his favorite poet, so he started talking about Dante's idea of paradise. Dante's heaven was bright lights and burning flames. I perked up when he started talking about souls as flames, how heaven was filled with burning flames so bright a person couldn't look at them. I think my inside self is a gigantic, blinding soul flame. Knowing this flame is inside really gnaws at me, if you want to know the truth.*

*I sound like Holden Caulfield, but I don't mean to. There's no escape from being a kid. I hate it – believe me. I know how I feel, but when it comes to expressing how I feel, I get all confused. If I tried to tell the story of myself, it'd make no sense.*

*Teachers are always reminding us kids that we aren't adults yet. They never miss a chance to dump on our heads that we're immature, clueless, that we're selfish, that we don't think.*

*When I was a freshman, Coccinella told me to read books about someone like myself. He called it adolescent literature. Mr. Resnick called it YAL when he talked to teachers about books for students. As if reading about someone my age will help me know who I am. I've been told to do that since I was in the fifth grade. Teachers think that reading these books will help us understand who we are. I've read a lot of these type of books. Some are really good. Like Cormier. I really like Eric in the novel* Tenderness. *He's a strange character. I like some science fiction.*

*There's a pretty good library in here, so I can get books. The librarian is an old guy who limps. I heard that he was a Vietnam vet who got his leg busted up going back into heavy fire to save a soldier. He's like Resnick because he's always reading. He takes care of the books. Dr. P says I should try and work in the library. She's been on my case about it. I'm not feeling comfortable yet. I do go in the library, but I'm careful because when I come out to go back to my room or to the general area I don't want some guys to see me with a book. Carrying a book can be dangerous.*

⁂

"How long has he been doing this?" asked Dr. Proctor. She peered into the cell.

The guard took another peak and turned to face Dr. Proctor. "I've been watching him for close to fifteen minutes. He's mumbling. He's been sitting on the edge of his cot, talking to himself, moving his arms, giggling. You name it."

"Has he eaten lunch?" asked the doctor.

"He ate his meal. No problem."

"Good. Thanks, Herman. Keep an eye on him. He has a session with me at four o'clock."

⁂

Dr. Proctor observed Zeke. He sat in the chair, looking at nothing in particular. He surveyed the room, snuck a look at Dr. Proctor, and began to fidget. "Zeke, what's up? The guard and I saw you apparently talking to yourself."

"Whadduyuh mean?" Zeke began rubbing his hands as though he was washing them.

"Were you talking to anyone in particular? What were you talking about?"

"I was just playing around."

"The guard watched you. You were quite involved. Would you like to tell me what you were talking about? What was on your mind?"

"I was just pretending. I won't do it again."

"I think we need to talk about this type of behavior. You haven't done this before. What were you pretending?"

"When I get mad sometimes, I start pretending that I'm talking to my father, to Atwood, to that asshole math teacher who made a fool out of me, to my mother…." Zeke's voice trailed off.

"To your sister?" asked Dr. Proctor.

"Maybe."

"You've started swearing these last few weeks. Why? That's not like you."

"Everybody here swears. I've gotta fit in with them."

"Everybody swore in your high school, too, and you didn't swear."

"Here it's different."

"You don't have to swear if you don't want to."

"I know."

Dr. Proctor switched gears. "What's getting you angry, Zeke?"

"You always ask me that. How come?"

"We have to get you to talk about how you feel and why you feel the way you do. We've been working a long time."

"It doesn't make any difference, does it?"

"It does. It makes a lot of difference."

"Nothing makes any difference. This place, I don't like it. I'm sick of talking. What good does it do? I don't feel any better. I feel like crap." Zeke folded his arms, leaned back in the chair, and stared at the floor. He pictured Dr. Proctor's desk in flames.

"You didn't bring your journal today."

"I didn't write in it. I'm not writing in it much. I don't want to do that. It's a waste of time." Zeke did not dare to tell her that he'd been writing poems in the journal, which he kept under his library books in his small room. They were his secret, for now.

# Chapter 37

*I shouldn't swear, I know, but everyone in here does...so I do. I have to. Swearing does nothing for a person. It releases emotions and all that stuff. Swear words aren't the best words to use necessarily. Mr. C and Mr. Resnick spoke about swearing once. Mr. C did a class on the F word. We all thought he was crazy, but the class was interesting. He took risks. The class was sure that he was going to get fired. No one said a word.*

*It's funny about some teachers, how the students respect them enough not to make a big deal out of things. Mr. C was one of those teachers, the kind that kids respected because of his fairness and his ability to actually listen, the type of teacher that goes to bat for you. If you do have problems with them, they work everything out so that things are okay and you don't have to worry about stuff. Funny, the good teachers are the ones that the administration doesn't get along with. Mr. C was always rubbing against school rules.*

*Then there are the mean teachers who no one respects. The kids wait for them to make some stupid mistake so they can turn them in. The trouble is the principal and vice-principal are often friendly with these types and they always side with them. These teachers never volunteer or do anything with us. They are out the door with seniors. They can't wait to leave the place. They're worse than the students.*

*My father and mother did not like swearing. When Michelle was in the seventh grade, my mother had to wash Michelle's mouth out with soap. My father held her down. I just sat at the kitchen table and didn't move. I didn't dare. Michelle screamed to beat the band. It was a very scary scene.*

*We had lots of scary scenes when I was in grade school and Michelle was in junior high school. Michelle twisting and yelling, screaming, my father holding her down, practically sitting on her when she fell off the kitchen chair. My mother, a look of horror on her face, trying to push this soapy, bubbly glass of soapy water into her mouth, liquid flying all over the floor from near misses and Michelle's constant twisting in my father's arms. She spit the stuff out at him and hit him directly in the face. He didn't swear, but he yelled, "You're gonna learn what we teach you!"*

*Michelle slowed her twisting enough for my mother to pour the concoction into her mouth. Suddenly Michelle stopped trying to escape. She stopped moving and sat on the floor as though she had no spine. She went limp. My father bent down to lift her up and that's when Michelle struck again. She spit out a mouthful at my father, hitting him in the eyes.*

*He slapped her across the face, stood up, and yelled for my mother to bring him a washcloth because his eyes were burning. Michelle flew up to her room, screaming, "You asshole! What kind of father are you! I hate you!" My mother came back from the downstairs bathroom with a hot washcloth and began wiping my father's eyes. He grumbled at her, "For God's sake, Peg, be careful, will you." She said, "I'm sorry, Eben. But you've got to hold still." My mother is always sorry. For everything. That's why I'm not sorry for what I've done. Being sorry gets you nowhere.*

*What Michelle said at the kitchen table caused the situation. We were all eating and I thought everything was okay because the four of us were talking about some stupid thing, like school or something. The conversation ended up about some guy at school who had been hassling Michelle. I guess that he had said some naughty things to her between classes and in the cafeteria. My father perked up at this and asked her what he said and wanted to know what was going on.*

*I thought that Michelle was too smart to fall into that trap, because she just looked at her food and acted all calm and everything. She took a forkful of beans, ate them, then, after a few chews, casually said, "Oh, it's nothing. He just said he wanted to get in my pants." I never knew what to expect from my father when Michelle said something like that. She said things like that all the time starting in seventh grade. That's when she developed, using make-up and wearing clothes that made her look like she was eighteen instead of thirteen. High school guys started driving her home and she started getting rebellious.*

*She added, offhand, "Today in school, Richie Hilton grabbed my ass and whispered that he wanted to see me naked." I sat and stared at my beans.*

*My mother's comment was, "Oh, dear," and set her fork down on her plate. My father stayed calm and said, "What?" He stared at Michelle. Finally, he said, "The Hiltons. They're white trash. Their kids are outta control. I'll tell you this. They're not going to treat my children like that. I'll see to it, by God that they don't. I'll call the principal tomorrow. I'll call the Hiltons if I have to." I thought that was the end of it. But it wasn't. In our house, with my father, there was never an end to it.*

*After he finished blowing steam, Michelle made a comment that seemed so innocent. But it wasn't because she swore. She said, "He's stupid. He's just being a royal asshole." I think she said it innocently. It was a statement that was "innocuous." Not a bad swear word. My father lost it.*

*Swearing. I do it a little. I've used "asshole" a lot. I do it to show the other guys here that I'm normal. If my father knew that I swore, he'd probably come down here some night, tug me out of bed, and skin me alive. As they say here, He'd be supremely pissed.*

*My father never liked us to take the Lord's name in vain, either. He was really religious. We had to say prayers before every meal. He made us attend Baptist bible school Sunday mornings, and I did until the eighth grade. Michelle never went after grade school. She'd skip out.*

*I don't read the bible much now. I probably should, especially since I'm in this place.*

*There's plenty of time to read it because there's plenty of bible study groups in here. I don't go. Bunch of losers. Goody goodies. Fake good. I do not want to be a fake. That gets you nowhere. I know I need to be a good person. I want to be good in a natural way, that doesn't advertise myself. That's how I feel about religion. What you believe in must be natural. No one should show off their religion, and the guys in the bible study groups here come around like a parade asking me and other kids if we love Jesus and, if we do, we should let him in into our life.*

*I haven't let anyone into my life, as Dr. P has pointed out to me. I'm supposed to think about that and "work on it."*

Dr. Proctor looked at her notebook. It was early May, almost time for black flies. Dr. Proctor lifted her hands, cupped them behind her head, and leaned back in her chair. Adolescents, tomorrow they'll be just like they are today, she mused, except when they aren't. Perhaps today Zeke will have a breakthrough, though yesterday his eyes told her he wouldn't. She wondered when that special day for Zeke would come. Here I am today, she thought, waiting for Zeke.

"I'm not a bad person," Zeke mumbled.

"Explain yourself."

Zeke fidgeted in his seat.

"Come on," Proctor prodded, "Look at me. Talk. You've been saying insightful and important things lately. We can really move forward. Cooperate." Dr. Proctor reminded herself to be careful in pressing the boy.

Zeke looked at her. "So I did light the fires. That doesn't make me all bad. No one got hurt."

"You were extremely lucky, young man."

"I know."

"You burned down a school, tried to burn down two others. We've talked about the other fires, about your family."

"I told you that stuff in confidence. All I'm saying is I'm not ba
I did bad things, sure. Inside I'm not bad. Everyone thinks I'm a monster."

"You don't."

"No, I don't." Zeke's shoulders tightened. He sat up straight. He stared at the coffee table.

"You're getting angry."

"So what if I am. Nobody listens to me. You don't. No one does." The boy folded his arms across his chest.

Dr. Proctor rolled her chair to her desk. She rested the elbows of both arms on the desktop and rested her face in the palm of her hands. "Listen, I hear that you were reading a bible in your room yesterday."

"Who told you? Herman?"

"It's his job. This isn't a criticism." She smiled at Zeke, who caught the smile when he raised his eyes from the coffee table to sneak a peek at his doctor. "He says you've been spending a lot of time writing in your journal. What gives? I thought you gave that up."

"I started again. I like to write in it."

"When did you start?"

"I started a few weeks ago. I kept it secret."

"Why?"

"I don't want anyone here to know what I do."

"Are you ready to share any of it?"

"The stuff's private. If I show you, you'll think I'm crazy, which is what you think anyway."

"Zeke, come on. That was unfair."

"It wasn't. Everything's unfair."

"What's unfair?"

"Kids like me never have a chance."

"What do you mean 'never had a chance'?"

Zeke slunk down in his chair, arms once again crossed on his chest, and pouted. Dr. Proctor reminded herself that he was just a was a dangerous kid.

ıobody." Zeke smirked, "but I'm not a nobody now.
self came out like the flames came out of me."

ꕥ

"I'll consider it, Dr. Proctor," said David Coccinella. "The seniors are leaving next week, then graduation, then school ends. It's a hectic time. Let me finish up and I'll get in touch. How does that sound?"

"Fine. I'll expect a call."

Coccinella hung up. That's a twist, he thought. Wait until Morris hears about this. "One never knows do one," he said softly to himself as he put one some water for tea. Coccinella looked out the window over the stove. He noticed that Harold Cashen had dumped another load of chicken manure on the corner of the alfalfa field. He'd start spreading and plowing the adjacent field of old corn stalks soon.

# Chapter 38

*I am Ezekiel. I have seen heaven burning. I have seen a tornado cloud of flame, as if the firestorm of all firestorms whirled so vast in the sky that the light of the flames blinded every human being and their children and their children's children for ten thousand generations. Only I can see the truth.*

*I am Ezekiel. Inside the firestorm I have seen my enemies, and they are blazing with a heat so intense they might as well be molten metal. They are screaming mad in unbearable pain. Their wings gleam like armor and their heads look like bronze and ripple in the heat. I laughed at them and hoped for more flames to burn them like melted gold. And lightening flashed around their heads. And their eyes were yellow-orange charcoals and tears of molten lead flowed from them. They were torches writhing in agony and they flew like sparks in the whirling, burning wind.*

*I am Ezekiel. I have peered deep into the flames and I have seen beyond my enemies, into the firmament, into the glorious blinding light beyond all. And I have seen there the gleaming shape of one man, in complete agony, shining radiantly alone. And the man is me.*

*I am Ezekiel and you'd better leave me alone.*

Kingdom: Animalia; Phylum: Anthropoda; Class: INSECTA; Order: Diptera; Family: simuliidae. Common name: THE BLACK

FLY. Black fly season in Maine is mythic. Their appearance in late spring is a bane for every resident of Maine, especially the initial infestation come the end of May.

These damned bugs even drive the mighty moose crazy. Hounded out of the woods by black fly swarms, they have been seen fleeing into pastures, bogs, and lakes in order to gain relief. Summer is gauged by the severity of the infestation the way winter is gauged by the snow and cold.

Local farmers and woodcutters swear Avon's *Skin So Soft* keeps the flies at bay. The problem is that it dilutes with sweat, so one has to keep on applying it in thick quantities. Others try *Woodsman's Fly Dope* or bear grease. The truth is that nothing keeps black flies away except a screen or a closed window...with luck.

A second truth is that the first appearance of black flies indicates spring is giving way to the lengthy, languid days of the short Maine summer. A third truth is imaginative strings of invectives have been invented by Maine citizens, who shout at them when attacked by the thick swarms. Rumor has it that a professor from Orono, a recently hired anthropologist in pursuit of tenure, traveled around the state in an attempt to record some for a book.

~

"Dr. Proctor, a pleasure," Coccinella put out his hand. "Your call caught me off guard. The request intrigued me."

"Thanks for coming down today, Mr. Coccinella. I've heard a lot of good things about you from Zeke. He's fond of you. You and Mr. Resnick. Have a seat, please."

"Thanks." Coccinella smiled. "You need to fill me in on my role in working with Zeke. I'll be more than happy to help Zeke in any way that I can. But I must say I have qualms."

"Qualms are understandable. You do know teens, and your

work with them is respected. Zeke seems comfortable with you."

"That's a bit of a surprise. He never said a whole helluva lot in class. I can count the number of times he came after class to hang around and chat. He's peculiar. Kept to himself. I could never read him. I knew that his family was...problematic. He was the last kid I would have suspected to set fires."

"I can understand that. But, that's where you come in. Zeke has been secretly writing. We think that some mentoring by a trusted teacher would benefit him. I, personally, think he'll drop his guard with you."

"What has he been writing?"

"We know he's been writing extensively in the journal that he brought with him down to the Youth Center. He won't show anyone. He did tell me that two of the journals were from your English class."

"They would be poetry journals."

"My thinking is that you create a writing session with him, once a week, for an hour. Having Zeke work with you will affect his rehabilitation in terms of communication skills, problem solving, even cognitive restructuring."

"I can work on his writing with him, for sure." Coccinella smiled. "Do I have free rein with materials? Can I use whatever material I see fit? I don't want to be censored."

"I have no trouble with your request, Mr. Coccinella, but the material you use must be approved by his parents."

"I understand that. You know Mr. Titcomb. Though I don't have the inclination to deal with him, I will, of course." Damn, he thought, how much are teachers asked and expected to do anyway? The free time I spend outside of class on student related issues.

"Excellent. Send me a prospective list of books and poems so that I can have the Titcomb's okay it, should you decide to work with Zeke."

"I'll call you in a day or two. I need to think about this."

Dr. Proctor stood up behind her desk. "I appreciate your taking the time to see me. Sorry for the brief meeting, but I have two others today."

"Don't thank me yet." Mr. Coccinella shook hands and left.

He walked down the hallway toward the stairwell. He really did want to work with this kid. By the time he got to his car he knew his summer would be busy in a completely different way than he expected. After all, if I don't help the kid, he thought, no one will. A gentle breeze caught the tips of several white pines clustered at the southern end of Pratt Street. The afternoon light was right out of a Fairfield Porter painting. Coccinella took a deep breath.

He recognized this day in May as a gift of spring, the type of day that appeared suddenly, now and again out of nowhere, a day that warmed the earth and warmed the hearts of all who lived up here even more, a "Gloriosa daisy of a day." He loved that phrase. He also remembered a Frost poem as the first two lines popped into his mind: "Nature's first green is gold/Her hardest hue to hold." He opened the door of his truck knowing that he would try to do the best work that he could with the boy.

Zeke scrunched up his face. Why did he say that, he wondered.

"Don't be upset, honey," Peggy Titcomb urged. "Your father didn't mean what he said." She looked at her husband, brows furrowed.

Eben Titcomb caught the look and turned to his son. "What I meant, Zeke, is that there are criminals in here, real bad kids, so please be careful. I don't want anything to happen to you."

"I'm fine. Some kids in here are alright. I'm taking care of myself." He looked at his father. For the first time, he noticed a steel blue sadness in his father's eyes.

"I guess that your work with Mr. Coccinella is going well. Dr.

Proctor said you look forward to the meetings. She says that you're doing a lot of writing with him. When are you going to show us what you are writing?"

"I dunno."

"What kind of answer is that?" snapped Mr. Titcomb. "Are you going to show us the stuff or not. It's only poetry crap. It isn't really important, is it, explaining how you feel about all this stuff?"

"I don't have to show you anything," Zeke blurted. "And poetry isn't crap. Mr. C says it's good. We talk about what I write and how to make it better. He even shows my stuff to Mr. Resnick and he comments on it, too. I get to see what he says when Mr. C comes back and then we talk about it."

"What? I didn't know that Resnick was involved. Peg, did you know this? Nobody notified me. I'm the one who needs to give permission about what goes on with my son."

"No, Eben, but it doesn't make any difference. They're both helping Zeke. That's a good thing, isn't it?" Peggy Titcomb pushed her hands along her thighs.

Titcomb wasn't mollified by his wife's response. He stood up. "Next thing," he began, "everyone one in town will know what our kid is thinking. Why if anyone gets a hold of what he writes, they'll probably publish it in *The Sentinel*. Then what do you think will happen? I sure as hell hope Proctor is in her office. I'm going to give her a piece of my mind." Eben moved to the window and gazed out at the warm May afternoon. He turned to his wife.

"What my kid says and does is private. It's bad enough that she's drilling and grilling the kid. Now Coccinella and his poet friend are participating in this crap. Imagine what they'll say to all the high school teachers about Zeke. That's just what I need. I never should have let that teacher in to see Zeke. He's a troublemaker, anyway. He's from away and he puts all kinds of ideas into the kids' heads. I knew something like this would happen." Eben Titcomb strode back and forth in the tiny meeting room, ignoring his son. Zeke's eyes followed him though his head and body did not move.

# Chapter 39

*I am Daniel. And though Kings condemn me to burn in their fiery furnaces, I walk out unscathed. Though King Atwood's rage sends me into his white-hot furnace, I dance amid the flames. Though King Father's demands cast me bound into his fiery furnace, I smile as I stand amidst the towering flames that sweep above and past me. I walk through them and stand still as upon a golden coastal sea in the furnace fire of the world and remained untouched.*

*I am Daniel. I am here to promise that I will deliver divine sparks and lightning to anyone who berates those who are afraid, who berates those who live in fear and cannot speak their words with confidence and hope. Standing amid the furnace flames, I have seen the molten future where every lonely teenager stands tall and is spoken to with respect. I have seen the blistering urge for acceptance reveal itself in the eyes from those who are stronger and more fortunate than those who are not.*

*And I have seen an eternal peace fostered through the universal hope to be popular whose heat burns within the heart of every ungainly adolescent. And this popularity rises with angels who, shrouded in leaden smoke, sing the praises of those teens who have never attended the prom, who have never tried out for basketball, and who remain invisible throughout their high school years. In fiery sparks of exclamation, they repulse the punches on the shoulder and the nasty comments in the hallway suffered by the hordes of invisible teens who wander the hallways between classes.*

*I am Daniel. I dream spectacular dreams in my cell room. And I carry these dreams during the day. My visions appear to me unannounced and they cause me to tremble with confidence. They are burning hot and foretell of a conflagration so great that hell will be forged into a mighty sword that will destroy even the mightiest of mills and the smallest of towns.*

*I am Daniel and I'm a real person, so you'd better listen to me when I speak.*

ණ

"Lionel, he's a son of a bitch, that's all there is to it." For the first time in a long while, Elizabeth Proctor was angry, and a tad nervous. "This meeting better go properly or I'll have him for lunch. I'm serious."

Lionel Avery laughed deeply. He moved the phone away from his ear and looked at the receiver. "Go get 'em, tiger. Don't take any crap from him. He really doesn't have a leg to stand on, does he?"

"You trying to bait me? You want to tangle?" She laughed.

"I'll tangle with you. But later, after the meeting. You do still want to head down to Portland?"

"Yes, Chief, I do, and you are buying me a real martini."

"You'll get no resistance from me."

"Good. Gotta run. Call me by six, okay?"

ණ

Eben Titcomb was riled up. Shibles had ordered the parties to iron out the Resnik problem. Eben Titcomb strutted around the meeting room like a farmyard rooster, chest pushed out, arms flailing, saliva building slightly at the corners of his mouth.

"You have no right, Coccinella! No right at all! That stuff is private. That stuff is my boy's and no one else's. You high school teachers are all alike; you think you can do whatever you want to do with our kid's work. Well, you ain't getting away with this." He stopped by Coccinella's seat and looked at him. The English teacher put his left hand up to his jaw and rubbed it. Titcomb thought he had put this high school teacher in his place. In fact, Coccinella was stifling the urge to laugh.

"Did you call Zeke a sissy for writing poetry, Mr. Titcomb?" asked Coccinella.

"What?"

"You heard me. Zeke told me at our last meeting that you called him a sissy for writing poetry, that you told him to write 'real stuff' in his journal. He told me that you said if he wrote 'real stuff' then he could get out of the Youth Center on time."

Eben Titcomb glared at the English teacher. He sat down in his seat, rubbed his face with his hands, leaned on the table with his elbows, and said directly to Coccinella, "Listen, mister, don't you try to get fancy with me, you hear? I can have you fired. You and your ideas. Ever since you came up here, you thought you knew it all. Teaching *Catcher in the Rye*. Having students read Indian treaties. And God knows what else."

Coccinella looked over at Proctor, then at Rust, and then at Gardiner. He really wanted to put Titcomb in his place. Instead, he thought of Zeke. After a pause, he sat up and answered Zeke's father. "You're welcome to try, but you won't get anywhere. I think you know that. Zeke is working quite well with me. Since you know nothing about creative writing, let me tell you something about it. There's a collaborative component. Zeke and I were sharing our poems. I remind you that Zeke was the one, after only three of our meetings, who asked if Mr. Resnick was around and whether he would like to look at his poems. I was helping Zeke. He was reaching out, to a reputable published poet, I might add. And you know that your son respects both me and Mr. Resnick." Coccinella, disgusted and about to get angry, exhaled a long breath loudly, and sat back in his chair.

Eben Titcomb did not respond. He turned to his lawyer. "Ron, I want this guy kept away from my son, is that clear. I do not want Resnick near him, either. I want another teacher, someone like Mr. James, the math teacher. He runs a tight ship. He grew up in Chaldea. He's dependable, trustworthy."

David Coccinella shook his head, laughed, and then grinned at Eben Titcomb.

Zeke was writing in his journal when Coccinella came in for what was to be their last session. "Hey, Zeke. What's up? Whatcha got there?"

"Nothing, I started a poem last night and I am trying to finish it. I can't show it to you."

"That's true. Sorry, kiddo. Your father's orders."

Zeke looked up at Coccinella, now standing in front of him. He noticed that his teacher's face looked tight and tired, like the teacher had just had a long argument with Mr. Rowell about G Period study or with a student. "Yeah, I know." Zeke continued to write in the journal. Suddenly, he crossed out a line his pencil. He kept crossing out harder and harder until the page ripped. He flung the pencil past Coccinella against the wall.

# Chapter 40

*There's never an easy ending to a particular experience. That's because a new experience begins before the older, previous ones can end, before those earlier experiences totally affect you. Look at me here, in this place, having the new experience of dealing with being here in the Youth Center where I am trying to deal with what I did last fall in Chaldea.*

*I'm a fire setter, a pyromaniac. Dr. Proctor says that I set the fires for a reason, that I think about flames for a reason. We've been doing better with each other in the last month or so. Maybe it's the warmer weather.*

*Things don't end easily. I've done a lot of reading in here. More than I did secretly in my room back when I lit the fires. I've found out one thing. Life is not a novel. Life is life. I don't know what's going to happen to me, but I want to change.*

*I think every character in any so-called young adult book comes to that conclusion. Go ahead and read any of them. You'll see what I mean. Even Caulfield was not sure about what would happen to him. Arnold Spirit, same thing. Sam, the skateboarder. You know, the character that had the poster of the famous skateboarder, Tony Hawk. Same thing.*

*Even the kid who was autistic, Christopher, after all he went through, ran away to London to look for his mother. He was great in math, though, so maybe he doesn't count. I think he does count because I think he didn't know what would happen to him except he had to take this tremendous math test.*

*Same with Alex D. over in Italy. He loved that girl from the U. S. and he was confused at the end of the story. And, the kid, that boy soldier, Agu, in Africa. He had the most traumatic experience of anyone. Now, what happened to him was scary. I'd be afraid to meet him, but I'd like to. He was all messed up at the end of his story. Then there's that soccer player, Robbie. He goes through a lot, but at least he had help. He had his girlfriend to help him understand his life and what was happening to him.*

*I depend mostly on myself and I'm used to that, but I have been trying hard to talk more to the other guys in here, to the assistants, and to the doctors, especially Dr. Proctor. I talk with her almost the entire session time now. She wants me not to stay inside my head so much. That's tough because I am not the kind of kid to make friends easily. You can't make real friends in here. I told Dr. Proctor that I don't look like a person whom anyone would want to be friends with. She gets angry with me when I say that, but I think she knows it's true. I don't look special.*

*My experience down here isn't going to end nice and neat, like the ending of a bad novel. Mr. C taught us about ambiguous endings. Life is ambiguous. I am ambiguous. All the books about teenagers that I read are supposed to have some kind of optimistic ending, but I think that's really bogus because who says a person will learn good things from an experience at the end of it? Besides, how do you know when an experience ends? It seems to me that life is a series of experiences, where one experience tumbles into another until you die. You never know what the ending of an experience is going to be. How can you know?*

*Look at me. Look at my experience. I am down here in this Youth Center. I never expected to be here after I set those fires. I didn't even know that this place existed. I sure know it exists now. Before that there was the arrest, the arraignment, court, and the trial. Having all these experiences makes me who I am, and I am trying to figure that part, the who I am part, out.*

*When I try to figure things out, I start thinking that the way I'll turn out from all this can't be good. Maybe something good will happen.*

*How I turn out can't be predicted. If that's the case, maybe I can keep hoping that I'll turn out okay.*

*Good novels have real endings. A good ending is a natural one, one that makes sense. I want my life to make sense, though it doesn't make much sense at the moment. Although, I am beginning to think that where I am and what is happening to me makes sense.*

*I think too much in this place. I would love to see the ocean.*

❧

"Aren't you going to have a cookie, Zeke? They're tollhouse, you're favorite," asked his mother. She sat forward on her chair in the visitor's room and rubbed her hands against her knees. She gazed out the window at the patch of deep blue sky above the low, flat roof of the adjacent outbuilding. "It's such a lovely day," she said softly.

"A lot of good that does him." Eben stood near the door. He had not moved from the spot since coming into the room. He looked over to his son.

Zeke sat at the table in the centre of the sparse room. He looked at the thick, circular stack of cookies covered by Saran Wrap sitting on green plate. He did not move to take one.

❧

"Why'd you call my father?" Zeke focused on the mole on Mr. James's cheek. "I didn't do anything wrong last time."

"Zeke, you know that's not true. You weren't paying attention to me when I was explaining the math problem."

"I sat there. I was listening."

"No Zeke, you weren't. You were moving around in your seat. You looked out the window all the time, and you never gave me an answer to any question I asked."

"I don't have to talk to you. All I have to do is my math. I did my work."

"Yes, but we are supposed to talk, too, you know. I expect you to pay attention and talk to me when I speak to you. I'm your teacher now. Remember that."

"Don't worry. I know that." Zeke let a smirk appear.

"Don't be uppity with me, young man." James sat up in his chair.

"I'm not. I don't have to talk to you, if I don't want to."

"Okay, that's it. I'm calling you father tonight. Read the rest of the chapter and do the first problem."

Zeke crossed his arms on his chest and a smile crept over his face.

"Lose it, mister," James snapped.

"You aren't my father," Zeke snapped back.

# Embers

*There's this kid that's just like the Eric character in Cormier's book. I mean he isn't actually a serial killer like Eric was because he hasn't killed anyone yet. But he tried. At least that's what I heard. I heard he attacked his parents. Rumor has it that he's vicious. He's the quiet type, like me. I haven't talked to him yet, but I want to. I've watched him many times sitting in the cafeteria. He never looks to his left or his right. He never talks. He eats his food.*

*You can't really sit alone here when you eat. I sit and try to mind my own business. Which is hard to do because of who I am. Guys just unload on me. I bring out the worst in people. The story of my life. Here, I've only been beat up really bad twice. 'Really bad' means that I was sent to the infirmary to recover.*

*I learned fast how to only get punched and shoved and hurt in a real quick way so the authorities never find out. Geez, there are mean kids here who really don't give a shit. They'd hammer Billy Atwood. Now that I'm down here I see Billy as a guy that was simply afraid of himself. So he picked on me. He'll never pick on me again. But I won't see him again anyway. I can't go back to Chaldea. Obviously. I guarantee no one will ever do the stuff to me that he did.*

*The secret to only getting hit, say twice a week, instead of getting whacked steadily on a regular basis, is to shut up. Which I am a master at. I look away and let it happen. People get tired of the pleasure. I don't respond. My outside self takes the punishment. The puncher gets nothing out of me. My inside self stays tucked away. It's a trade-off. I take the pain until they lose interest.*

*I know this is not the best way to deal with life, but that's what I've got to do here. I've started to talk to Dr. Proctor about this stuff. She's pleased. I can tell because she gets all active, writing notes and asking me questions with this serious and caring look on her face. She gets all upset when she hears about what happens to me. I know she speaks with people, but she can't protect me. Nobody can protect anyone else. Life has to be lived alone, by yourself, unprotected.*

*That's real scary to think about, but it's not so bad if you think that means you've got to be yourself. That means you've got to know what kind of person you are. Then, after you know, if you ever do or ever can, you've got to be who you are. Being who you are means living life as yourself. Which means accepting who you are. That's what I mean.*

*I think a lot about stuff like this because someday I'll get out of here. The sooner the better, as far as I'm concerned. Dr. P says I am starting to accept who I am. I guess that's true. She's been great, really. I've stopped giving her such a hard time. Now that we really talk, I've started to make a plan. I've talked to her about it. A lot, actually. I know she's told my parents about what I've said. That's okay though.*

*I'm looking to go college when I get out. I can get my GED in here. That's why I've been reading so much. Besides, reading relaxes me in one sense. In another sense it gets me excited about my life, even though I'm cooped up here. Reading helps me figure things out, things like who I am. Which means that reading helps me think about my life and the way I act.*

*Don't get me wrong, reading won't make me turn into an all-American teenager. And while it doesn't answer any questions about why I lit those fires, it helps me to think about what I did. And maybe that thinking about what I did will lead me to begin to understand why I did it.*

*I can't answer that question yet. I'm circling around it, as Dr. P says. It's going to take some time. I've only been here six months. There's going to be plenty of time for me to try and straighten myself out.*

*She always tries to get me to talk about my father, but I can't just yet. Dr. P says I am going to have to talk a lot about him and my whole family, even Michelle, wherever she is. I know this is true, but I can't do it. I get all upset inside and I want to explode.*

*I've been writing lots of stuff, mostly poetry. I'm not showing it to anyone except Mr. C, who comes down here once a month to work with me. My father agreed. One day, James grabbed me up off my chair and pushed me against the wall. My mother stood her ground when that happened. Coccinella came back. I still have to deal with James, the jerk. Everything is a trade-off. Can you believe that? I couldn't, at first. My father even agreed to let Mr. Resnick see the poems and go over them, too.*

*I never thought that I would connect with those two guys, of all people, after what I did. Talk about "irony." You never know what's going to happen in life. I think about that a lot.*

*There was a second meeting about me with my parents, Mr. C, the lawyers, Dr. P and the judge. I wasn't there, but my mother told me about it. Dr. P told me some, and eventually Mr. C told me some. I put the pieces together as best I could. I would have liked to have been there. Adults are funny. They want to tell you stuff, but they're afraid to because they think you can't handle it. To talk directly to you is like breaking some unspoken rule.*

*If you're looking for a cool ending, you're in for a surprise because there are no surprises to stories like mine. You knew that, right? Here I am in the South Portland Youth Center. I'll be sixteen soon, and if I make good progress, then I can get out when I'm eighteen. I have no idea what "make good progress" means, except talking with Dr. P and doing my GED work and not getting into any trouble. Adults want you to make good progress. I think it means to behave myself, to do what they want. But Mr. C said it could mean to start taking responsibility for my actions. He said that would mean beginning to talk about my family and about how I feel about everything, including the fires.*

*When I am alone, lying on my cot, staring up at the ceiling of my room, I daydream. I daydream about all sorts of things, fly fishing, skiing, things that I have never done.*

*What I haven't daydreamed about is starting fires. I have been talking with Dr. P so much about them. She's relentless. I do think about flames. I think about them when I talk to Dr. P about my inside self, my invisible self. I don't daydream about them.*

*Sometimes I daydream that I am like Resnick, that I write a book of poems. That seems like a joke when I think about all I've been through. Deep down it isn't a joke to me. Poetry has become part of my life. Life is a joke that isn't really a joke. I've got to take life seriously in a different way than I have. I don't have much of a choice.*

*I know that I'm Zeke. I feel like I'm Zeke, only different. I know that I'm a pyromaniac. I don't feel like one. I know what I did. I'm trying to figure out why. I'm confused. I am writing some poems about my confusion. Just the other day, I wrote a short poem about my father. For an exercise that Mr. C gave me. The exercise involved asking an important question when you were somewhere specific, and I remembered a time with my father. I wasn't planning on writing about my father at all. It sort of came out. I can't explain it. I don't have a title yet. Only Mr. Coccinella has seen it so far. He's going to show it to Mr. Resnick and then get back to me. This is the poem:*

*Standing beside my father*
*Underneath the old Elm*
*Out at the edge of Davis's pasture*
*To catch a look at some moose*
*As they come out to graze,*
*I wonder what it is about watching*
*These animals that calms him?*
*I stare down at my mukluks*
*Where I rub the muddy orange dirt*
*Just so to trace a smiley face.*
*In the late afternoon sun*
*I look over at Dad, he looks back at me,*
*Rests a hand on my shoulder and says,*
*"Zeke, it's better....hunting with your eyes."*

*Coccinella told me Mr. Resnick's going to come down and talk about it with me. I can't wait.*

*I feel like all those flames that grew inside me have died down into burning coals. I'm wondering when those hot coals will die out into cold ash. I wonder what will happen when they do. Maybe, I can just clean them out of me like I used to clean them out of the wood stove in the living room with the big ash bucket and shovel when I lived at home, before I burned it down. We've all got to clean out the old ashes from the burnt out fires that are left inside of our selves.*

*I know that I have to let this fire inside me burn out. I can only do that by figuring out what caused it. That should suck the heat out of its burning coals so I can clean them out of me. Once they're cleaned out, if I work at these recent experiences with Dr. P and keep writing my poems, then maybe I can ignite a new fire inside me, one that burns steadily, contained, clean and safe, that gives me strength to be a new Zeke. You know, everyone keeps this type of fire in them. And these types must be tended.*

David Cappella is a poet and Professor of English at Central Connecticut State University where he teaches creative writing and literature. He has co-authored two widely used poetry textbooks, *Teaching the Art of Poetry: The Moves* and *A Surge of Language: Teaching Poetry Day to Day*. His *Gobbo: A Solitaire's Opera*, won the Bright Hill Press Poetry Chapbook Competition in 2006. His poems and essays have appeared in various literary journals and anthologies in the US and Europe.

Visit his university web page for more information:
http://web.ccsu.edu/english/faculty/cappella

CPSIA information can be obtained at www.ICGtesting.com
Printed in the USA
BVOW08s0820170216

437018BV00002B/42/P